THE JOY OF SORCERY

THE JOY OF SORCERY

STEN NADOLNY

TRANSLATED BY

Breon and Lynda Mitchell

PAUL DRY BOOKS

Philadelphia 2020

The translation of this work was supported by a grant from the
German Federal Foreign Office and the Goethe-Institut.

 Auswärtiges Amt

First Paul Dry Books edition, 2020

Paul Dry Books, Inc.
Philadelphia, Pennsylvania
www.pauldrybooks.com

Printed in the United States of America

Library of Congress Control Number: 2020937389

ISBN-13: 978-1-58988-146-4

*"Sorcerers don't have it easy
when they're given a hard time"*

Kurt Kusenberg (1904–1983)

Contents

THE JOY OF SORCERY

Rejlander's Cover Letter

Stockholm, 28 July 2017

Dear Iris, Dear Stephan,

Pahroc named me executor of his estate. I enclose, in confidence, twelve long letters he wrote at various intervals between 2012 and 2017 to his granddaughter Mathilda—meant to be read when she came of age, of course, for she was only three months old when he wrote the first, and five and a half when he wrote the last, which lay unfinished on the eve of his death.

That means the letters, amounting to almost a book, won't be delivered to Mathilda until at least the year 2030, in accordance with Pahroc's wishes. Except for Waldemar III and Waldemar IV, Pahroc's most recent servants, you're the only ones receiving copies of the letters now. I'm sharing them with you because you were among those who understood my history with Pahroc, and I want to discuss him and the letters with you.

He told me himself why he started writing these letters, and if I ever make a film about him it will begin on that day—with Mathilda:

A baby asleep. An old man gazes at the child intently, having pulled a chair up beside the little bed to do so. He looks neither left nor right, but seems to be waiting for the baby to awaken. The room is quiet—the only sound the ticking of the wall clock. The old man murmurs something now and then in a friendly tone, perhaps a question, but what answer could the little one possibly give? On this day in late March, Mathilda is barely three months old, born on Christmas Eve. A mixed blessing since children generally receive only half the normal number of gifts if their birthday falls on Christmas.

The old man's hair is snow white and slightly disheveled, his face deeply wrinkled. Friendly wrinkles, not ill-tempered—it's clear he hasn't forgotten how to laugh. His body is slim and light. He sits upright, spine straight. He watches, murmurs, smiles, seems curious but not impatient.

It's a large apartment, meant for a family with children, expensive, spacious and bright, high above the city. Gabled roofs can be seen through the window, and in the distance a broadcast tower. No street noise reaches this high, only now and then the drone of a passing airplane. The wall clock rattles, then strikes twelve times. The child stirs. Will it wake? It opens one eye, its right hand slips from under the blanket, jerks upward, but then falls back and remains motionless. The little one sleeps on.

The old man's glasses have fallen from his nose to the floor. He bends down for them with a groan, then sees that a lens is missing. This doesn't seem to bother him. In fact he chuckles to himself, amused. Now he gets up to look for the lens, but it's only when he hears a small cracking sound that he discovers where it is—or rather, was. The old man wags a warning finger at the baby and smiles: "I've caught you now. I know you, you're an open book to me." He approaches the bed, places his hand gently on the baby's head, and whispers, "You little devil. You have my blessing—and Emma's too."

The old man fetches a small dustpan and brush from the kitchen and sweeps up the glass from the carpet. Then he walks down a long hall lined with framed awards and photos. The photos aren't of him, however. They show an actor on stage and in films, a virile man with a strong chin, a cool gaze, and the nose of an Indian chief. The name "John Parrock" appears on one of the awards, we're in the Parrock family apartment. The old man enters a small room that seems to be his own. This, too, is filled with photos, most of them showing a smiling woman, often with him, the old man, at her side when they were younger. He sits down at a Biedermeier desk, its writing surface shielded from prying eyes by a roll top that can be locked. He slides it up, presses both thumbs near the back wall, and a secret compartment opens. A small flask of whiskey shimmers inside. He pulls it out, but only to retrieve what lies behind, a large envelope from which he draws a letter several pages long. He reads the first page, which opens with "Johann, my dear son," lifts the lid of the inkwell and selects a quill from a cup—yes, he writes with quill and ink, the way children were taught to do a hundred years ago in grade school. His first stroke crosses out the salutation, above which he now writes: "My dear granddaughter Mathilda." And in the margin: "When you read this, I'll be dead. Perhaps for so long you'll no longer remember your grandfather Pahroc." He spends a moment or two revising what he's written, draws an arrow from the added text to its place below the new salutation, then continues reading the earlier letter to see if further deletions or additions are required.

Now something important occurs to him. He pulls down the wooden roll top, stands, goes back to the hall, and dons a thick overcoat, for it's the coldest March in years. The coat is a roomy, protective hull with a hood—a duffel coat. The old man looks himself over in the mirror on the door and is satisfied. A duffel coat and a Basque beret—enough in themselves to make him love winter. "Trevor Howard," he murmurs, pleased. Yes, his memory is still not bad. He would never have dreamed of buying a coat like this sixty years ago if the

British investigator in *The Third Man* hadn't worn one. Without that film, the duffel coat would never have had its day in the sun. "Major Calloway," he says, sets his beret at a slightly greater angle, leaves the apartment, descends, and emerges from the building. The missing lens is no real hindrance. He buys a newspaper on the way.

On the tram, he has to stand. No one lifts his bottom from a seat for a hundred-year-old man these days, but that doesn't bother him. Let them sit there, these sickly sixteen-year-olds, he has no wish to watch them struggle to their feet and then collapse before his eyes from the strain. He himself can spend hours standing or walking. The stretch from the tram stop to the cemetery poses no problem for him, even over trampled snow, flattened here and there to sheets of ice—only two weeks till Easter and it's still snowing. When he reaches the gravesite he brushes the snow from the bench, spreads his newspaper out on it—no, just the classifieds, but they're thick enough—sits down and gazes at the headstone. Beneath the photo in its small oval frame stand the words "Emma Pahroc, née von Schroffenstein, eternally beloved sorceress, 1912–1955."

Perhaps it really happened that way, on a day in March 2012, five and a half years ago. And that's how the film might begin—with a mystery. And then the long flashback, in which it becomes clear why a letter the old man first meant for his son in 1955 is being revised now, sixty years later, and addressed to his still tiny granddaughter, along with other letters yet to come.

It remains to be seen if they'll ever be published. Pahroc meant them for his granddaughter alone, and once she's come of age and read them it will be up to her to answer that question. For the time being, let's keep all this to ourselves. I'm sharing them with you for another reason: In case something happens to me (and the original manuscript), please keep in touch with Mathilda and deliver your copy of the letters to her at the intended time. Pahroc gave you pleasure while he lived, and I'm sure you'll find equal pleasure in these letters—at any rate, I love equally the true and the invented in them.

Some letters were composed on the computer, others were written by hand. Deciphering and copying the hand-written ones was difficult. Pahroc didn't need a secret code—if you haven't struggled as long as I have to learn it, his Sütterlin script is impossible to read. But the letters have been accurately transcribed now. I've added nothing to them, nor offered any explanations, save one. Where Pahroc chose not to mention a historical figure by name, for example, I've re-spected his decision.

As you know, he didn't use his own first name, so it doesn't appear in the manuscript, nor do I think it will be missed.

Although you knew Pahroc, you may not know his fam-ily history. He was born in 1905 to John Pahroc, a Paiute Indian from the Pahranagat tribe in Nevada who became a naturalized German citizen in 1899, and a woman from Ber-lin named Marianne. John had arrived in Berlin in 1890 as a horseman and dancer with Buffalo Bill's Wild West Show and fell in love with the young woman, who, so the story goes, wanted to learn the war dance from him and offered to teach him how to waltz in return. It seems he was a quick learner. Evidently the Ghost Dance of the Paiutes offers a good start-ing point for standard European dances. When Marianne received a small inheritance, they married and moved to Ber-lin-Pankow, where in 1902 they bought a former restaurant with a large dining hall and opened a dance school. Nowhere in Germany do they dance more enthusiastically than they did back then in Pankow. The business took off and did quite well in the years leading up to the First World War. The fam-ily lived at a genteel upper middle-class address on Hartwig-strasse, and eventually had four children—our Pahroc the youngest among them. He seems to have had a happy childhood. His parents were quiet and good-natured and he had playmates in the neighborhood—among them a little boy named Schneidebein who, like Pahroc, was always up to pranks of one sort or another—in Schneidebein's case the beginning of an unfortunate career, which you can read about in Pahroc's letters.

Everything about his own life is there as well, including a retirement that lasted for fifty years after his pension began, though you could hardly call it retirement. Since Glasgow in 2012, the two of you shared aspects of that life with him. That's where I met and came to love him. You were there too. And your story began that same day, in the same hotel. He writes about that in one of his letters. He was around 100 years old at the time—in fact already heading toward 200. He played a piece by Chopin for me, and I was amazed at how well he played. He had practiced the organ a little in the thirties, but he only took up the piano when he was in his nineties.

At the end of 2011, Mathilda arrived as the youngest daughter of his son John and Adele Reuter. She was Pahroc's last grandchild, with great-grandchildren already around. At three and a half months, the little one broke the old man's glasses, but won his heart completely. Now he took the letter he had addressed to his son in 1955, when he was seriously ill, and revised it for Mathilda. Together with many letters that followed, it grew into a lengthy manuscript. His last servant—you know him as Waldemar IV—passed it on to me, and I'm charged with delivering it to Mathilda sometime after her eighteenth birthday. She's now five and a half. So a lot can happen to her before she comes of age.

Pahroc didn't always act sensibly over his long lifetime (111 years!). Apart from the criminal activity that landed him in jail (something I found totally forgivable), he led an orderly and remarkably modest life by normal bourgeois standards. What will be remembered most about him was his happy marriage with Emma, along with his unusual gift for bringing out the best in people and his lively imagination. Of all he wrote, only his letters to Mathilda are likely to survive, and even those only if, as I've said, she decides to publish them.

I think a film might be easier to follow than the book. As professionals, you'll see what I mean when you read the letters. From the first scene of the film, where the old man sits writing beside the child, it's clear that the letters retelling his life are meant for the young woman the child will one day become. In the book, readers may wonder whether it will be a dialogue with Mathilda.

But we can discuss such questions in more detail. Perhaps there will only be a film, and if we're all still alive in 2030, Iris will do makeup, Stephan will handle sound, and I'll direct—as always.

Hugs to both of you. Tomorrow morning I fly to Reykjavik for Waldemar III's seventy-fifth birthday party, and I still haven't packed. He's invited you too, but I hear you can't come. Too bad, but we'll see each other again in Berlin!

Yours,
Rejlander

THE LONG ARM

March 2012

My dear granddaughter Mathilda,

When you read this you will be at least eighteen, the year will be 2031 or thereabouts, and I will have been dead a long time. Perhaps for so long you'll no longer remember your grandfather Pahroc. Starting today, I'll be writing you letters from time to time. You won't receive them as I write them, but in a single packet when you've grown up. In fact you've already received them, since you're looking at the first page and beginning to read. I want to tell you the most important things I've learned about magic. Each letter will have one type of magic as a theme.

Today, in March 2012, not yet four months old, you made your little arm long, reached from your crib and knocked the glasses off my nose. That made me very happy. We call that the "Long Arm." It's how we recognize a talent for sorcery, even in a baby. It happens unconsciously, in half sleep, and is forgotten at first, reappearing only five or six years later. You were certainly no exception to the rule. I hope that Waldemar arranges a meeting for you with my colleague Rejlander, as

I've instructed. Then you, too, will learn the techniques. As I write this, Rejlander is already a master of the art, though still young in years. I haven't met her in person yet, but if I feel strong enough, I hope to look her up some time this summer and suggest that she take you under her wing. She's said to be a good film director too.

As for the techniques of sorcery, I don't want to put anything in writing that might fall into the wrong hands. Moreover, the precise procedure must be demonstrated personally by a master. What is written can only enlarge upon it. I imagine you've already learned how to concentrate on the visual center of a specific thought and sink simultaneously into a state of magical twilight—sorcery isn't just a matter of talent, it takes a skilled hand. I assume that you know that, and that you've already mastered to some degree the arts that are possible at a young age. In which case you can skip this letter and the ones directly following. Or read them anyway, to learn how I dealt with all this (at least you'll get to know your grandfather that way).

One thing is true, in any case: Take your time, Mathilda! Don't expect to climb immediately to art's highest summit. Don't be sad if you wake up tomorrow and still can't turn invisible or walk through walls, to say nothing of sorcery's heavier artillery. That's simply the way it is: higher level techniques can only be acquired gradually; they arrive at different stages in life. Many are beyond the young, no matter how gifted they are. I myself was over forty before I understood how to produce money instantly. And even when you've practiced and mastered a spell, the advice of an older colleague is always of value.

As a teenager, I had the great good fortune that the sorcerer Schlosseck lived in a building directly across from us on Hartwigstrasse. He occupied the fourth floor with his servants. Schlosseck was my first teacher.

There's no way to know under what conditions and with

what prior knowledge you will be reading this. You'll run across passages that at first you can't understand. Eventually you'll understand them all. You're a sorceress.

You're also part Indian, but that has nothing to do with your magical abilities. My father, John, was a full-blooded Indian. He could ride bareback, shoot a bow and arrow, and dance like a god, but mind you he was no sorcerer! The fact that I myself was—or could become one—was something I didn't realize as a child, and at first there was no one to tell me. My siblings and parents had no idea. I only knew I wasn't normal, and suffered because of it. I was introverted, highly imaginative, basically obedient, but everything they warned me about or asked me to do was immediately forgotten, and I wept easily when scolded.

My parents were not overly strict. Even when I'd misbehaved I could count on their affection. They loved me, and they sensed I needed help whenever I felt I'd somehow failed. Other children often teased me because I was different. Little sorcerers are always getting in the way and don't look where they're going. I would stand motionless for minutes at a time in a meadow or in the bushes, watching birds or insects. I studied the movement of leaves and blades of grass in the wind. Sometimes I didn't hear someone calling me and they thought I was just being contrary. But it wasn't that, I was simply somewhere else. Concentration means shutting out everything around you. When I saw a cherry ten feet away and plucked it without taking a step toward it, I was aware of nothing else, not even any kind of pain. Back then I didn't even realize it was magic. I was concentrating far too hard to think about what I was doing.

Even when it gradually dawns on someone that they might be a sorcerer, it's not necessarily a matter of joy. You've surely felt that yourself over the course of time. Your gift separates you from others, from your classmates, your circle, your best friends. Who can you talk with about it except other sorcerers? One thing is clear to us all: we must keep this art secret.

There was only one other little boy in our neighborhood with the gene for magic—his name was Schneidebein. We sensed immediately that we had something in common and spent a good deal of time together later, mostly playing tricks on others. At school, Schneidebein decided to use the Long Arm to undo some button or other on a classmate's shirt and then call out, "Why are you running around like that, man?" I laughed at his pranks and mischievous tricks, like shattering flower vases or sending hairpieces flying. But as inseparable as we sometimes seemed back then, in the end Schneidebein proved to be more a competitor than a friend. As a child, I was glad he was there—a child needs someone to share secrets with. When Schneidebein visited my teacher Schlosseck and asked if he would mentor him, too, the master declined. He had too many students already, he said, and was busy with other things. But I knew he simply didn't like my playmate. He didn't like most people, including sorcerers. I tried to bring him around.

"He's just a little odd because his father beats him all the time."

It was true—Farmer Schneidebein's riding whip didn't just dance on his horse's back, least of all there, in fact. The Schneidebeins had sold enough land to the city to make themselves rich, their meadows and fields were now irrigated with sewage. That was all fine, but the money hadn't done them much good: the family was still joyless.

Nevertheless, Schlosseck was not ready to teach anyone he considered suspect. That gnawed away at Schneidebein, and he took it out on me. He placed me in dangerous situations on more than one occasion, and did so deliberately. He gladly courted danger himself. That can end badly, and so it did. He eventually joined an unopposed ruling party—dangerous types like to do that—and plunged into the abyss along with them. I'll describe that in more detail later.

I had another playmate and true friend, little Jakob, who lived on Eintrachtstrasse. He was nicer than Schneidebein, and cleverer too. But he had no gift for magic.

Sorcerers are no worse than most other people, nor are we any better. There are sensible old men among us and good mothers, but also compulsive troublemakers and utterly nasty tricksters. What we call "witches" don't exist—there is no Devil who might lead them.

When my father, John Pahroc, had to go off to war because he'd longed so to be a German, my mother wept. He himself didn't—Indians never cry, as everyone knows. But he surely felt like it. He wanted to join the cavalry, but was assigned to the infantry instead. No one else cried either, at least none of the men. I did, though, and felt ashamed of it. Sorcerers have strong premonitions. But I didn't know that yet, I just had a queasy feeling. That always indicates the presence of a strong premonition, but you have to gaze deeper into yourself to find it.

My father taught me to dance, to shoot a bow and arrow, and to ride horseback. We kept a horse in a stall near our street, close to Schloss Niederschönhausen. My father told me about the Paiutes, his nation in Nevada, and his tribe, the Pahranagat. He even told me his true Indian name, but it was nearly impossible to pronounce. That's why Buffalo Bill called him Pahroc, after the mountain the Pahranagat lived near, and "John" because performers always have to have a first name in the program.

Meanwhile, my father had long since become a fervent German citizen. His goal was to be more German than the Germans, something he never quite succeeded in doing. Nevertheless, he attained a certain fame: an article about him in the *Berliner Zeitung* (entitled "The Prussian Indian") hung framed on our wall for years. His German was some-what idiosyncratic, but always easy to understand. His view of Germans, for all his admiration, remained tinged with amusement. Except when they spoke of "consequences"—that worried him. And all that, he passed on to me.

He was assigned as a runner in his regiment, since Indians were supposed to be good at that sort of thing—his superior officers had been reading too much Karl May. He made friends with an artist who had attended a Buffalo Bill show years earlier and painted a picture of Indians on horse-back. Father mentioned in a letter that he'd seen a photo of the painting. Pahroc was clearly recognizable on one of the horses. This fellow August—Father mentioned his name—was apparently a friendly and thoughtful man. He was killed by enemy fire at Perthe-lès-Hurlus in September 1914, my father at Fort Douaumont in the summer of 1916. My memory is something, isn't it?

My mother sold the dance school then, under unfavor-able circumstances, the most unfavorable of which was that she never received the money.

Back to the Long Arm. It's the first trick we can do and corresponds to what every baby wants: to grab something, stick it in its mouth if possible, play with it, or merely hold on to it. It's a good thing the Long Arm disappears soon after babyhood, but at some point it returns and can be used con-sciously. Then nothing is safe anymore. When I was eleven years old, in the midst of the war, it was a real advantage, since we were starving.

Things were particularly hard during the "Turnip Win-ter," when we had nothing to eat but those bland, tasteless tubers, and all Berlin was wandering around the countryside from farm to farm, trying to find something edible. I had bet-ter luck than my siblings when we went out foraging, though I wasn't as good at begging—I just grabbed things and stuffed them in my rucksack. Bread, potatoes, soap, and eggs, and on one occasion a whole smoked ham. Of course I didn't dare let the others know about my magic spell. To their admiring comments I simply replied: "They were just lying around." Once, one of the farmers saw what I was up to. In Stahnsdorf, it was. He must have known about sorcerers and the Long Arm, and he sensed this little boy was one. He came at me with a pitchfork, and since I didn't know any other spells I ran for my life. I had to leave the rucksack with its precious cargo behind, including five good wax candles I needed to read by at night. I was twenty before I learned to see in the dark. Later, I even learned the Light spell, which allowed others to see a few things too.

There are many words to make stealing sound less serious: to pocket, to pilfer, to forage, to have sticky fingers. When I told the story about the pitchfork, Schlosseck added a new term. "When you're hungry and have no money for food, there's nothing wrong with petty theft. The owners are mad even then; they're mad most of the time. But you have a right to survive." He went on, "Of course, stealing is easier for a sorcerer, and it must be admitted there's a certain pleasure in stolen goods. But follow one rule: be just. That doesn't mean adhering slavishly to the owners' laws, or to those of the owners' owners—the State. But be fundamentally just."

To clarify his concept of justice, Schlosseck used the English term "fairness." It's difficult to render in German, but my father used it, so I know what it entails. "Be fair" means to take from others only what they have in abundance, not the necessities of life, and nothing they've worked long and hard for. Don't lower someone else's chances merely to increase your own. The temptation to steal is often strong, particularly when you're clever and quick enough to do it. But resist it if the result would be unfair. When foraging, for example, you mustn't steal the hard-won goods of those who are begging or trying to find something to eat themselves. If you do, you'll feel shabby and mean, and with good reason. You'll hate yourself, whether you admit it or not.

My skills as a thief would never have sufficed to feed my family, and without Schlosseck we would never have made it. He always brought a large basket filled with food when he came. He owned his building and other tracts of land, and told my mother (swearing her to secrecy) that he was raising fruit and vegetables on the quiet behind high walls. He even claimed to be keeping chickens. But he had no real need for all that—after all, he could cast spells. That became clear years after the war, when inflation set in and money could fall to a tenth of its value overnight. I remember how my mother wept when she'd waited too long to go shopping. The money that was supposed to feed us all hadn't been enough for even a quarter liter of milk. I can still see Schlosseck standing in our kitchen, reaching in his pocket with slight embarrassment, and pulling out a million Mark bill. "Go back again, I just happen to have sold a plot of land."

Even as a child, I liked making things. When Schlosseck was about to conjure up a doghouse for Ulf, his sheepdog, I objected:

"Can I build one? Please, Herr Schlosseck!"

"All right then, there are plenty of boards lying around."

I drew up plans, found a hammer and saw, all I lacked were nails.

"That's your affair," he said. "You took over, now solve your problem."

Using the Long Arm to open drawers and take out nails proved very difficult in a hardware store. Hardware store owners keep a particularly sharp watch. Then I remembered that a wooden statue of General Hindenburg had been placed in front of the Reichstag, next to the Victory Column on Königsplatz, to raise money for the war effort: For one Mark, a person could buy a nail and then pound it into the statue, anywhere he wanted. Thousands of nails lay ready in small boxes, and one was open. The hammer was hanging on a long chain—they knew their Berliners—but I only needed nails. One week later, Ulf was comfortably ensconced in a pristine doghouse and the nails were serving more effectively than the ones in Hindenburg.

I have a lot more to tell you about Schlosseck, and, by way of a detour through me, you'll profit from his advice.

He recognized me from across the street when I was still a baby—he could see me in my crib on the balcony. He noticed that I stretched out a little long arm while half asleep and plucked petunias from a flower vase no normal child could have reached. So he took me under his wing in later years and, when I could do a few things, he showed me samples of his own great art.

Schlosseck was the most conservative of all my teachers. The others were all convinced cosmopolitans, though almost parochial compared to him, for he was a true philosopher. He was constructing a powerful mental edifice of sorcery that was not only global, but universal. He's said to have understood the curvature of space and the changing sum of angles, and in doing so helped Albert Einstein develop a theory. I don't know any details about that—he couldn't possibly teach me all he knew.

Schlosseck had a large flagpole on his roof, and ran up the flag on the Kaiser's birthday and other holidays. In 1916, he was standing beside me in the garden when the report of yet another victory arrived—there were many back then. The cries of the newsboys reached us from Breite Strasse. He sighed, for he now felt it his duty to mount to his attic and raise the flag. At that moment, a pigeon sailed in and settled on top of the pole. Schlosseck's eyes brightened, then narrowed to slits with superhuman concentration, and within ten seconds the pigeon disappeared: it had unfurled into a large war banner and waved with the same certainty of final victory as the others. "Was that hard to do?" I asked. He replied: "With a pigeon, yes."

Another thing about the Long Arm: It can barely be seen by ordinary people, but those with quick eyes notice. So it's even more important to wait for the right moment, when no one's looking. Now simply because the arm is long doesn't mean it's more muscular. It's slender, light, and quick, but the moment you want to move something heavy with it, or if the object is too far away, it moves with stubborn slowness. When I was thirteen I tried to extinguish the street lamp from our balcony, but the ten meters involved proved too far. My hand failed to reach its goal and sank down into the front garden area, forcing me to reel it in laboriously. Nor is the Long Arm incorporeal. That means it can get stuck. That can be quite embarrassing in certain circumstances—I know what I'm talking about. For example, when I got on the tram, I would usually snatch a ticket from someone who had just shown it and was about to put it away. That went fine until one day when the tram was too full. I had trouble pulling my hand back through the crowd. When I finally managed to, the ticket was gone and I had to pay. People are jostled about so suddenly. They bump into each other, or are even thrown into a spontaneous embrace—with my arm sticking between them of course! And be careful with doors that might close, particularly revolving doors and swinging ones. I hope this advice doesn't come too late, and that your arms are OK.

Schlosseck even gave me extra tutorials, since I was so busy with sorcery that I didn't exactly shine in school. Schlosseck saw that he would have to help me if I expected to move up to the next grade. After some hesitation, he taught me a few tricks that would help me cheat on work in class. He didn't like to admit it, but he himself had been forced to employ the Round-the-Corner spell, a masterful way of copying someone else's paper, to pass the written Greek exam. No matter how principled he was in his own life, he made exceptions now and then in my case, and to this day I'm thankful that he did so. Without Schlosseck I would never have completed my final exams, and without them I would never have been employed at Telefunken.

Most important of all, he encouraged me by sharing his own joy in sorcery and offering invaluable advice on various methods and procedures.

He accompanied me on my first attempts to hover in the air and fly over obstacles. Had I not achieved a certain proficiency in this area I would have been trapped in the Stalingrad pocket and no doubt died there at age thirty-six. Then your father would never have existed, nor you, not as Mathilda at any rate—I'll return to the subject of flying later.

It's important to get to know experienced sorcerers personally. Since, sad to say, we die like everyone else at some point, you should make every effort to watch a few famous old sorcerers at work. One shouldn't forget that practitioners of our art stand on the shoulders of the great figures who came before us. I mention only Caspar, Melchior, and Balthazar, those magi from the East. They didn't follow the Star of Bethlehem, as people say, but instead drew it along after them on high, like a paper dragon, without wind or string. Christianity somewhat embarrassedly styled these great sorcerers "Kings," though they clearly had no court of any kind with them. Fine, let people call it Three Kings Day, it's our day even so! Emma and I always gave each other presents then—in secret, since it was still Christmas for the children. It worked out well that I was born on what they called the Holy Night, like you. And like other important sorcerers throughout history too—that date seems to have something about it.

If I could travel back in time—some of us can, but alas I'm not among them—I would visit Bachstelz in Munich, known back then as "The Great Bachstelz," one of my Swabian ancestors on my mother's side. And once I was in the early nineteenth century, I would travel to Sweden to see Arfwedson, who wasn't just a sorcerer but discovered lithium as well, an element whose medicinal effects enabled me to reach my seventies and beyond. Or I would take a bouquet of flowers to Fatma Pertschy, the legendary sorceress from an Austrian-Ottoman family, who invented far more than the vanilla crescent cookie. And I would certainly visit Racing Turtle, the only Native American at the Boston Tea Party in 1773, though he didn't remain a friend of the White Man for long, becoming a famous medicine man instead. And I would gladly see again two excellent colleagues who tried to breathe a little magic into Socialism. They weren't forgiven for that, and their story is a tragic one.

Dear Mathilda, be patient while you're learning. You'll develop all your abilities if you keep trying. Sometimes it will seem you're making no progress at all, and then suddenly there it will be, like a gift. In the meantime, enjoy what you can do, and don't feel too bad about what you still can't. Ambition is worthless in sorcery. Doors to magic either open or they don't, you can't force them. We can't learn everything possible anyway. Of thousands of magical spells, an individual sorcerer develops a standard repertoire of only twenty to fifty, an equal number of the more exotic, and you keep adding new ones as long as you live. In my case, I learned over 200, far more than average, but of course I can't employ a lot of them as well as I did years ago. I'm slowing down.

When you've reached that point in your life when a new field of sorcery opens up to you—and you'll realize it—then read everything you can about it. But reading can't replace personal experience gained by working with a master—my colleague Rejlander for example. Consult the works in her library, there may even be a few of my old books there. By the way, you can sniff out older treatises that conceal something on sorcery beneath their apparently innocuous content: they smell ever so faintly of Gorgonzola.

It's best not to make reading too easy. There's a spell, to be sure, that allows you to place two fingers on the book's spine and know its entire contents in a minute. Some even do that from their couch, using the Long Arm, but I think that's a terribly bad habit. Knowledge is processed better when one is active, and laziness in general poses a serious danger for the sorcerer. If you simply extend your arm for anything you need, at some point you may never rise. Make it a habit to get up and go outside from time to time. You can use the Long Arm to put what you want by your chair and go back to it later. Move around even when you don't have to, exercise your arms and legs, take detours, make things more difficult. Read books page by page, unless it's an emergency. And don't make a text magically appear on paper—write or type it out carefully, letter by letter, then you'll weigh every word. All weight, like gravity itself, leads to effort, but it grounds you. I'll write more later on the theme of flight.

The Great Bachstelz, by the way, was called "Piggy" in his final years, much to his annoyance, because he'd turned truly obese due to lack of exercise. That highly talented sorcerer died much too soon because his heart couldn't take the extra weight and retired from service. How much he could have taught younger sorcerers!

Read books that have nothing to do with sorcery, too. Read widely, read almost anything, read novels! Reading develops the ability to separate the wheat from the chaff. If you've read a lot, you can tell within a few pages whether you should lay the book aside at once or only later.

And there's something else I should mention at this point: fear. Every sorcerer feels it. The moment he begins to feel his gift, he fears that he might not do it justice, which would be a shame. Then there's the fear of attracting attention, of awakening envy, of growing lonely, of being persecuted. Or the fear of committing some evil act, simply because it would be so easy—the temptations are numerous. You may have already experienced all of these fears. Fear isn't bad, as long as you don't let it become a beast of prey. Then it can twist your mind. People who live in fear eventually begin to hate those who don't. But don't ever think you're totally free of it. Let it live, give it its place, keep it as a pet. Let it hiss and scratch from time to time, but keep it in line, don't spoil or overfeed it. Then it will be useful, and will keep you from underestimating risks. But never panic, even when Death has you in his sights. Look him in the eye and remain calm, consider the moves still open to you, and watch for the gifts chance offers.

You'll need courage, that's certain. And I'm sure you have it—we're related after all. Courage shouldn't degenerate into excess (or it too will become a beast of prey), but it can push things along a bit faster now and then. How would I ever have approached Emma if I'd lacked courage? I knew the spells for both beauty and desire back then, but I could see my only chance with her was to forego them. So courage was needed to declare myself. And at times we humans have it in decisive moments. We sense somehow that this is no foolish foray, but a necessity, that the step we are about to take is not premature, but perfectly timed. It's tremendously invigorating to take heart and see the courage you called on arrive in a flash. You know at once when a rush of fresh courage comes over you. It's time to act, to speak! Don't make courage wait around, or it may take to its heels.

Emma and I badly wanted to have a little sorcerer, by the way. It was by no means certain we would, since the ability is not directly inherited but rises unpredictably from the no man's land of the genetic pool. Nevertheless, we wanted a child with magical talents and tried time and again to have one. Just count all your aunts and uncles and you'll get some idea of how hard we tried. And once, with our last child, it seemed that we had succeeded: your father Johann, who calls himself John now.

In 1955 I was firmly convinced he would be a sorcerer, because when he was only three months old he pulled out my pocket watch. I know now that it was Emma who lengthened his arm—she'd fallen seriously ill after the hard birth, but could do magic as well as ever. She wanted to give me some temporary hope that we'd finally produced a little sorcerer. I believed it only too gladly, since I fell ill myself after Emma's death. Johann never saw the letter I wrote to him about sorcery—first, because I recovered, and second, because it became clear at some point that he was a born actor, not a sorcerer. My wonderful Emma! How gladly I forgave her that final sleight of hand. True love alone can pull a trick like that.

My little Mathilda, reading this letter as a grown young woman, there's so much I want to tell you. I hope I still have time to get it all down. I'm 106 now. There's no way to fool Death, though for several years a few of my colleagues have thought I've found one. Only Pospischil in Vienna is older— and still the beautiful woman she always was. You'll hear about her later.

I still enjoy life. It's true that mail no longer arrives from many of those I knew and liked, even loved. But when special moments grow rarer, they become even more precious. I'm not lonely. I still speak often with your mother, with my servant Waldemar IV and my former servant Waldemar III, who writes books now, and with your father when he's not making films.

I still have the address books I kept over the years. Handwritten on paper, only circled names remain, followed by two vertical strokes, one thick and one thin. That's the final notation that closes a musical score. No crosses in my address books! Many of my dead were Muslims or Jews anyway.

For years now I've also been updating my computer files and cell phone by deleting the names of those who can no longer be reached. It saddens me, because I know that names digitally removed will be forgotten more quickly than the ones I circled.

But that's what's so wonderful about life—new people are constantly appearing, the world teems with them. With luck you can make friends with them, even if you're a little old yourself.

As I write this, you're the youngest of those teeming forth. I'll check on you in a minute or so. But I'll leave my new glasses on the desk.

Your grandfather Pahroc.

SECOND LETTER

BE BEAUTIFUL,
BE CHANGED

April 2012

Dear Mathilda, you're my favorite grandchild. So I wish you a long life, filled with beauty, and personal beauty too. If not, I'm still not worried—you're a sorceress!

I've been thinking over what aspect of our art I should cover next. I'm trying to treat them in the order they come to us in life. But that differs from case to case. I had a colleague whose Long Arm was not followed by Beauty or Love—in fact nothing new came for years, then all at once Nurturing appeared. Nurturing children is one of the most difficult arts of all, and almost no one masters it fully. Another colleague learned Credibility early on. He couldn't change shape, make himself invisible, or fly, but he told such good stories about doing so that everyone believed him. Credibility doesn't come to everyone, and it's somewhat controversial—some call it the "Beautiful Lie." I never learned it myself, and so I've always stuck to the truth.

I'll begin with Beauty (if you already know the essentials, you can skip ahead). There are two quite different techniques associated with it, the actual production of objective beauty, and the enchantment of individual observers. In the one case you transform yourself, in the other only those who look at you.

In my day, teenage sorcerers were mostly interested in casting a spell on young women who looked at them; young sorceresses, on the other hand, all wanted to look like Greta Garbo, and that was far from simple, since it required great effort.

A child has no idea as yet what beauty is. It appears first in human form as their father and mother, and for a long time that's all it is. Meanwhile all sorts of things are being called "beautiful," children hear the word constantly. A fairy tale, the weather, a horse, a day off from school, or the view of the countryside from the window of an inn—they're all beautiful—or more simply, we find them appealing. They please us. Human beauty appears at first to be similar: it's no lofty summit on which only a few stand, it's a visage that pleases because there's nothing disturbing in it—measure and proportion correspond to the ideal type. Everything that runs counter to the rule is ugly. A baby is beautiful if it looks like a baby should (and cries like one, and thrusts its feet out, and does a beautiful job of filling its diapers). But if a mature man looked like a gigantic baby he would be ugly indeed—a different rule applies to grownups. Facial beauty depends on the current ideal. Not too little and not too much anywhere and we start talking about pristine beauty. Even more—and I find this touching: people are thrilled, they use terms like "divine" and "diva." Some fall into a sort of paralyzed worship, one that mustn't be confused with happiness or love. Almost everyone, young or old, male or female, beautiful or not, wants to be loved, and love is often associated with beauty. But in reality, love is a far different kind of magic.

Regularity (balanced features in a face) has no particular charm in itself. To avoid boredom it requires a few small faults as spice—a birthmark, an impudent gap in the front teeth, a perky nose, or a slight squint. If it weren't for Nefertiti's blind eye, people wouldn't look at her for long. Ideal beauty makes human beings interchangeable. I have a hard time telling young women on television apart these days. I'm always pleased when one's homely—because then I can remember her.

They say that beauty and youth are nearly synonymous. That's only because a young face has not yet been etched by all the things that make it ugly: apathy, greed, arrogance, pedantry, or physical illness. These may have already begun to destroy the face, but we can't see it yet. On the other hand, there are old faces that were quite unremarkable in youth but now shine with beauty. Here, other forces are at work: sincerity, humor, or a good heart.

Schneidebein was handsome and tall as a tree, with blond hair and blue eyes. I saw that and found it distinctly unfair that he was good-looking and I wasn't, for his soul was ugly. I could tell from the constant jibes he made about my physical shortcomings. It's true they were in clear evidence: a nose too large, legs too short and slightly bowed. He once described me as "an equestrian statue minus the horse." "Well put!" I replied. "And where did you get an idiotic name like Schneidebein?—Cut Leg—sounds like cutlet!" The exchange soon ceased to be merely verbal, and at some point I attempted to rearrange Schneidebein's regular features with a straight right to the nose. Unfortunately, I failed—he wasn't as good at sorcery as I was, but he was a better boxer.

I discovered beauty as something sensual, as a force in real life, when I was a teenager. My admiration for beautiful people almost took my breath away. I was surprised by this. What produced this effect? Did some slim figure with an elongated face simply have the right proportions and symmetry, was it because the lips curved a certain way, the hair was thick, the eyes large, the lashes long? If someone had asked me back then what caused my reaction, I would no doubt have blushed and said something about "love." But beauty has a power of its own. Love is by no means the only emotion it produces. It can chain, humiliate, enslave. Men want to "serve" it somehow. Its power affects all things: good-looking young women get higher grades, unless their teachers want to show how fair they are—then they lower their grades. But all this is probably nothing new to you. Good-looking people are trusted more (till there's proof to the contrary). They're elected class president (like Schneidebein!) or some artist wants to paint them in the nude. It works the other way around too: we have no real idea what Jesus looked like, but no one seems to think he was ugly.

Admiration can change to hate and envy. It's true that beauty is distributed unfairly, which can be annoying. But unlike property or wealth, it can't be distributed more fairly. We can hardly hope to achieve it in the future, like happiness or wisdom.

The evening after the fight, I asked Schlosseck how I could lengthen my legs and make them a bit straighter. A smaller nose, I said, could wait for now. My request gave him no pleasure.

"It can be done, but you'll have to practice for weeks. And then what? What do you expect to gain? It's not permanent." He showed me how it could be done, but only reluctantly.

I practiced diligently, even when I was at school, and a month later I succeeded for the first time. My legs stretched out and I was a little taller too. I rushed onto the street to show myself. But I had concentrated so hard on the bow in my legs that I was now slightly knock-kneed. My right knee got hung up on the back of my left and I fell while running full speed. I bloodied one knee, and my nose too. I returned to my perplexed master and asked him how to make a wound disappear. "Nonsense," he muttered, and put something called a "Hansaplast" on my knee, the latest thing for patching scrapes and cuts. But I didn't want to wear one on my nose, so I wound up learning how to make my nose look better after all. I soon succeeded: it grew smaller and the scratch disappeared. I ventured forth again to test the effect. Neighbors and schoolmates saw and recognized me, but only Schneidebein, who practiced sorcery himself, noticed that my figure and nose had improved. The others saw nothing, since they considered the change impossible. Their accustomed image of me was stronger than the new one. What a disappointment! What's more, I soon realized that I'd spent so much effort on my nose that I'd forgotten my legs. They were still straighter than normal, but they had shortened again.

Yes, we can flatten ears that stick out for a few hours, make birthmarks disappear temporarily, or straighten a nose that dips in the middle for a time. Corrective sorcery is strenuous because the new appearance is so like the old—everything slips back easily to its original state. Even a well-trained sorcerer can't keep up the effort for long. Moreover, Beauty gets harder to cast as one grows older, and of course there's less need for it. One simply gets too lazy. It's been twenty years, for example, since I've bothered to make my wrinkles disappear for the woman who delivers the daily mail.

If you think it's truly necessary, it's much easier to become a totally different person; you can maintain that state longer. Someone whose beauty lasts for only a short time disappoints anyone who's around them for long. Using Beauty only makes sense in one situation: If you want to annoy someone who wishes you'd go to the devil—I'm thinking of rivals.

In most cases, it's better to be beautiful in ordinary ways, through graceful movements and fine posture, unless the latter gives you a double chin. A small smile helps too. Almost anyone who's been photographed knows how to make herself look a little more attractive. And the standard methods: lipstick, makeup, a nice dress or even a fancy one, high heels. None of that is too tiring. It lets you approach others and practice a completely different sort of charm. When the world knows the source of your beauty, that you've dressed up and applied makeup, they're pleased both by the way you look and the effort you've made—the result is always touching.

These days many budding sorcerers would gladly make braces disappear for a few hours. Unfortunately, they can't, because, like plaster casts and handcuffs, braces are not part of your body. Their disappearance requires other arts, ones that come only later. I'd like to speak sometime with the person in charge of the whole sorcery and miracles business— there may even be a god or goddess for it. I'd point out the annoying delay of some magical skills. Some of them don't become available until they're no longer necessary. I'd bring up the matter of braces, too.

I assume you can already turn yourself into a totally different person, if you know the Turn and have practiced it. The drawback is that you always need a real model. You can't just appear as a person you've made up—you would always be lacking something you hadn't thought about. There are certainly enough real people running about. Schlosseck liked to go shopping as Kaiser Wilhelm. The Kaiser was still alive of course, but he was living in exile, far away in Holland, which was a good thing. The disappointment was that no one in the milk shop took any notice of the Kaiser, since he looked just like the cobbler on Florastrasse, and always had.

If you can transform yourself, you can bluff very effectively. Schlosseck told me how he once saved a communist. They'd been shooting at the fellow as he fled toward the S-Bahn. Schlosseck turned himself into a large man with a strong chin, a man in a leather coat, and called out gruffly: "Hold your fire!" Gruff commands were obeyed instantly in Germany at the time, and this one was too.

Schlosseck also brought the dead back to apparent life. He visited the zoo as Gottlieb Daimler and the city library as

Karl May. He could even turn himself into an animal. He greeted me once in his garden as a crocodile. Of course I recognized him:

"Good morning, Herr Schlosseck!"

"Hello Pahroc," replied the crocodile and revealed a wealth of teeth. "You look quite delicious today."

He'd taken care that no one but me could recognize him, which meant he could have devoured me in peace. But I could rely on him, something of great importance among sorcerers. You have to take care not to misuse your abilities. I answered quite calmly:

"You're the perfect picture of a crocodile, Herr Schlosseck, my compliments!"

Then he grinned. It's amazing how many parts of his huge jaw a crocodile can grin with at once.

But always be aware of the dangers in transforming yourself. Never create a magical state you can't reverse at any time. To remain a crocodile or Karl May too long is no pleasant matter, and if you happen to be a frog, no prince's kiss can bring you back—that's just in fairy tales. And remember this: We can't hide in some other shape or remain invisible for years on end. It starts to be a strain after just a few hours, and no one has managed to last more than two months, even with short breaks. If it's for a longer period, reckon with suddenly becoming yourself again at some point—perhaps at a very unfavorable moment.

Another thing: when you appear as another specific person, it can't be someone in your immediate vicinity. If the model and original are too close to each another, the spell is broken. You're suddenly standing there as yourself and have to answer embarrassing questions. The original is always stronger than your magic, so be sure to keep a safe distance between you. Photographers are dangerous too, since they can document your altered appearance. Don't let them near you when you're casting spells.

Those weren't good times back then. Many people were murdered, though the war was over; murdered simply out of hate. There were street demonstrations, the forces of class consciousness struggling for a world of greater justice while the nationalists battled for an unjust one, where their own country would always fare best.

There was also a general strike that forced everyone in Berlin to go on foot, including me, since I couldn't fly yet. The political parties had all split into factions at war with themselves. Every poster showed good-looking people on one side, and stubby, fat people with crooked noses on the other.

In those days everyone seemed insulted or upset by something. Those who returned from the war emaciated and crippled, those who were broke and couldn't find a job, those who felt Germany was being deliberately humiliated, forced unfairly to pay for all war damages, those who had lost a son—almost everyone was in some sort of turmoil or despair, and many went to political meetings and sought out others in similar despair and turmoil. I attended many such meetings, though I was slightly horrified by them. But they were an ideal place to practice, because no one knew or suspected I was there. I changed my face and my name and joined practically every party, even if they made jerky gestures and saluted one another oddly. Although I had always "forgotten" my I.D. papers, a free beer or pea soup with sausage duly appeared, and then I quickly disappeared—never to be seen again, for the model for my transformation indeed existed somewhere, a person who looked just like me, but had a different name and could (one hoped) prove he had never been in party headquarters. I must admit, I acted somewhat thoughtlessly. But I was always hungry. Other sorcerers took part in much greater public mischief. My somewhat older colleague Blüthner had himself photographed as the Reichspräsident in a bathing suit. That was a painful attack on the young democracy, for the true president was a tub and could disclaim that part of it weakly at best. Blüthner was later ashamed of himself, but appearing as another person was always the thing he enjoyed most, just like Schlosseck.

In all self-transformations, one thing is important: A sorcerer can look like a woman and a sorceress like a man, we can alter the pitch of our voices, but we're never able to change our sex, briefly or permanently. Not by magic, at least—to the distress of colleagues of both genders throughout the whole of human history who have deeply desired to do so. The same is true for transformations into animals. When Schlosseck became a crocodile, it was a male. On this point the universal constitution of sorcery permits no discussion.

There is, as I've mentioned, a second spell that doesn't turn you into a true beauty, but simply renders you more attractive and makes for greater happiness in the long run. I'd be surprised if you didn't already know it; in any case it's one you can use. It falls in the area of influence, and often, though not always, leads to love. Your allure is selective, affecting one person alone, rather than charming all those who see you. You have to feel you're pretty, or at least find yourself attractive, or you'll lack an essential aspect of the effect. It happens that most people in good spirits find themselves "nice looking," certainly prettier than what they see in the mirror.

So I convinced myself I was a good-looking fellow and, combined with the spell, managed to make another person see me that way too. Yes, actually see! It wasn't a matter of faith, it was fact. Schlosseck said I had a quite a decent gift for awakening the interest of young girls. He'd already noticed that watching me playing with them in the front yard.

Eroticism is a powerful force; it can be reinforced to some extent with spells, but it achieves its full effect on its own. When desire is aroused, beauty becomes merely ornamental. The first time it happened to me, no magic was involved, we just wanted to kiss and so we did, even though sharp-eyed people were strolling around us in Schlosspark Nieder-schönhausen. The girl's name was Wiltraud, an innkeeper's daughter from Pankow, and she was shy at first. She turned shy again when she noticed that something stood between us when we embraced. "Oh, him," I said. "That's just a lit-tle sorcerer. He's always getting in the way." This explanation seemed to calm her, and at some point he managed to hide again.

I might have stayed with the young lady longer, she was open and cheerful and liked me as I was. Not so her father, the innkeeper. I was probably not nice-looking enough for him, or I was, but not in the right way: too foreign, too Indian, brown eyes instead of blue. At any rate, he insisted she stop seeing me. As I sit here writing while you suck contentedly on your pacifier, crowds of people are arriving in Germany, fleeing strife and civil war in their own countries. Many of them are clearly handsome. And some people feel awkward and ugly in their presence. That's probably how Wiltraud's father, the brawny innkeeper, felt around me.

I wasn't downcast for long, nor inclined to be faithful, in any case. Since Schlosseck was refining my skill at charm-ing young women just then, I sought out new ones and prac-ticed all the relevant arts diligently. Schneidebein, who was often my rival in such matters, kept getting the short end of the stick. They would have their eye on him at first, but then found me more interesting. My magic spell was a great help, and I had great fun constantly stealing away his latest flame. He made his own mistakes. Although he was already quite appealing, he wanted to be even more so when he met a girl, so he was constantly busy with spells that made him look like a movie star. That left a negative impression. He concen-trated so hard that he lost his appeal. What's more, Schneide-bein was incapable of a true smile from within. He simply made a face and showed a row of white teeth. His muscles and teeth smiled, but his eyes didn't. It was the fixed smile of a victor, and it gave no pleasure.

I had my successes, but I still didn't know how to switch off the magnetism. Basically, only time can do that. So for a few years I broke hearts, caused tears to flow, and then felt remorse. But there are spells to ease the pain of breakups too. They should be learned right along with the others.

I've just received a fax inviting me to Glasgow for a "Berg-fest"—a party celebrating the halfway point in shooting a film. Rejlander is the director (so I'll get to meet her), and your father plays a great statesman and lord. How glad I am they still make films. I know and love hundreds of them, probably thousands. It's the third time your father has played a wise older man. I'm always trying to do that myself, but without your father's success.

Who knows if they'll still have fax machines by the time you're reading this. Even smartphones may be gone by then. I enjoy picturing the future, even if it makes me uneasy. For example, I imagine a universal chip implanted in each person's head that outperforms their own brain. If you want to speak with a friend in New York, you just start talking. You don't need to hold anything up to your ear, you just press a button on your watch and you're connected. You might say the only difference between technology and sorcery is that in the latter case you don't have to press buttons or flip switches.

Schlosseck foresaw technology's attempt to replace sorcery. Far from believing in its triumph, he thought it would fail, and found most technology ugly, automobiles in particular. I differed with him on that score.

If you wonder what I did all day when I was seventeen, my dear Mathilda, the answer is certainly not that I was busy all the time with girls or sorcery. I was crazy about technology. I read everything I could get my hands on, assembled gadgets, screwed and welded—much to the displeasure of

Schlosseck, who made a face and raised his eyes to the heavens from whence cometh our help at the very notion of technological "achievements." He would say things like:

"Technology is sorcery's little sister, ready to prostitute itself in all sorts of ways. Or to put it differently: technology is nothing more than the attempt of non-sorcerers to imitate our art with machines!"

I tried to defend myself:

"But technology has its uses. I think the slow, and non-sorcerers most of all, need something resembling sorcery to help them keep up!"

"Sounds like the Social Democrats," growled Schlosseck.

"And I think automobiles are beautiful!"

"They're a plague!"

"But all these devices expand our possibilities. What's wrong with that?"

"Well, fine. We ward off attacks, protect ourselves from hunger and cold. We no longer travel on foot, that's fine too. But why by train, when the tick-tack of the steel rails is already starting to ruin music? Why drive cars that make noise and stink things up? Horse-drawn carriages are more attractive and the postman's greeting is more pleasant than the 'plop' of a capsule from a pneumatic tube!"

I was enthused by all technology and grew angry. I remember our argument as if it took place this morning.

"Should the streets remain dark then, should water cease to flow from the tap? Should my mother trudge to the village well in Pankow? Should we burn down the forests because we won't allow coal?"

Schlosseck lifted his hand to stop me. "I'm willing to talk about such things! But technology serves superfluous purposes as well, ones of its own creation, and that should be stopped. Sorcery serves the beauty of the world as it was meant to be."

"As it was meant to be?"

"From its original source. And all sorcery"—yes, here comes the famous phrase—"all sorcery flows from the Source."

He was a wise and highly educated man, but that didn't keep him from casting a longing eye back to world of the druids, who exercised their arts to shield their tribes from misfortune. Sorcery and miracles have less to do with physics than they do with the human soul, and Schlosseck believed many modern skeptics dreamed inwardly of such things. He repeated that phrase on sorcery and its source often, and wrote it down as well. A writer by the name of Hesse picked it up at some point and made use of it.

We were poor back then, and Schlosseck was rich. That didn't bother him or us: he helped us out. He'd taken a liking to me, and to my mother too, because she was bold and honest and always friendly. She'd been living in Wedding with me, her youngest, since 1924, and worked as a seamstress. Without an allowance provided by my older brother, who was now a brewer, our family couldn't have made ends meet. Nor could we have made it without Schlosseck.

I liked him and enjoyed being his guest, most of all in the evening, when his servant Wladimir had already lit the candles, and the flagpole on the small tower outside the window still gleamed in the last rays of the sun. It was a beautiful house. He'd built it in 1906, but the tower had been added later. I gazed through the window of his fourth-floor study at our former home across the way and knew I wanted to live there again some day, even if thirty years passed in the meantime. It turned into ninety, but I have a small elevator to make up for that.

At some point I asked Schlosseck if there were masters who were better at sorcery than he was. He nodded.

"There's definitely one."

"What's his name?"

"Babenzeller."

"And where does he live?"

"No one knows for sure. I've never met him myself. They say he's unbearable, but interesting."

"And what can he do?"

"Kill. Sorcerers aren't allowed to kill with spells, nor can they. But apparently Babenzeller is an exception on both counts. Some people say he's evil."

"And can he kill sorcerers?"

"From what I've heard, yes."

"And why does he kill?"

"How should I know? Perhaps to amuse himself."

I made up my mind to give this Babenzeller a wide berth. But I was young and my head was filled with other thoughts. Who bothers to contemplate death? By the time I finally met that notorious figure I'd almost forgotten his name.

My mother had no idea that Schlosseck was a sorcerer. "Say hello to the Professor," she would say when I set out to visit him. And she knew nothing about my special skills. For all my dreaminess and occasional fits of rebellion, she was fond of me, and without her I might have turned out a nasty fellow, in spite of, or perhaps because of, my rare gift. We often spoke of my father, whose photo hung above the sewing machine. He too had been unaware of my magical talents. Or perhaps he did sense them, for once, long before he went away to war, he told me of a great cliff in Nevada, in the Pahroc mountain range, on which the future of the tribe stood written in the Indian script. And in that script, he said, was a special sign that foreshadowed my coming. I would live a long life and write a book—all this was carved on the cliff. I believed him then, and still do. Perhaps when I've told you everything important I have to say, I'll go to Nevada and ask an Indian to explain the signs to me. I expect to find something about you there too, Mathilda. Somehow, sorcerers are always foretold.

FLOATING AND FLYING

August 2012

All flight, Mathilda, is a revolt against the authority of gravity, an impertinent uprising, but a legitimate part of sorcery. The art of flying announces itself when we are fifteen to eighteen years of age—you will have already experienced it, or will soon.

In my case, the first signs I could fly appeared during Advent of 1923. I was almost eighteen, and Schlosseck had shown me how to weigh less on a good, well-calibrated scale. He'd wisely refrained from mentioning flying, but spoke instead of health checks at school, for when it came to portions at lunch, it was better to be classified as undernourished. I learned how to concentrate on weighing less, and tried to do so while standing on the scale, but no matter how hard I focused, I was at most four pounds lighter. "You'll get the hang of it!" Schlosseck said encouragingly. A little later on I headed toward Reinickendorf with a group of Pankow students to slide about on Schäfersee, or to try out the new ice skates Schneidebein had been given. The ice was still thin, he and I were the only ones who dared go out onto it. He tried moving quickly, racing along on his ice skates as cracks kept appearing beneath him, but he soon grew frightened by the steady crackling of the ice and returned to the bank. Things went differently for me: I was lighter than him and the ice crackled less insistently beneath me. But suddenly I broke through and felt icy water filling my shoes. It's almost impossible to cast a newly learned spell when you're badly frightened, but for a split second I managed to hover in the air over open water. I reached the solid edge of the ice hole with one foot and my remaining momentum carried me to safety. No one realized what had happened.

I was quite proud of the ability that arrived at that moment, and practiced it whenever I could. It worked best with the aid of a ladder, in the lavatory located in the stairwell. This room was shared by two floors, but at least it could be locked. I set our ladder by the toilet and floated up along it. When my power fluctuated or lessened I could quickly find a hold. In the end, I could reach the ceiling without hands or feet touching the ladder. Entering the loo with a ladder led to a few wisecracks, but I told my detractors some story about spiders that couldn't be removed any other way.

A rapid loss of weight has many uses, even if you're not yet ready to fly. If you stumble and fall, for example, it can lessen the force of the impact—you go flying instead of falling. I used it in schoolyard fights as well: there has to be weight behind a blow, but if you're on the receiving end and can turn light as a feather for a split second, you avoid cuts and bruises. The great Muhammad Ali came close to this art, but despite all the rumors, he was no sorcerer. Since you're female, I hope you won't be getting into fights, but a spontaneous loss of weight serves well in other situations too. I'm thinking of the day when some likeable but not particularly athletic groom has to carry you across the threshold in front of everyone—you could really help him out. But control the dose. Some weight is always necessary. It becomes truly problematic in sports. In 1926, I was the best long jumper on the Telefunken staff because I made myself lighter in the last third of the jump and stayed in the air that tiny bit longer. Only a camera could have revealed it. Or a keen-eyed fellow sorcerer, but he would have said nothing. Today I'm ashamed of the medals I won.

As soon as you can lift off the ground and hover, practice in the woods where no one can see you, and if it's too windy, tie yourself to a long rope. Don't be too adventurous, watch out for power lines, windmills, and anything else you might get hung up on. You'd better wear trousers, too. If someone's after you and you need to get away quickly, don't try to ascend vertically if you haven't mastered that art yet. Nothing is more embarrassing than being grabbed by the feet and pulled back down. Play the track star instead and take off running!

Opinions differ on how best to reinforce your concentration when taking off. Some find it helps to flap their arms. I liked to pull on my nose with my right hand; my famous colleague Münchhausen did the same thing with his hair. Schneidebein had no talent for flying. He would flap hard and pull at anything he could, but he was always barely off the ground when he would wipe out and land on his butt—as pilots say.

Before I get to Flight proper, let me reemphasize one piece of advice: keep your magical powers under wraps, or more specifically, don't let anyone know it was you who cast a spell here or there. Make no exceptions, don't tell even your closest friend, unless he or she is a sorcerer. Don't get caught! Use Beauty, for example, in inconspicuous ways. If you really want to show how good you are, be the mysterious stranger, the unknown beauty never seen again. Always find a moment when no one's looking to use the Long Arm, never float when others can see you, and only fly late at night, or when you're sure you can make yourself invisible as well.

Of course, you can seem to be walking on water, but that's all just show, and fairly difficult as well, since you have to pretend you're walking while floating along. All that it does is let them know you're a sorceress. Nothing against small miracles now and then, but don't overdo it. In later years you can make a Madonna weep on occasion, or restore sight to the blind if you want, but stay in the background. People shouldn't revere you as a saint, they should simply imagine what it would be like if miracles were real—that's the right dose for their spiritual health and the only sensible reason to provide some kind of "miracle" now and then.

When humankind was still young and listened to us, we didn't need to hide ourselves. We gave advice openly, healed and consoled, led entire tribes. A word from us would dampen brawls, unless they were unavoidable. Back then people's brains were set up differently, leaving little room for self-determination. When they were deciding what to do, they listened only to their bodies and to their shamans. We led them like a shepherd leads his flock. We disguised the fact that sorcery was nothing but a rare gift, claiming we had special knowledge of what the spirit world desired. And we brewed magic potions. That was pure quackery, but also the beginning of medicine. And we murmured magic formulas, but that was just to keep our image up—all we really needed was to repeat them silently. In fact speaking them aloud hindered more than it helped.

Later we appeared in fairy tales, always with various magical implements, a sort of technology of the marvelous: lamps, rings, hats, tables that set themselves, genies in bottles, magic wands—all mere fiddle-faddle. And flying carpets only exist if you take a carpet along when you fly. Most people these days still believe there's magic inherent in physical objects (that's why they buy more stuff than they need). But only one object in the world is truly magical—the blanket on a bed. It can hold a person down against his will, even long after the alarm has gone off.

Our practice is a hidden one, no other course remains to

us in this day and age. So, dear Mathilda, never cast a spell so openly that people realize you made something strange happen. The things you do in front of others should never disturb normal reality. Everything must remain explicable to a middle school physics student. If that's not possible, operate behind closed doors or in the dark. Don't get involved in sorcery contests. Such affairs lead to carelessness. It's easy to forget that others are around, or how many are watching. If you ever wind up in jail (these things can happen) and you can already fly over walls or walk through them, do it only at night and return to your cell by early morning like a good girl. Some of my colleagues who spent years as political prisoners exited freely without the guards ever noticing. But they were patient and worked on more refined spells to gain their actual release. That went on till the government fell—always the best way to end a prison sentence.

While we're on the subject: it's both necessary and preferable to lead an ordinary, inconspicuous life. I didn't undertake my various professions simply because I enjoyed them—they were camouflage, too. If your neighbors think you're a person of substance you can own nice things or take long pleasure trips without arousing suspicion. Any standard, well-paid profession will do, one that doesn't require special abilities. I hate to say it, but, as a rule, those with the gift of sorcery (and I don't mean stage tricks) have no special genius in other areas like art or science. Very few of us have discovered or invented anything. The famous sorcerer Biro created the ballpoint pen and the scooter. I invented the Schacktograph and the satellite antennae navigation system (I'll explain both later). But we're often successful entrepreneurs: I'm thinking of the sorceress Clicquot-Ponsardin in the Champagne. For the rest, the power of sorcery itself is a sufficient gift. It's normal men and women who turn out to be shooting stars.

Now that I've retired, I run a bed and breakfast place, one that seems to make enough money to explain the expensive cruises I take. I enjoy it thoroughly—where else can a hundred-year-old man meet so many young people on a regular basis? And some of them are truly delightful: there was even a sorceress from China, and a promising young colleague from Venezuela, a dangerous place to live for someone who posed riddles to the authorities. I was able to teach the young man a few useful tricks—for example, how to use Switchclothes when being chased through a crowded square. I could do that at sixteen: suddenly someone else is wearing your clothes and you have on his. The agents arrest the wrong man and are forced to let him go. And they lose confidence in their own eyes, which is the best part.

Schlosseck drove home the fact that an experienced sorcerer needs a servant, someone who knows about sorcery, but does not have the gift himself and is thus no rival. A "number two man," so to speak, who provides whatever's needed, but with whom one can also discuss things. Such servants are rare, most people want to be number one. Schlosseck called all his series of servants "Wladimir." I called each of mine "Waldemar." One of them, Waldemar III, wrote a seafaring novel. I've "forgotten" their real names—which just means I won't reveal them.

Back to flying. As soon as you can float, you have to check which way the wind is blowing—always test that in advance. Don't be caught by surprise as I was the first time I tried to fly. I was practicing one morning in March when it was still dark enough. But I took too long getting a short distance off the ground. The eastern sky was brightening and a thunderstorm I hadn't noticed was rolling up in the west—who expects a storm so early in the day? A sudden squall lifted me high in the air and blew me a few kilometers to the southeast. I was terrified. The houses beneath me grew smaller and smaller, and before long I could see the Weissensee glittering in the morning light. I tried in vain to regain weight—

I was blown onward like a scrap of paper. Directly over the lake I was caught in a down draft, or perhaps my concentrated desire to land was taking delayed effect—in any case, I plunged toward the broad surface and must have lost consciousness, for I have no memory of a splash or being under water. All I know is that at some point two strong arms pulled me into a boat. The beach was still closed, but the lifeguard was an early riser and had seen my fall and set out in a rowboat in spite of the storm.

"How in the world did you get here—in a Zeppelin?" he asked, as he rowed back toward shore. I postponed my answer and focused on chattering my teeth. Mathilda, it's always important to prepare ready explanations for whatever might happen.

"A wind spout," I finally stammered. "It lifted me off my balcony and carried me away!"

"Where?"

"At home."

"I know that, kid, but where do you live?"

I decided on Berlin-Tegel. That seemed like a good place to set out on flights. In any case, I didn't want anyone in Pankow looking for me—they might find more than they expected. Moreover, I felt like boasting a bit and heightening the sensation of my first flight. That wasn't very bright of me.

"What a story for the newspaper!" the lifeguard cried, and wanted to telephone the morning edition of the *Berliner-Zeitung* right away. He gave me a towel and a bathrobe and said he was heading for a phone booth. *For heaven's sake, not in the newspaper!* I thought. I had to get away. The dear fellow had some sense of what he was doing: he'd locked me in. But he'd left the key in the lock and it was a door with slats—no problem for the Long Arm. I used Switchclothes and borrowed the outfit of a Weissensee newspaper boy for a quarter hour. I walked away calmly. Unfortunately, the spell didn't dry clothes—in spite of my changed appearance I was still soaking wet, but the rain was streaming down anyway. Walking along the street five minutes later I met the returning lifeguard, gave him a friendly nod, and handed him a dripping copy of the Berlin morning paper. I'll never forget his face.

It took me an hour to reach home, but I was happy and confident. Not only had I lifted off, I'd been high above the town, had seen city life from above. Anyone who's had that experience quickly develops high-flown plans.

Back to practical matters: flying is only worthwhile when you can keep to a particular course. But how? Not the way airplanes do, and not like Dumbo the Elephant, who uses his ears both as wings and to change direction. Flight functions in a totally different way for us. You ascend vertically as far as you can. That's 4000 meters at most, birds can fly much higher. Then you let yourself fall, holding your body flat while you concentrate on something you see below—you work with the magnetic attraction between your eyes and what you see. And what you see becomes your next goal— you fly by sight. Of course, you can glance around, but you always return your gaze to your goal. When you draw near it, switch your gaze to another goal you can glide toward. Hold your hands and arms like a ski jumper, as if they're small fixed wings. They aren't, of course, nor will they be, but any waggling or waving about will cause problems.

If you're floating or gliding but can't yet use Sight Mark (a strenuous spell) for longer periods of time, you'll have to make stopovers, rest your eyes, and then ascend vertically again. How long it takes to get from A to B is difficult to say. Count on a good three hours from Berlin to Munich, if it's nonstop. And always keep in mind that flying humans tend to be noticed. So if you can't make yourself invisible or shrink to the size of a bird, fly only at night. One further thing to keep in mind: other sorcerers sense that you're in flight, and if they know you personally, they'll almost certainly recognize you by your flight echo—every sorcerer's is unmistakable. So if you have a sorcerer for an enemy, you're in danger while flying: if you're not too far away, he can locate you precisely.

A word about things you might want to carry along: they can't be made smaller. Medications, cell phones, and food all have to be taken with you, so decide in advance what you need most. If you have to deliver tools or weapons to someone, don't overload yourself. Make several flights and carry one thing at a time. If at all possible, take nothing for yourself. When I flew out of the deathtrap on the Volga during the war, supplies wouldn't have saved me—on the contrary, I would never have made it that far with the extra weight. I had to find everything as I went along, nor could I fly very high, due to the cold. But the ability to rise into the air, the escape into the broad countryside, was one of the greatest moments of freedom in my life. Stars, clouds, forests, animals, and the hope of finding those who would help me—it seemed like returning from hell to the dawn of creation. The feeling of happiness didn't last long, in part because the frost was already creeping into my bones. Later on my flight home I lost years of my life to a Heisterbach Time Crack, an as yet unexplained misfortune to which sorcerers are susceptible only in flight. It's rare, but I should mention it. We drop out of time in the midst of flight—time goes on without us, we remain behind without noticing. It's like a long sleep. When we come to ourselves again a great deal has happened, to us as well, but we were not there, we didn't experience it. It may be a matter of months, years, or, in extreme cases, even centuries. One no longer recognizes the world, or is recognized by it. In my case, I got off fairly lightly with a loss of two years. Schlosseck was familiar with this danger; he called it "The Monk of Heisterbach Effect," after a poem from the Romantic period that he recited by heart with obvious pleasure. I have a theory, by the way, as to when and why this misfortune strikes us—but I'll wait to tell you about it when we come to the war. For now, I'd rather stay in the twenties, when I was still as wonderfully young as the person reading this now.

Flying gives a tremendous sense of freedom; it fulfills one of humankind's greatest dreams. Those trapped behind walls and barbed wire are not the only ones longing to fly up and away, it's the dream of the young who wish to leave their family homes behind, who long to spread their wings like strong young birds. In my day, boys were more eager to do this than girls, mostly because of disagreements with their fathers—but perhaps that's changed in the meantime.

My father died before I reached the age of rebellion. But my mother had to put up with a few things on my part, though I tried to be a good son. Young sorcerers, and as I am well aware, young sorceresses, too, are often extremely difficult because they can't talk about their special gifts—it would only worry their parents. They would think their child was crazy.

I remember my dear Indian father with nothing but gratitude. He was so different from all the other fathers. He wanted me to be independent; he wanted a son who knew how to take care of himself, who didn't ask others what to do and then blame them if things went wrong. I remember how he taught me to swim: he held me above water briefly, then let go. As I yelled and flailed about, he swam backward and watched me calmly. I couldn't sink because I was wearing a cork-lined vest, and he stayed close by. I was still scared, but I understood his look: "Sometimes there's no one else there and you have to deal with things on your own. That's what you're feeling now. Learn to live with it, learn to swim!" He didn't need to say a word, it was all in his kind, solemn gaze. I became a good swimmer, too, and never had to conjure up an invisible lifebuoy. Schlosseck had nothing to teach me in

50

this area—he feared water like a cat. Even as a crocodile, he was afraid to get his feet wet.

Before I start the next letter about love, I'd like to add a few lines on how to recognize colleagues. Our art is and must remain secret, for the State still searches for us and keeps track of us with increasingly refined methods. But secrecy makes it harder for us to find each other.

There are a few qualities, habits, even certain sensitivities that most sorcerers share. I'm thinking of the way we close our eyes almost every time we shift our gaze, or our dislike of nutmeg. But such things alone don't serve as means of recognition. In each individual case, it takes an active personal effort to be sure he or she is one of us. That can be done with small magical effects only we notice. After all, our greatest strength is our close attention to things. A sorcerer notices if the sugar bowl is suddenly half a centimeter closer to your cup. A normal person believes in the unreliability of sense perceptions, and his brain immediately suppresses what he's just seen. A sorcerer responds with a small signal in return. He pours a little cream in his coffee, for example, without tipping the little canister. It's important that none of the signals repeat each other. Invent a new one each time. When agents are looking for us, they're fixated on their checklists and only recognize what's listed. Security cameras can be an annoyance, of course, but even then the video would have to be examined frame by frame. But that doesn't happen if your magic signal is small and inconspicuous. Never try to impress the person you're with by some sensational trick or other—you can do that later when you're sure. When you've recognized each other as sorcerers, turn off your cell phones and go for a walk. One of the deeper purposes of a park is to allow you to converse freely.

I don't know if I've already mentioned St. Polykarp—and I don't want to leaf back a long way to see right now. So forgive me if I've already written this, I'm a bit scatterbrained at times. At any rate, there was a monastic library at St. Polykarp that held a famous collection of early cookbooks with ancient recipes and other mysteries no longer known outside its walls. You have no idea what a revelation a Gugelhupf marble cake or a cap of rump is when it's prepared according to a recipe from Bachstelz's book *Complete Instructions in the Art of Cookery for the Noble and Upper Class Dining Table*, published in Munich in 1858. But the interesting thing about these cookbooks was that they included between the lines magical instructions that only we could read, and detailed the experiences and experiments of our colleagues through the centuries. Sorcery includes research of a sort, simply because our greatest masters wished to discover if even more powerful magic was possible. Read correctly, Bachstelz's cookbook also reveals his major thoughts on how magic might alter the entire course of history, alter it after the fact, mind you. One may reject such ideas—modesty has its place after all. But Bachstelz, disguised as a nondescript, obsequious chef in the royal Bavarian court, took a position as sorcerer and philosopher that these days we might call "thinking big"—he took a daring stand. You should definitely read him some day. In my opinion, altering even small details of past history is prohibitively difficult. I'm relatively certain that even if the great Bachstelz had lived longer, he could never have done so.

Dear Mathilda, I've just reread what I've written. My admonitions and suggestions are somewhat copious, but please be patient with me. Take what you can use and treat the rest with good humor. All I hope is this: if one day you face your century as a successful woman, and perhaps even help shape it, it would please me, even if I am dead, to have offered a few words of helpful advice.

I've just returned from Scotland, where I finally met my colleague Rejlander. She's making a movie with your father playing the lead, but I've already told you that. She's something else as a director. She's the smartest woman I've ever met, not counting your mother and Emma. She's also beautiful, and even her voice delights me.

The producer invited the entire team to a restaurant in Glasgow, and asked me to join them. I sat with Iris, the make-up artist, and Stephan, the sound man. They struck me as newly in love. For my part, I couldn't take my eyes off Rejlander. I think I may be in love, too. For someone 106 years old that probably sounds a bit unusual, but what do people know about sorcerers anyway?

When Waldemar III introduced us, he said, "You've seen this little one before, Herr Pahroc." This little one? I had no idea what he meant, but she helped me out:

"When we first met, you were Uncle Boom-Boom."

As a little girl in the seventies, Rejlander had played a role in a film for which I provided the pyrotechnics of a splendid First World War. Waldemar III told her how I'd learned to play the piano at ninety, so she asked me to play something for her. The hotel even had a well-tuned grand piano. She acted delighted, and I may indeed have impressed her a little. Then we spoke about you at some length—after all, that was the point of our meeting.

So: Rejlander will come to Berlin at some time and look you over. You won't get much out of it at first, you'll only get to know her properly later on. You'll surely come to like her. She's promised to train you in sorcery, and by the time you read this that will be long underway.

I took a plane to Glasgow, since I wasn't about to wear myself out flying solo across the waters. I'll leave that to sorcerers like old Henry Grund, who's nuts about sports. But I do wonder who he thinks will praise him for it—he'll never make the newspapers that way, no matter how many times he's crossed the Atlantic.

FINDING LOVE

January 2013

The thing I loved most in life (next to your grandmother) was electricity. As a young man I was more curious about benefits and research in this area than I was about sorcery. Someone who masters sorcery has little need for mechanical aids. But I was attracted by anything new in technology. To this was added my inclination toward socialist ideas. I imagined a world in which technology rendered war unnecessary, brought nations together, and eliminated most of our ills. But my appetite for technological progress outlasted my desire for a classless society.

These days I'm thankful, for example, for a fitted hearing aid that allows me to distinguish between the sound of *s* and *f.* I don't have to cup my hand behind my ear, I don't have to maintain an audio spell for the whole of a concert, or struggle constantly with an ear trumpet. Those could still be seen after the Second World War, tin funnels that channeled sound into your ear.

There are so many reasons to be thankful for technology, and in particular for electronic devices. I just don't understand people who make use of these magnificent aids and still claim morosely that things were better in the old days.

Machines, engines and automobiles, dirigibles and air-planes, the telegraph and all things electrical, that was the new world in those days, the brighter future. All we young boys were crazy about technology, including Jakob from Ein-trachtstrasse, but I was most of all. I wanted to be an "elec-trician." The very concept seemed magnificent, filled with promise. To anyone who would listen, or even to those who wouldn't, I would explain Ohm's Law, the difference between voltage and amperage, low and high voltage current, alter-nate and direct current. I even tried to convince my master Schlosseck of the magical qualities of radio technology: Braun tubes, amplitude modulation, Thomas Alva Edison, and the USA, the land of unlimited opportunities. At some point he called for his dog—not to sic him on me, but to throw him a ball. He praised Ulf warmly and at length each time he brought the ball back—he'd simply heard enough from me.

Other new areas of sorcery were, in fact, opening up to me, such as the Credibility spell, but that one went against my grain. I couldn't imagine feeling good lying, even if some-one believed me. That's generally how it is when you're young—and you should remain young as long as possible.

After graduating from high school, I was taken on as an unpaid intern at Telefunken. I underwent basic training first, which I didn't really need, since I'd already taught myself soldering, wiring, and gauging. After being shocked a few times, I even learned to unplug an appliance before repair-ing it. A totally new concept was the assembly line—it didn't reflect my vision of human freedom, but I hoped to eventu-ally work my way up to departments where such ideas were sought. In the evening, after work, I was my own electrical apprentice, or even engineer: I constructed a modulator re-ceiver and listened in on the outside world. By the light of a battery lamp I'd built myself, I read everything I could bor-row from the Pankow library about electrification, radio, broadcasting technology, and all sorts of other technical areas. It was a good thing I'd finally learned from Schlosseck how to read books more quickly than normal by placing two fingers on their spines to master their contents.

I also tried my hand at inventions. Unlike most sorcerers, I've never needed much sleep, but I've always enjoyed lying in bed mornings, thinking about things. That often drew me back into the realm of dreams, so that I was rated the tardiest intern at the firm, but also the most eager to learn and the quickest to understand. So not only was I kept on, but I was soon functioning as a quality-test engineer. I inspected gramophones and records all day long—they even flooded my dreams at night. Records were made of shellac back then, which in turn was prepared from a resin secreted by lac bugs from the Philippines. I couldn't imagine how those tiny insects could secrete enough raw material for millions of records, how there could be so many of them, and a sufficient number of people to gather the resin. Lac bugs filled my dreams. They were the size of oxen and shat shellac without end.

My stay at Telefunken was pleasant. They valued me; they even paid for my studies at the technical university. That's what I call a good employer. "Graduate Engineer" is the only title in life that I actually earned, by the way, even though it didn't take that long. All my other titles were conjured.

My natural inclination to meet new girls was hampered somewhat by the urge I felt to study day and night. I didn't have a single female friend in 1926. The only pleasure I indulged in other than learning was singing along with others. I'd met a young man sitting on a bench in the castle park who sang Russian songs. He'd come to Berlin with a young woman named Alissa, but they were apparently just friends, not a couple. Both were from the wrong class in revolutionary Russia. Sergej's parents had been shot, Alissa's stripped of their property and forced into exile. They lived on Neue Schönholzer Strasse, near my former school, sang Russian songs together, and learned German ones too. Alissa even played the balalaika. I chipped in as well: I'd learned all I needed to know about sound recording by then, so I could repair their record player and, with my Long Arm, provide the foundation for Sergej's famous record collection. I couldn't read music back then as well as I do now, but I had a good voice and ear. I played a few records over and over and tried to sing along. I was at my best with "I Kiss Your Hand, Madame." Sergej's German wasn't very good yet, but Alissa spoke it almost perfectly. We discussed politics once, but soon dropped the topic. I sympathized at the time with Lenin's phrase "Communism is Soviet power plus electrification," but preferred not to say so to Alissa, the victim of the revolution.

One summer evening I accompanied Sergej, Alissa, and Jakob from Eintrachtstrasse, no longer little but now tall, to a dance at the city park pavilion, something I rarely did otherwise. We ran into Schneidebein there, who'd arrived with a very young redhead named Emma von Schroffenstein. She came from the nobility, and there was something noble, even eternal, about her beauty. She seemed to have stepped out of a Renaissance painting. I wondered how Schneidebein had managed to meet someone like her. But he was crazy about the nobility in those days (and later too) and did all he could to break into their circles. He probably didn't know why himself. Incidentally, he collected beautiful women like trophies. He'd made himself as handsome as possible with spells— at first I hardly recognized him. But he danced worse than ever. He could just manage a waltz, but he looked like someone badly in need of a restroom when doing the Charleston. I talked all evening about America, the land of dreams and technology, and my father's homeland. Those rhapsodic flights may have strengthened Alissa's decision to go to America. She worked as a screenwriter in Hollywood, married an American, and to top it all off became a famous writer. In the music pavilion, she asked me sternly if I planned to just talk and not dance.

Since we were all sitting at the same table, I asked Schneidebein's companion if she'd like to dance too. She was very young, at least five years younger than me, and she carried herself well. But the truly remarkable thing about her was her voice: it was unbelievable, stunning—to me. It's strange: a voice can electrify a person like nothing else without being what's called a "beautiful voice." It needn't be melodic or darkly pleasing, it can even be squeaky. Yet it's still the one voice that awakens a deep resonance in another person. Her entire being strikes him as open and generous, her smile sincere and enchanting. He can't help it—he wants to be near her forever. Was Emma truly a beauty? She was to me, at any rate, and to Schneidebein. It was her voice that drew me, that forced me to forget everything else. I didn't want to at first, in fact, I tried my best not to look at her too often, but her attraction was far too strong for me to resist.

It was easy to spirit her away from my old rival. She had long since realized that she would simply be one more trophy in his collection. He got quite angry with me, but that didn't bother me in the least. Within a few days, Emma and I had become inseparable. We planned to grow old together, but to postpone that part as far as possible into the future. Why, why? Love needs no justification.

Emma's father, Count Schroffenstein, had married a commoner, Dorothea Haidle. Perhaps that's why he was so understanding when we fell head over heels in love. He found my Indian heritage interesting and me sufficiently likeable. One day he showed me the von Schroffenstein family tree and the Haidles' too. The latter included a name I actually knew—Bachstelz! Not only was Emma descended from Swabian robber barons, but from the personal chef of the Royal Bavarian Court as well, a man to whom I myself was distantly related on my mother's side. I mention this because you should know the few sorcerers in your family background: Bachstelz, Emma, myself, and you. That's all there are—the list is a short one. The gift of sorcery does not come through one's family, it arrives like an escaped parakeet from some other realm.

By the way, I didn't know at the time that Bachstelz was a sorcerer. And at first I was equally unaware that Emma was. I only knew that her strange birdlike voice set something profound in motion within me. I soon loved that voice more than anything borne to me on the airwaves, more than the words and sounds that reached me from short, medium, and long wave radio stations at Vox-Haus, Nauen, or Norddeich. Not even the maritime weather reports from Newfoundland could delight me so.

Your voice, too, awakens something in me, although in a different way. Mathilda, you have the most beautiful voice since Emma and Rejlander. Yesterday you said, "Opa!" That told me right away that you are intelligent enough to see to whom to turn for what you need. I've been called Opa by so many grandchildren I can't remember all their names. But that word from you filled me with tenderness; it spread so intensely that I passed by the elevator and took the stairs instead—two at time! I haven't done that in decades. You cast a spell without my help, a greater charm.

Not long ago, I tried using voice recognition software to write because I'd pinched my right hand installing a satellite dish. I spoke aloud and Notebook reproduced what it thought I had said. But the result made so little sense I had to laugh—and now I've gone back to writing by hand. By the time you're grown the programs will no doubt work better. And there will be endless new things—I would so like to know what. The *Curiosity* landed on Mars not long ago and took photos. I'd like to know if colonies were actually established on Mars, which the current reckoning places around 2036. I'd like to live to see solar panels that produce a hundred times more energy than today's, and rechargeable batteries that are much lighter and longer lasting. I'd like to know about advances in processors, and how fast chips can become. In your era, Mathilda, life will be much easier, unimaginably easier in present day terms. I learned only a few years ago how the World Wide Web works, and only recently saw my first 3D printer—I still find it creepy, but it fascinates me. So many people miss this pleasure, they don't even know what goes on inside a TV set, and see digitalization in general as the work of the devil. What algorithms are, how The Cloud works—Terra Incognita. And if they're told medical telemonitoring might help keep them alive, the first thing they want to know is: is that really legal? Far too many try to stand up to technological civilization by despising and ignoring it. But I say do your best to learn how to use it, understand it, deal with it. Then if you still have objections, at least they'll be well-founded.

I love technology, even though I see the sacrifices it entails. For its sake we have to say farewell to much that was familiar. It's true I've grown more skeptical too, given the stupidity and devilry that positively swirls in the midst of innovation's splendor. I no longer have the same faith in technology I had as a young man—that's due in large part to the war.

But back then, in the twenties, I was a true missionary for all things technical. I tried to explain to Emma's parents at dinner the blessings that would flow from the Hollerith electrical punch-card tabulating system—it would revolutionize the entire administrative world. When that failed to send them into transports of joy, I told them all about the radio: rectifiers, resistance, transformers, variable capacitors. I got nowhere until dessert, when I came to the railroad's electrical signaling system. That prompted Emma's father to ask if I could repair the bell they used in the Schroffenstein household to call the maid. It took me only a minute to fix it, at which point he offered me cigars, cognac, and continued conversation on a first name basis (his was Pankraz, as I'm sure you know). To shine even brighter following the cognac, I shared with him an idea I had for a new enterprise. Because I found Emma's voice so beautiful, I wanted to record it electrically. My device would be similar to Edison's Phonograph, but you could make your own recording on a disk of hard wax (there were no tape recorders yet, let alone computers to record with). From there I could go into mass production. I'd picked out a name for the machine: the Schallograph. In fact, working nights, I had produced a prototype that functioned fairly well. My invention wasn't totally new, but it opened Count von Schroffenstein's ears and heart to me.

"Make your own recordings—that could be a real winner. Lovers would immortalize the voice of their beloved, young fathers catch their child's first cry. It's an invention with a great future, like photography was."

He said he'd start a company immediately and finance the development of the recording device, if only—yes, if only he had the money. Unfortunately, ancient nobility did not protect one from poverty. After the inflation he was, for all practical purposes, broke. But he recommended me to another Count by the name of Schack von Wittenau who was still well off and who was willing to step in on the condition that the device be named the Schacktograph instead of Schallograph. I went along, although I'd already been thinking of calling it the Emmagraph.

It was all fine with me, as long as I could keep tinkering around with it and strike the Schroffensteins as a young man with good prospects while doing so. For one thing had long since become clear to me: I wanted to spend my life with Emma and to support her accordingly. A solid position as an engineer at Telefunken was still a long way off, so I set my hopes, and that of others, on a bright future as a manufacturer.

I still haven't told you how Emma and I finally realized that we were sorcerers, something neither of us knew at first. I stumbled over the root of a tree one evening in the fading twilight. Emma gave a frightened cry and tried to keep me from falling by grabbing my belt. But at that very moment I reduced my weight by fifty kilos to avoid a hard fall. To her astonishment, Emma not only kept me from falling, but jerked me up in the air and set me back down again like an empty cardboard box. I was sure she'd be frightened and find it uncanny. We walked on a while in silent thought. Then she said:

"I can do that too."

"Do what?"

Instead of answering she took a small running start, leaped into the air, and grabbed the branch of a birch tree almost three meters off the ground. I clearly saw her leap merge into floating flight. She swung on the branch a moment or two, then let go and, light as a feather, floated down into my outstretched arms.

"I'll be damned," I said.

"That's nice," she replied.

"What?"

"That we can talk about it now."

"Yes, that's wonderful."

She restored her normal weight, we followed the path on through the woods in silence, and we both knew that the life we were to share would never be boring.

The times weren't boring back then either, but sadly they were far from peaceful. There was dancing and jazz, research and witty arguments. But for many that wasn't exciting enough—they longed for battle. They swarmed forth in countless numbers, bursting with the desire to attack something—to stir things up even more. They were constantly discussing guilt, whose fault this all was. Who started the war, who was responsible for the way it ended, whose fault it was another war was coming. And everywhere the word humiliation, the humiliation of our fathers, that must be expunged and revenged—but revenged how and against whom? Against anyone not of one's own party. And anyone who was, but was a "traitor." The wheel of history had to be reversed. But only sorcerers can do that, and then only with the strongest misgivings. Those furious men, young and old alike, thought they could do it too. How? By building up armaments and a particular form of fanatic belief. I heard the slogan "final victory" for the first time. It meant that the loss of the First World War could be annulled by a second, victorious one, if one only believed more firmly this time. But the vast majority didn't think that way. They went along with anything that cost them nothing, but war and death weren't in that category.

Emma and I weren't too worried about all that. When we heard hoarse shouts in the streets we closed the windows and withdrew to the place whose magic was stronger than any uprising—our bed.

Love craftily resists the question Why (and thus can never be digitized). Anyone who tries to explain why he loves someone winds up tongue-tied. I didn't even try. Sorcerers know what they can't do, and electricians avoid the illogical. All I knew back then was that I wanted to hear Emma's voice for the rest of my life, and watch her move about each day. The way she poured tea, or picked something up, or stepped down from the tram! The word "grace" comes to mind—because it's not used often, and for Emma only rarely-used words seem appropriate. Grace: that's a magic words can't describe. All the poets who've tried didn't know Emma.

I've read that fish and birds have a special sense organ that allows them to move in unison with a school or flock.

Since I've often turned myself into a flock of birds in my old age, I can confirm that fact. Love provides something quite similar—an invisible bond, perhaps even an electrical path from brain to brain. I always knew immediately what Emma was going to say. Of course I never interrupted her, because I loved to hear her voice. If our voices hadn't been the purest music to each other, we would hardly have spoken—we sensed almost everything wordlessly.

If you expected this letter to describe some magic method to find the right person, a Search spell that would lead infallibly to the great love of your life, I'm afraid it won't. I don't want to discuss things that don't exist, that would be irresponsible. And there's no point in applying all sorts of filters to find the ideal person. Someone who's searching seldom finds the right person—he's too busy searching. The one who finds doesn't search, or not for very long. Love comes to him and he recognizes it.

Of course there are spells that can be employed in the general vicinity of love—I'm sure you've learned some of them. But they're not guaranteed to bring you any closer to your own great love.

The man or woman of your life: that gift comes from a place where our sort don't have much to say. And love can do something no sorcerer can: turn someone into a better person. You can turn yourself or someone else into a crocodile, but you can't make them good or even trustworthy. Love can. Someone who has richly received gladly returns a portion of those riches later—to others.

Nearly every person to whom you speak may offer that most important gift. Don't exclude anyone! Love, true love, sweeps aside preconceived criteria. And listen to a person's voice. They don't necessarily have to know how to sing. Great love exists for the unmusical too—and for those who are never lucky.

In the spring of 1931 we moved into a rundown apartment at the back of a building on Breitenbachstrasse and fixed it up ourselves. I fixed the wiring, the plumbing, and the lock on the door. Emma would gladly have papered the walls and painted, but she was several months pregnant at the time, so she cast everything on the walls with a spell and was finished before I was. She said she'd be glad to explain the trick to me in more detail, and she did. Those were spells I hadn't learned from Schlosseck, since he neither needed nor liked them. He was passionate about employing others, not doing things himself. He would call workers in, then sit down and watch them work. If one of them dropped a tool, he'd catch it in midair with the Long Arm and hand it back to the surprised worker, saying something like, "There it goes again—gravity!" Then he would continue watching, taking pleasure in every small mistake. When I witnessed this, I knew why he'd turned himself into a crocodile back then: he was one! But by far the kindest and most helpful of all vertebrates to me.

There was one point on which Emma and I could never reach a peaceful agreement, despite all our efforts at compromise: the room temperature was always too low for her and too high for me. When I was warm, she was freezing. When she was warm, I had to flee. But since I seemed like an oven to her, she followed to be near me. Her need to be entwined was insatiable, only reptiles seem to have a similar need. Even in movie theaters, we sat with our arms wrapped around each other, and not just at *S.O.S. Iceberg*, where you could get cold just watching.

We went to the movies three or four times a week. We knew at once, without speaking, if we liked the film or were ready to leave. We soon had seen so many unforgettable films that on certain evenings we would settle on a title and watch the film together in our heads. No conversation was necessary, nothing could be heard but our shared laughter or perhaps an occasional remark like, "Wait, you've left out the Indian attack!"

We did not get engaged, because I declared it a feudal, bourgeois, unnecessary, illogical, and moreover, un-Indian custom. "Anything but a reactionary!" I said. Emma agreed, but not from any sense of obedience. Her opinions were modern and progressive, perhaps precisely because she'd attended a domestic science school and not one for the humanities. Papa Schroffenstein had intended for her to make a good marriage. That's how the nobility are, especially the impoverished ones. So he had no objections to our love—how could he? He was a great believer in miraculous inventions and already envisioned me—because of the Schacktograph, which didn't exist yet—as a well-to-do industrialist.

Emma liked beautiful things. She loved porcelain dishes, jewelry, mother-of-pearl boxes, brass containers, anything that was finely wrought and delicate. I bought the samovar that Sergej had brought along with him, although I had barely any money myself. That enabled him to go to France—he no longer felt politically comfortable in Berlin. Emma loved the samovar, but she said when times were better we should give it back to Sergej—after all, it was the only piece he still had from his parents.

Life wasn't easy in those days, even for people with our abilities. I wasn't able to conjure money yet—that would have helped. Emma was younger, so she was even further behind than I was. I think it's unfair that that spell develops at such a late date in life. You need money most when your family is young. But old Schlosseck was still there. He helped us, just as he had helped my mother. Of course, I had to go to him— he no longer left his house, because of the rabble, as he put it. There were marches in Pankow like everywhere else. The democracy, forced to defend itself against the marchers, was becoming increasingly undemocratic itself. Its enemy, mostly fat fellows in jodhpurs who'd never been near a horse, were more brutal than the State dared to be, for it remained, with some effort, guided by its laws. So there it stood, in properly regulated helplessness, dignified to the end.

A young art historian by the name of Kusenberg lived in our neighborhood. He wrote articles for the newspapers now and then about exhibitions and auctions. He not only knew the names of all the artists who'd painted the pictures, he also sensed that we were sorcerers—how I don't know, for he wasn't one himself. At any rate, after having had tea with us one day, he wrote a very realistic story about a quarrel between two sorcerers named Pahroc and Schneidebein. He read it aloud to us the following week. I was shocked at first— I knew I'd said nothing about sorcery and had only mentioned Schneidebein in passing as a schoolmate. I liked the story, since Pahroc was portrayed as the nicer of the two sorcerers. The idea that the story might be published some day warmed my heart. Nevertheless, I asked him not to do so, and explained that it might cause harm and that it came dangerously near to reality. Then I told him everything, which I could do because he moved in a different world than I did and was completely trustworthy. A few years later I actually encouraged him to put the story in his book, since I hoped it would annoy Schneidebein. Kusenberg did so, changing my name a little, of course, and ended the story on a conciliatory note.

That, in part, led me to learn the Name Eradication spell. It guarantees that other people will forget your name. If they ask you again, you tell them and they forget it again. I used it later with my first name—many sorcerers do. No one on earth knows my first name now. It's in my papers, my will, everywhere. Everyone thinks they know it—as long as no one asks them. But when they have to repeat it or write it—it's gone! "And your first name was . . . ? Oh, just write it down yourself, please." I've written it in by hand on thousands of forms and lists. Computers either don't react to sorcery at all, or they crash, so my first name causes me less trouble these days than ever. I'd like to know what they'll carve on the tombstone I'll share with Emma in Luisenfriedhof. Some spells outlast the death of the spell caster, others don't. In my case, I'm not sure.

Schlosseck started in again urging me to get a servant. Sorcery was hard work and required extra sleep. It made you absent minded, too, so you needed someone loyal to handle your everyday affairs. You couldn't ask a wife to do it, certainly not if she was a sorceress herself. A good servant protects his master, but is also protected by him. He will never betray you, looks up to you, makes personal sacrifices for you, handles your problems, knows everything, will do anything, and in return is loved only with reserve—the relationship must remain business-like. Emotions or rivalry are out of the question, they would poison everything. A servant who can't abide serving, who conceals envy or even hate behind his servile façade, is more dangerous than helpful.

I looked far and wide and found no one who fulfilled all these criteria. Kusenberg was aware of our sorcery and was an independent fellow, but he couldn't take on the position. He was in love with Emma, more so than he wished to admit, even to himself. A sorcerer's servant constantly thinking about his master's wife was unthinkable. He would have suffered and so would we. It was a good thing we had no money—servants have to be paid.

We finally married to prevent our first child from being born out of wedlock. This struck me as a narrow bourgeois perspective, but Emma felt we couldn't just set aside all social conventions—we'd always have to be explaining why we did so. The wedding was very churchy, very noble, and terribly expensive, but I was now widely considered to be an ambitious young entrepreneur and a good match. My mother was moved more by our love than by the ceremony, but when von Schroffenstein called his fellow father-in-law, John Pahroc, a German patriot who, had he not fallen at Douaumont, would surely have enjoyed that day, she both laughed and cried. My dear, wonderful mother! She was not intimidated by these fine people. Anyone brave enough to marry a dancing Indian had no fear of a few nobles around a wedding table. She found most of them "basically nice people," but she couldn't say they danced any better than ordinary folk. She was unreservedly delighted by Emma and offered her advice, which Emma accepted with tactful good will. After the first glass of champagne, for example, she revealed that under proper guidance, I would turn out to be quite a good boy.

Schlosseck was also among the wedding guests. He didn't say much, the only person he exchanged more than a few words with was Count Schack von Wittenau, about technology, of all things. It must have been what these days we call "a frank discussion" in politics, one that grows increasingly heated. He preferred dancing with the bride at that point. Up to that time I had only introduced her to him briefly, and as they danced he realized that she was a sorceress. Of course, I had already told her that he was my mentor. They sat together afterwards while I danced, mostly with my mother. Not long after, Emma told me what Schlosseck had said to her—that with proper guidance I would turn out to be a good boy, and that he hoped love would serve to dampen my questionable infatuation with technology.

After the wedding, he said of Emma: "She's fantastic!" He was particularly pleased that she read so much and with such pleasure, and that she preferred to do so in the normal way, rather than with two fingers on the book's spine.

He took the occasion to remind me again to seek a servant. I replied that there was a financial crisis, I'd been laid off Telefunken, I was getting nowhere with my invention, and everyone was flat broke now. My only source of income was repairing radios. He shook his head.

"Do you want to be a sorcerer or not? Without a servant you'll have to deal with banal, everyday matters, surely you see that. Do something to make some money. Go to work for someone who's rich and getting richer. Market your ideas, write a book, a bestseller like Karl May or Karl Marx. Or give flying lessons, if you have to."

Flying lessons! That sounded like a good idea, something technical. I studied everything about mechanical flight, passed all the exams, and was soon chauffeuring a Düsseldorf millionaire through the air. He planned to invest heavily in transforming the old Germany into a brand new one. Fortunately he didn't mention politics.

So I earned enough money to hire a servant after all, and found a clever, modest young man I trusted named Waldemar. I was even able to buy a house in Frohnau that I hoped my mother would move into later.

I was often away from Emma for days at a time now, but that didn't bother her. She knew I would survive any crash. Once the contraption did take a dive—a prop on one of the wings gave out, pure bad luck. My parachute failed to open, but it didn't matter. I floated for a while till I spotted a wagon loaded with hay. I used it to explain to eye witnesses why I hadn't died from the impact. The millionaire floated down gently, too—his parachute had opened.

So things were going fairly well for us after all as the thirties began. Waldemar was a great help because he understood legal matters, could fill out tax returns, and wasn't a bad liar, either. He didn't lie to me, of course, only to my enemies. He saw at once how important secrecy and camouflage were to a sorcerer, especially in those days.

I noticed that Schneidebein had also had a servant for some time, more than one, in fact. He was deeply involved with administration in the party of arms raised stiffly in salute, and he had three servants. They all looked alike, which was reinforced by their pale brown uniforms, and their names all started with "H," so I didn't consider them separate individuals. To me, they were Schneidebein's "HamHamHam."

A frightening number of people had voted for Schneidebein's party in the recent elections. He urged me to join the Party, he could put in a good word for me, and the Party was well supplied, thanks to major industrial donations. He said he'd been making himself useful to them for some time, as an informer and investigator—of course his fellow party members had no idea about his hidden skills. I could tell it was Emma he was interested in. Perhaps he wanted to get back in her favor, although she was now married and no longer among the nobility. Her beauty attracted him, and the fact that she was a sorceress. I felt he would gladly take her over, together with our son. Little Felix was already on the scene by that time, your uncle (whom you won't ever know, he died twelve years ago). Schneidebein pawed the little boy awkwardly. Felix didn't like it at all and started crying. Meanwhile, Schneidebein was talking like a waterfall about the New Germany and the "Gleichschaltung" of businesses, associations, and administrations.

"What does that mean?" I asked.

"Come on, who's the electrician here?" he replied. "Surely you know what 'Gleichschaltung' means!"

"Never heard of it. Do you mean a parallel connection? Or switching from alternating to direct current?"

He got annoyed and growled something about petty objections. Gleichschaltung was a matter of bringing everything in line with the Party. I could still become a member. Once the Party was in power it would be more difficult to get in.

"Just drop it, Schneidebein."

"Listen, you'll be contributing to Germany's salvation."

"I would like to do that, truly."

"Well, then!"

"But at the moment, that means saving it from you people, Schneidebein."

"Well look here, that's very interesting. The gentleman objects to pulling the cart out of the mud. He's comfortable in the old swamp and filth. Fine then! I just wanted to help you, but I won't repeat my offer, you can be sure of that!"

He stood up, clicked his heels, and shot an arm into the air. I stayed seated and looked at him in as friendly a manner as I could muster.

"Ludolf, thank you!" I said. "I'm truly grateful for your good intentions."

I called him by his first name, something sorcerers never do among themselves except when they're children. It was no accident, for I could no longer respect him as a colleague. I'd hoped to conceal the way I felt, but he understood at once and alas made a note of it.

When I recounted this conversation to Schlosseck, he grimaced with disgust. "He's eager to join those filthy manservants," he said. "I could see it coming when he was ten years old."

Filthy manservants! Only an arch conservative could use such a phrase, but it was a deeply felt insult.

I couldn't stand the stiff-armed enthusiasts either, and I was worried that their idol, the man with the square little mustache, might be named chancellor. And indeed he was: Reichspräsident Hindenburg, whose resemblance to the wooden statue on Königsplatz had increased over time, appointed the shady character to run the government. I had to fly my millionaire to Potsdam to take part in a national celebration. He invited me to come along with him—a high but doubtful honor. The high point of the celebration came when the elderly wooden giant descended alone into the crypt of the Hohenzollerns to converse with the spirit of Prussia. Since Prussia had been dissolved politically a few months earlier, this was the only way this conversation could take place. After a brief but no doubt lively conversation, Hindenburg ascended again to greet several important gentlemen. The new Chancellor stood ready among them. Recalling a trick I'd played on Schneidebein when we were in school, I used the Long Arm so quickly no one saw a thing. As the two were shaking hands, the following exchange was heard:

Hindenburg: "Why are you running around like that, man?"

"What do you mean, Herr Reichspräsident?"

"Take a look down."

At that moment, a camera clicked. You'll find that famous image in your schoolbooks or on the internet. Of course, it doesn't show the embarrassing sight the shady character always thereafter associated with "Potsdam Day"—his unbuttoned fly. To be on the safe side, he kept his hands clasped over the troublesome spot on all future official occasions.

I was a little too sure that no one would notice my prank. As I opened my eyes again—having disguised my snort of laughter as a sneeze—I met a sharp look. Schneidebein was there and had seen everything. The only reason I wasn't arrested immediately was that denouncing me as a sorcerer would probably have blown his own cover. But he must have poisoned the well with my millionaire boss, for I was let go from one day to the next on some flimsy pretext.

Schlosseck had to keep out of sight. The fanatics claimed he belonged to a noxious race. They let Jakob know that too— Jakob from Eintrachtstrasse, though he was over six feet tall with incurably blonde hair.

I was working as an electrical engineer again, at Deho-mag, Deutsche Hollerith Maschinen GmbH, in Lichterfelde Ost. It was an American firm. To disguise that fact some-what, the business operated in the distinctly "new" fashion, with clicking boots, jagged salutes, and a barracks room at-mosphere at company meetings. The political "Gleichschal-tung" Schneidebein had been going on about was now in full swing.

I was a great admirer of the punch-card tabulating sys-tem, and I read all I could about it, including its history and inventor. In the *Hollerith Messenger* I ran across the following: "Human thought ends the moment the cards are punched. Then the machines take over." That was undeniably true, but I sensed that the system harbored dangers. It might develop into a weapon whose main purpose was to defend itself—against the threat of "human thought."

I was less bothered by the daily trip back and forth be-tween Frohnau and Lichterfelde Ost, since I loved the S-Bahn. On the way home I would occasionally visit our friend Kusen-berg, who had married a clever young woman called Grete (that probably wasn't her real name). Wherever he went, he established a world in which he felt at home, which often in-cluded adopting new names. When I asked him how he was, he replied, "I can't complain." It occurred to me later that he might have meant, "I don't know how to complain"—that he couldn't complain the way others can't dance, or cook.

Emma and I could do it all: dance, cook, even complain when necessary, but we were happy whatever we were doing. Regardless of how philosophers define happiness, above all it seems to me something wonderfully calm, with a sweet tug at the center of the nervous system (what we call the "solar plexus") when you're lying next to her and hear her breathe, a pleasant shiver. That's my experience, and I think others have felt that same joy, whether or not they're sorcerers. We weren't always calm, by the way. We wanted another child, one who might use the Long Arm at last.

As I write this, Mathilda, I'm looking forward to seeing you again soon. You're a full year old now, in a little white cap with a purple pompom, and you can already say several words, though they're all your own invention. Only your mother understands them—but I do too, since I'm a sorcerer. "Buf ein da" means "there's a book," and "featat" means "finished," when you've done your business. To your great joy, you've discovered you have a belly button, just like your mother and father—you were always a little sad when you saw a belly button, because you thought you didn't have one. Welcome to the club, little Mathilda!

Our happiness didn't last long. In the summer of 1933 Schloss- eck disappeared. We were worried about him—had he moved away, or perhaps been arrested? The latter seemed more likely, since apparently he could no longer contact us. Shortly thereafter I was given notice by Dehomag, and soon learned that Schneidebein was behind it. We were forced to sell the house in Frohnau and considered the possibility of emigrat- ing, to America of course. We soon gave up the idea. Tak- ing my elderly mother along was impossible, and leaving her behind unthinkable. And I wanted to find Schlosseck. At the very least, I wanted to know where he was and whether he was still alive.

But how could we make any headway when a powerful enemy like Schneidebein blocked every path? I even thought of joining the air force, which was being created then in open secrecy. His arm probably reached that far as well—at any rate, I was turned down. At heart I was happy, since I had no wish to drop bombs or kill anyone.

Life grew increasingly difficult for anyone who opposed the regime, or was thought to do so. Commands, punishments, and a cruel unpredictable power were the rule of the day. The regime wanted to show its determination, and so did many individuals who became activists. They committed acts of cruelty and murder to prove to themselves that they no longer had doubts, that they were determined, that there was no turning back. But it did no good—there were just more dead bodies scattered about and the doubts returned.

Many would gladly have given free rein to their disgust at all these horrors, but in the end they preferred not to come across to the thugs as too unpleasant.

When necessary, and if their skills are sufficiently developed, sorcerers can turn invisible. That's the most effective means of escaping notice. I had only recently learned to do so. Emma was on her way there, but that path was not open to our children. We had to be there for them. As visibly as possible.

TURNING INVISIBLE

October 2013

Becoming a sorcerer is like climbing a mountain starting from the valley floor: first gently rolling slopes, then foothills, then higher inclines; it gets rockier and more difficult, but at some point you've reached the top, and the air is fairly cold. You have a splendid view, and the rest is all downhill.

First we sorcerers learn all the varieties of self-transformation: the Long Arm, Beauty or Change, Weightlessness, and finally Invisibility, all self-altering. Only at the peak of maturity are we able to begin transforming objects other than ourselves. Onions turn into chocolates, maple leaves become Canadian dollars, cars become helicopters, and enemies suckling pigs. Unfortunately, some of these abilities are not yet available when they're most needed. In 1934 I wasn't that far advanced yet, but I managed to add Invisibility. It was the only spell I developed on my own, without a master's guidance. Emma gained it at almost the same time, although she was younger, and we both made good use of it, for there were situations in which it was advisable not to be seen in a particular place or with certain people. Those times may come again, Mathilda dear, we're never totally safe from them.

Before I tell you about the possible uses and dangers of Invisibility, there's one important point I mustn't forget—it's impossible to employ magic to end a human life. Not only is there no Death spell, no ordinary spell of any kind may be used for that purpose. For example, if you try to fly off to kill someone, you'll find you can't get an inch off the ground. I probably haven't brought this up before because you're still crawling about as a baby. It's never occurred to me that you might want to see anyone dead, but of course it's not unthinkable, so I need to tell you the basic rule: you cannot kill with magic. Not even in self-defense! It makes sense to me that magic itself blocks certain actions, but it's a mystery to me how it does it. The world's spiritual center, with which we are somewhat more closely allied than other people, seems to have both a mind and a will.

When it comes to giving aid and saving lives, the world-mind is not tightfisted. It's true that there is no spell to heal the dying nor awaken the dead, but I can fly in with the medicine that will save a patient on death's doorstep any time I wish. I approach his bed invisibly and administer the dose; the doctors notice nothing (they just think they've come up with the correct treatment yet again).

You're not even allowed to end your own life with a spell. A successful suicide requires traditional methods, as I learned when I was toying with the idea. The hour came in 1956, the year after Emma's death. I'd talked myself into testing what was possible, and tried to turn a steel fish kettle into a pistol and two 7-mm bullets. The pot didn't stir, but suddenly a wall-eyed pike lay there ready to cook. I prepared it Müllerin style, what else could I do? With no help on my part, potatoes, butter, and a sprig of rosemary appeared, and a cold bottle of Riesling stood on the table. The power of which we are a small part teaches us lessons occasionally—sometimes even with humor. We should take those lessons to heart.

Now to our theme. In case Rejlander, or someone else in the business, hasn't explained things yet and practiced with you: Invisibility is nearly the same spell that is used to turn yourself into some other being. If you've already assumed another form using that spell, you'll have noticed that there's an extremely narrow transition zone in which you no longer look like yourself, but not yet like the other being. Now, it's difficult but not impossible to halt the transformation in this no man's land long enough to remain in it—and that's Invisibility! My first servant Waldemar once watched me practice turning into a crocodile. He observed the paper thin invisibility phase between the Pahroc and the crocodile modes. He compared it to turning up the headlights in a car—before the landscape is fully illuminated there's a brief moment between dim and bright when darkness reigns.

The proper use of Invisibility requires a good deal of prior thought and training. For example, you become weaker when you're invisible. You can't expect to deliver hard blows or lift heavy weights. And if you plan to fly when invisible, take along as little as possible. Another question: what else turns invisible when you do?—everything?—your purse, the dog you have on a leash? The answer: everything that's yours in about a ten foot radius turns invisible along with you. So far so good. But what about a lively dog (or a horse, a parrot)? Sure, the horse is invisible as long as you're mounted on it, but it looks very odd if you dismount and a horse suddenly appears in the area. Or perhaps just its tail. You have to learn how to handle Invisibility. You have to realize you might not be able to remain precisely within the invisible zone at first. It awakens suspicion if you flicker on and off like a glowworm. That sort of puzzling behavior will make you seem uncanny.

And never forget the State! You must somehow avoid being exposed. If you're ever discovered you may have to abandon your carefully constructed bourgeois existence and start over as an entirely different person in some other country.

Of course, when you're invisible it's easier to enter and leave carefully guarded buildings, get to the bottom of mysteries, and listen in on conversations, that's only logical. You can enter a prison without being seen, appear in your friend's cell, then disappear again when you're ready to leave. Although that will require unlocked doors, if you haven't learned to walk through walls yet.

But remember one thing: other sorcerers can see you! Not clearly, but they know you're there, and may even be fairly certain who you are. And, of course, you see them too. It's like being in a murky aquarium: you don't recognize the other sorcerer till you're quite close to him. If you've fallen foul of some sorcerer who's now your adversary (I speak from experience), you'll only be invisible to his friends who aren't sorcerers: he himself will miss nothing—or almost nothing.

If one can remain unseen as long as one wishes, it's easy to commit a crime. So remember what I said about fairness. Our art can't help us kill, but it serves quite well for any other type of criminal mischief, unfair advantage, or covert enrichment. Whether you wish to obey the law or not is, of course, your own affair. In a corrupt State (here too I speak from experience) you have no duty to do so. The country in which you now play as a baby is a decent one, but it may have changed dramatically by the time you're grown and reading this. One should always hope the best for the future of one's country, but be prepared for the worst, and be thankful for each day that one is still safe and secure among friendly people.

Emma and I were happy from the start, in every situation, wherever we were. When, in 1934, we quietly moved to Gebhardswalde in the Uckermark district to be beyond easy reach of our adversary, we did so without bitterness. We knew our life would be glorious anywhere in the world. We were already a good-sized family; Felix was four and Felicitas (we called her Fay) three. My servant Waldemar pretended to be my brother "Wladimir." We claimed to be Russian exiles, and the samovar we'd bought from Sergej lent our story a note of authenticity. We also had impeccably falsified papers, under the name Schnittwitz. We told people we were descendants of a German family that had served in the court of Catherine the Great and came from Zerbst. That explained how I could be an electrician from St. Petersburg and still be a Lutheran.

After passing an exam, I assumed a newly opened post as sexton at the evangelical Lutheran congregation of St. Michael's. The entire subterfuge was based on the fact that sorcerers, good and bad alike, can barely bring themselves to cross the threshold of a church. Schneidebein would be no different in this respect. As members of a congregation, we were almost certain to escape detection.

I'd prepared well for the position and the exam by studying hard and attending church services regularly. Of course, to make our background credible we had to speak fluent Russian, but that was no problem. We learned the language before we moved, using the two-finger method in a Berlin library, without checking out a single grammar or dictionary. In Gebhardswalde, to our pleasure, we aroused general admiration for how well we knew German. We enjoyed that—undeserved praise provides a real lift.

We picked up the evangelical Lutheran rituals and texts relatively easily, the hardest chunk being the old-fashioned Bible, but even that was nearly memorized within three days. We kept quiet about it, to avoid arousing suspicion.

Even given my background, playing the organ proved a problem. That was one of the sexton's duties during church services. I learned to read music quickly enough, but playing the instrument placed great demands on me. I learned, in part, by repeated visits to empty churches when an organist was practicing there. I stood invisibly at the organist's side and watched his or her hands and feet in action. That, together with a few books I read and a lot of silent dry runs at night, allowed me to eventually accompany the awful multi-voiced hymns of the congregation and finally drown them out. As an engineer, I found it fairly easy to grasp the mechanics of the instrument. At one point, I even repaired the electro-pneumatic key action. It was a brand new Schuke organ with thirty-one stops on two manuals and pedalboard, standard couplers and four free combinations. I loved the second manual, the romantic one, more than the first, which seemed to me too bright and sharp. Who knows, Mathilda, you may want to learn to play the organ some day. It's well worth it, even if you don't need to go into hiding.

We didn't alter our appearance greatly; no magic spells were involved, at any rate. Gebhardswalde was far enough away from Berlin that no one was likely to recognize us. And my beard managed to attain a Russian fullness without magical aids.

I would have hated to miss our stay beneath the protective cover of the good and fortunately gullible Christians of Gebhardswalde. A few of them gained my special respect, particularly the pastor, who not only looked like Luther's double but shared his courage. I was impressed by Christians like him, because they remained nearly as independent and judicious in the face of all the lies the State told and the duties it placed upon them as we sorcerers did. But I didn't become a Christian. One shouldn't join too many churches. I'm a sorcerer, an electrician, and a melancholic—that's enough for me.

Friedrich Schnabel was our brave pastor's name. He hid those who were being tracked down, and we helped him. The German Chancellor—the one who kept his hands clasped in front of him—was now being called "Der Führer," and maintained to great applause that not all people were human. Some people were more like animals, worse than animals (the man was an animal lover). They were so dangerous, he said, they should be put behind bars, or sent as far away as possible. Since not all Germans grasped this right away, he appointed a Minister for Public Enlightenment, or "Volksaufklärung," who couldn't open his mouth without lying. Up till then, "enlightenment" had always been a favorite word of mine; Schlosseck called himself a man of the Enlightenment. He loved casting doubt on claims of all kinds, and was a firm believer in the progress of human thought (on that score he had no doubts). It's true he was contemptuous of technology-based communication. And he liked using the word "Volk." Sorcerers loved the Folk; they represented life. But combining "Volk" with "Aufklärung" as "public enlightenment" quickly became a totally loathsome concept.

Back then, I was enthusiastic about anything that converted electrical impulses into mechanical actions and vice versa, and I even came up with a few new ideas of my own. The most important of these was the "synchronizer," a device that coordinated the rotation angle of lift- and loading-bridges, canal lock gates, wheels, propeller blades, or spotlights. This enabled two or more machine parts to align at precisely the same angle without the necessity of gears or rods exerting mechanical pressure. I called my invention "Synchro Control with Parallel Resistant Diodes," and I was quite proud of it—unfortunately the only congratulations I ever received were my own. At some point someone else invented it officially and an American firm built it. Dear Mathilda, I was a rather ingenious fellow! But enough of that.

Schlosseck was still missing. No news from him, although he knew of our plans and new identities. Had he been arrested? Nonsense—he could easily have made his way out of any prison and let us know. Or had he been murdered in a surprise attack? He knew the spell for parrying a deadly assault, but he had to see it coming. Had he killed himself by some standard means, totally unlike a sorcerer? But why should he do that and leave no trace for us to follow? Had he fled to some pleasant corner of the world to escape the ugliness and noise of modern life? Hard to imagine in Schlosseck's case, a man who loved his country and preferred to study others through a magnifying glass (in the 1905 edition of *Stielers Hand-Atlas*, since he found it hard to give up the German colonies). And I just couldn't believe that he would have planned to disappear without saying goodbye.

I intended to fly cross-country to Berlin to fetch something from our apartment, taking precautions of course, including remaining invisible, but my main purpose was to search for Schlosseck. Emma advised me not to fly, but to take my bicycle instead and stay invisible all the way. She was right. There would surely be agents posted to watch both buildings, ours and Schlosseck's, and even if they couldn't see me, they'd notice doors opening and closing. I couldn't walk through walls yet, so I planned to float up to the balconies and peer in through the windows. Who was in our apartment now? Who was in Schlosseck's home? Perhaps Schneidebein himself, or some other corrupt sorcerer. There was a danger they might recognize me, follow me, and try to break my concentration. That can cause sorcerers to plunge suddenly to earth in full flight, unable to catch themselves, then hit the ground as hard as anyone.

On the other hand, Schneidebein was now a big shot, whose title started with "Reichs-." He spent all day at his headquarters, and it was unlikely he'd mastered the art of creating a convincing double, something only the oldest masters achieve. I was unsure of how far he'd advanced in sorcery—perhaps further than in electronics! He certainly hadn't received the same good training I had from Schlosseck. He might not be able to turn invisible or walk through walls yet, though he was slightly older than me—the Wall spell generally makes its appearance sometime after the age of thirty. I assumed I was a match for Schneidebein, but what if I was wrong? In any case, he'd be trying to ferret out our present location and keep us on the run. I bicycled off somewhat uneasily. I was underway for six hours, cursing the cobblestones. At least flying spared my bottom.

Yes, our former apartment was now occupied by "Ham-HamHam" types, and Schlosseck's was swarming with uniforms—the flagpole on the small tower was now adorned with a banner displaying that symbol reminiscent of a cattle brand. There weren't any guards posted, but since Party members were going from room to room, I was in no position to walk around, open drawers, or look for clues. Though a number of them were already tipsy at this early hour, someone would probably have noticed what I was doing. I had to get back to my churchly duties in Gebhardswalde soon, so I decided to resume my search at a later date. I also visited Kusenberg, approaching with caution and watching his house for some time first. As I expected, he was under surveillance—our adversary had surmised that we were acquainted. Kusenberg was a journalist, and still writing stories. His stories were just like him, and the opposite of everything the Sieg Heilers stood for—so completely opposite the Party didn't even realize it. They thought he was entertaining, which was true, and considered him harmless, which he wasn't. A fortunate error, for it kept him safe from persecution.

As I was peddling back, I saw five men in a side street chasing someone down. Their victim was an elderly man who could run fairly fast, but was trying in vain to escape into a side building. He rang at various entrances, but they kept catching up with him and none of the doors opened. Could I beat up the men? I would have liked to, but it would have been hard to avoid being revealed as a sorcerer. I recalled the story Schlosseck once told me about calling out "Hold your fire!" I leaned my bicycle against a lamppost, ran around the corner, turned myself into the six-foot-tall man in a leather coat I'd pictured mentally a few moments earlier, stuck my right hand in my pocket to make it bulge, and strode toward the group. They'd surrounded the old man and were shoving him back and forth. I saw one of them start to pull a steel baton from his belt.

"Halt, you!" I cried out. The band turned and looked at me.

"Not in my district!"

"What?"

"I think I've made myself clear!"

They were irritated.

"And you, come with me!" I said to the old man. "Name?"

"Meyer."

"Very original! I'll have a look at your apartment. Now march!" I turned to the thugs: "You, make yourself scarce! I didn't see you and I don't want to again—got it?"

They said nothing, but they already seemed scarcer.

I strode off with the old man, who willingly led the way. I took him home, turned invisible, readied myself for the return trip to Gebhardswalde, and headed back to my bicycle. That didn't go quite so well—my bicycle was missing, stolen. A spell of sorcerer's bad luck.

I was making night trips back then, too, mostly to falsify, steal, or exchange Hollerith punch cards. But an operation like that has to be well planned. Early on, I made mistakes, and they began, unfortunately, with Schlosseck's card. I still don't know if that contributed to his fate. Gradually, I became more adroit. I also sought documents I could get to by more ordinary means: crowbars or master keys. Other spells that would have provided more elegant entries had not yet appeared, but where there's a will, no sorcery is needed. I falsified whatever I could: orders, decrees, injunctions, everything. Death sentences vanished as I issued pardons on the typewriters at hand. Signatures posed no problem—they were nothing more than aggressive scrawls anyway. Things are going bad in a land where more and more people capable of writing quite clearly reduce their own good name to a palsied scratch when signing a letter. With a little practice, I wound up creating entire letters by hand. Every person in a position of power, high or low, employed a constant up and down zigzag motion that ruined pens and looked like they were erasing instead of writing.

Of course, there was no way I could check on the results of my work, since by day I was busy as a sexton.

One day, Emma and I asked Waldemar to look after the kids and flew off to see our colleague Blüthner in Saxony. By different routes, incidentally—I forgot to mention that sorcerers are unable to fly side by side; it produces a mutual disturbance, I have no idea why. You can't converse anyway, so it's no great loss if you take different paths to the same goal.

We were hoping that Blüthner had some news of Schlosseck. He too had studied with Schlosseck, and had long since developed into a master. He was a manufacturer and owned a villa with a terrace. The two grand pianos in his living room both bore his name in gold. He played them when he was alone, with up to eight hands. Many years earlier, as a high-spirited rascal, he'd had a beach photo taken of himself as the Reichspräsident. He'd become a little overweight himself, but in return he'd grown much wiser and more prudent. He'd thought of stepping up to the microphone as our sinister head of government, declaring the dissolution of the Party, and ordering the release of all prisoners. But he withstood the temptation, for he realized things would go badly— there were too many corrupt colleagues serving the regime who would have noticed at once, seen through his plan, and shot him on the spot. But I thought his idea would make a great film about dictatorships. That pleased him. He was eager to pass the idea on to a colleague who lived in America and made films. I've seen a few of them—his friend was a true artist, which, as I've mentioned, is rare among sorcerers.

Blüthner had heard nothing about Schlosseck's fate following his arrest, only that he had been interrogated a few weeks earlier due to an error in the registration office.

"I was afraid of that," I said. "I'm the one who messed that up. I slipped into the office and stole his punch card. In order to alter it, you cover two holes, add two new ones, and your ancestry can be whatever you wish. But when I went to return it the office had been moved to another part of town. I couldn't find the new office in time. They probably noticed the card was missing—and that wasn't good."

"Strange—who would miss a punch card? It's simply not there."

"The other cards miss it—the system, the registry. It was counted once, and now it's gone. That immediately raises suspicions."

"Too bad, we should have gone together: you as the Hollerith expert and I as the quick-change magic man. All I need to know is what things should look like when I'm done."

"Yes, I can't do that yet, I'm not far enough along."

A short time later, Blüthner said, Schlosseck was taken away in an armored car to Moabit Prison. How the government's henchmen were able to get him into the car wasn't clear. Blüthner didn't know if a sorcerer had a hand in it. I told him about my childhood and involvement with Schneidebein. He suspected that Schneidebein hated Schlosseck as much as he hated me.

"In any case, he felt he'd been treated poorly by Schlosseck. Schlosseck refused to mentor him."

"He just didn't like the boy. That's everyone's right."

"But it's a problem if you're a teacher. Being unloved leads to half of all murders," Blüthner said. I winced at the words.

"And what about the other half?" Emma asked.

Blüthner sat down at the piano. "They're in the way. They have something someone else wants. Perhaps the wrong religion . . ."

"Or the wrong ancestry," said Emma.

Blüthner fell silent for some time. Then he attacked the keys, plunging into a swinging ragtime that made you want to tap your feet. I knew he was not about to play anything sad. But my tears still came—and with them the thought that my father, for all he loved my mother, had not chosen the Germany we faced at present.

"I hope no one was listening! They call that 'Negermusik' and 'entartet,' degenerate," Emma said.

"This room is soundproof," Blüthner replied. "I can soundproof any room in which I speak or play. Schlosseck could do the same, but unfortunately he thought it unnecessary."

"What do you mean?"

"His servant Wladimir told me that he was standing by an open window when he referred to the Chancellor as 'an egocentric Herostratus.' And he referred to the German Reich as a 'secular Zealots State.' Whoever denounced him had to visit the library first to figure out what the names meant. And, of course, there was Schlosseck's ancestry. So one thing led to another."

"And his servant?"

"Also missing—presumably dead. Just like the dog."

"Ulf?"

"Yes, Ulf. No doubt he defended his master. At any rate, he was shot dead. Another thing: have you ever been to St. Polykarp cloister? No? You have to visit it sometime, both of you. I'll tell you how to get there, and exactly when you should go."

He'd invited a gathering of sorcerers to form what he called a "Mighty Handful." Schneidebein didn't know the cloister. No normal person could find it and it wasn't mentioned in any book. Sorcerers who had no mentor were unaware of its existence. On Three Kings Day a few friends who could be counted on would gather there from all over Europe.

Now Blüthner played something else: a piece for two pianos. He had no need for magic spells, since Emma accompanied him. In those days all daughters of the nobility could play an instrument, usually piano.

We returned by train because Emma felt unwell, which is no time to fly. Pregnant sorceresses shouldn't be casting too many spells, and she was in her sixth month. Train travel was risky too, but for a different reason: we might be recognized. We altered our appearance a good deal, which is more effective in a crowd than total invisibility—I forgot to mention that someone who is invisible is by no means bodiless. You have to prevent others from bumping into you. Keep your distance while you're invisible and be sure no one comes up behind you. Seats on a train are usually occupied solidly and unmistakably. It's customary in Germany to ask if an empty seat is free, but this doesn't protect invisible passengers from embarrassing moments.

In Gebhardswalde we could at least play the married Russian couple again. We were truly happy about that.

I'm telling you more and more stories that have nothing to do with sorcery directly, but that's how memories affect us. I simply want to pass on some of what I know, but it seems I have to tell the story of my life to do so. Bear with me a while. It's part of your family history.

Little Titus was born, and is still alive today, age seventy-seven. He lives alone on an alpine pasture in Tyrol and is called "Öhi," Swiss for grandpa—perhaps you'll meet him some day. Felix was already in primary school. And tall

Jakob visited us. I'd told him where we were living, and later learned he never gave us away, even under intense interrogation. Jakob brought the sad news that my dear mother had passed away. Attending her funeral was out of the question— it would be swarming with spies. Presumably Schneidebein himself would be there, assuming a sad face and keeping a lookout for us. Even if we were invisible, or had changed our appearance, he would have spotted us. I was in despair, tortured by the thought that this evil man might be standing, perhaps even in uniform, by my mother's grave.

I had underestimated the duties of a sexton. The job took everything I had. I could only compare it to being a captain whose ship threatens to go under every few hours. If I hadn't had Emma and Waldemar/Wladimir, and, of course, the occasional magic spell, I wouldn't have been up to the task. A real sexton is supported by his faith. We sorcerers can only pretend, and over months and years that's a real strain.

We lived in a house right beside the church, which was fortunate, since I had to supervise everyone who had a duty to perform there. These duties were manifold. In a church, someone is responsible for keeping things clean. The floor must be scrubbed, the organ dusted, the altar and processional crosses polished, along with the sacred vessels and implements. Someone must brush the pastor's cap and gown, not forgetting the collar with its hanging strips. The altar hanging and baptismal cloth must be laundered, the hymn numbers inserted into the slots on the board, the money in the collection bag and offertory box accounted for. Someone has to get out the candles and place them in their holders. A further specialist makes sure the wine and host are available and in the right spot. In winter, someone's in charge of the heating and also clears the ice from the entryway. Someone has to handle the floral arrangements. Then there's the electrician, who keeps the emergency lighting up to snuff and repairs loose connections on the podium reading lamp, and the orderly who makes sure the kit in the sacristy is stocked for all sorts of medical emergencies, and is trained in first aid (last aid is left to the pastor). Someone has to unlock the church at the right time, air it out, see that the Bible is opened to the correct passage and help the pastor on with his gown. There's the bell-ringer, who has to know exactly what to ring and when and how long each bell should be sounded. That's the heartbeat of every church, which is why they sometimes call the bell-ringer the "Beater." And someone has to see that the organist doesn't oversleep, is seated at the organ on time, and has the right music before him.

There were a vast number of festivals and services, and supervising the innumerable tasks outlined above severely tested both my strength and my nerves. Since I was now responsible for carrying them all out myself, I was essentially my own supervisor.

The most important thing about a sexton's job is that it's what is now called "results-oriented." Decades later, when I posed as a specialist in business management, I drew on my rich experience as a sexton. My young listeners learned a great deal—indeed several of them became successful managers, while never suspecting they'd been trained as sextons. What I'd conveyed, without using the words, was a sense of service and duty. Today those concepts are generally thought to run counter to self-determination, they sound like a form of imprisonment. And there's no doubt something in that— but are we truly free? At any rate freedom isn't worth much if you haven't developed something inside yourself that you'll always stand behind. And in doing so you've freely chosen— to no longer be free.

The year 1936 passed, Advent and Christmas meant hard work. Then our own celebration approached, the feast of the three holy sorcerers present at Christ's birth. I took a brief holiday and turned my duties over to Waldemar. We traveled to St. Polykarp, which, thanks to Blüthner's directions, we quickly found. It wasn't too cold that day, so we could fly (by separate routes naturally), taking pleasure in the splendor of the snowy landscape beneath us. No matter what terrible events were occurring in the State, it was beautiful when seen from above, even the large cities. So far.

We took a room for three days at an inn and headed straight for the Cloister library. It's an unbelievable place, and you can take that literally. They still have chained books there. Yes, in the Middle Ages chains were attached to precious books so that no one could steal them, be they negligent scholars or time-traveling rare book dealers from the late twenty-first century. The only other visitors in the library were three elderly men and a young woman, presumably sorcerers. We waited for Blüthner to appear and introduce us. We passed the time reading, particularly in the cookbook section, where I came across the great Bachstelz's work, which smelled distinctly of Gorgonzola. I've been back there a few times since then. No one becomes a great master without continued study.

St. Polykarp was also the name of the small town with a few shops and inns surrounding the cloister. People lived and died there like anyplace else. They studied and worked, strolled about, played games, married, and went to the dentist. And they loved the old cloister and its church, where services were still held. But one thing about this place was not normal. It couldn't be found by the rest of the world. It didn't appear on maps of Germany, nor in lexicons. The stranger who accidentally happened across it, having lost his way in the woods, or driven his car down a private road, found a friendly little town and made a mental note to buy a better map next time that showed it. But once he left the town he never found it again, nor even remembered it. And those who lived in St. Polykarp? They didn't feel the slightest urge to leave town, they had everything they needed (which didn't include cars and telephones). Perhaps they too sensed that if they left they would never come back. I don't think they suffered, but I don't know for sure. I would have to ask, and their answers would probably prove nothing.

Places that don't exist—I'm thinking of Kaisersaschern or Vineta—are particularly memorable. In St. Polykarp we felt a combination of total freedom and deep inner security. I wanted to go back there after the war, but the way was barred: even if the place wasn't real, it was in the East, and at the time that was difficult terrain, real or virtual, for sorcerers. I learned much later that during the final days of the war the library books were smuggled into the West by a sorcerer with ice in his veins (I'll say more about him later).

The martyr for whom the cloister is named was remarkable too. When they came to take him to be burned at the stake, the saint checked his calendar and offered the hangman a private appointment: a one-hour Introduction to Christianity, free, with further instruction by arrangement. That's my kind of saint.

Emma and I spent the first day sleeping, reading, and walking.

Blüthner was nowhere in sight.

The following day we visited the library again. The same people were there. Suddenly I thought I recognized one of the three elderly men as someone who once had tea with Schlosseck. I remembered his name only because it was so extraordinarily difficult to remember: Constable de Lesdiguières. I couldn't speak French, but I told Emma and she spoke to him: daughters of the nobility knew three or four languages in those days, and French was first in line. The reason? Every noble family dreamed of being admitted to the court of Louis XIV at Versailles. That hasn't changed much over the years.

Emma addressed the Constable by name. He sprang up,

kissed her hand, and said in French—Emma did the translating—"I knew I would meet you here, Countess! Then this must be Pahroc. Good day, my colleague. Never fear, there are no Kalagans, Hanussens, or"—he raised his eyes to the heavens—"oh mon dieu! Schneidebeins here!" And to me: "You see, I know everything, Monsieur Pahroc. But now a favor: be so good as to learn French to make things easier for me. I can speak German when I have to, but your brain is younger, and knowing French won't hurt you. You'll find everything you need over there." He pointed to one of the bookshelves. I went over and placed two fingers of my left hand on the spine of a French grammar and two fingers of my right on a French dictionary named Larousse, and learned as quickly as I could, since I didn't want to keep the Constable waiting too long. After four minutes we sat down and continued our conversation in French. My vocabulary was still somewhat limited, of course. I had no idea what a "toxic shaman" was in either French or German. As I now know, the phrase refers to colleagues who love evil, or at least act like they do. The Constable mentioned a French name—something like Bambin Zélé—presumably one of his adversaries in France.

He asked what abilities we possessed. We had little to offer beyond the Long Arm, Flight and Beauty, Change and Invisibility. Walking through walls and all the truly powerful spells had yet to come. But the Constable showed us one trick we were ready for: a spell that was the reverse of Invisibility.

"You can turn invisible, fine. But there's a way to make yourself appear somewhere else—without being there! For example, as I'm talking with you, I'm seated at a table in a café on the Seine, and anyone who knows me would swear I was there. Now this is important: If he questions my coffee-drinking alibi, I can employ a second spell that works in combination with the first. He immediately forgets what he meant to do, because he feels a pressing need to be elsewhere.

The combination itself isn't available at your present age, but I can teach you the basic spell."

We learned a lot that afternoon. The spells we discussed can be developed even further at a certain age. Not only can you make a visible double appear somewhere else, you can establish a true alter ego that someone can talk to, and that can speak and act almost as well as you do. Dear Mathilda, sorcery doesn't change the course of the world a great deal, but now and again it can offer a lot of everyday fun!

Gradually sorcerers and sorceresses arrived from all over Europe. They were all looking forward to what the conference would bring. Then Blüthner arrived and it was underway.

SIXTH LETTER

WALKING
THROUGH WALLS

January 2014

During lunch break at the St. Polykarp conference, I managed to walk through a brick wall for the first time. I immediately developed the ability further with the help of a few
older colleagues who were there, which I assume gave me an
even greater head start on Schneidebein. But first things first!

The circle that gathered on the seventh of January, 1937,
in St. Polykarp was not large, but I've never seen such a prom-
inent assembly of European colleagues again. As a rule, the
greatest experts among sorcerers do not employ first names.
It's been that way since Metternich's era, and remains so
today. Others, the younger ones, have normal names: Henry
Grund for example, Leonore Dreyser or Krine Profuso from
Zülpich, a pretty redhead with her dress cut a little too low
and a distinct squint (her gaze slightly askew, but in a cute
way), an elf named Raissa Pospischil from Vienna, and, of
course, my Emma.

We younger ones listened attentively for the most part.
When we spoke, we did so quickly, for the older ones were
prone to interrupt—they always knew at once where the
younger ones were heading. Sorcerers are like everyone else

in this respect, perhaps even worse, which has always disturbed me a little. Our elders should restrain themselves better, and not jump in at once just because they've heard it all before. I haven't let this bad habit grow as rankly as others have—at least I hope not.

The conversation was led by the elders: Blüthner, Lesdiguières and the Scottish sorceress Macintosh, who was privately referred to as "the praying mantis," because she was tall, angular, and remained almost always motionless. She spoke in a mellifluous, sparkling voice that carried a grim message, stressing the necessity of abandoning any illusions about the threat posed by the sole remaining German Party. Macintosh was a businesswoman and represented the unrelenting realist. Blüthner, who was a musician but also a businessman, agreed with almost everything she said at first, but at some point showed himself a respectful opponent. Lesdiguières was a knight through and through, stiffly erect and seemingly encased in armor, who gladly argued for attack. The others represented sentimentalists and idealists of various stripes, which enlivened the conversation: realism and strategizing make for a dull meeting if there's no one who dreams, speculates, or at least shows some enthusiasm.

We sat in the great hall of the library, which was "Closed for Inventory" that day. Of course, a moderator had been chosen and asked to remain neutral. That's the only way to counter the powerful self-confidence of those who are wise and experienced, and it's the essence of democracy. We settled on Kajetan Gnadl from Wasserburg am Inn, a jovial man who limped because of a stiff leg, but enjoyed hiking through the mountains. Bavarians make the best moderators, because they're not at all shy about admitting (or pretending to admit) that they haven't understood something. They admire superior intellects but have a quiet, friendly, and spirited way of forcing them to make themselves clearer. In his old age, by the way, Gnadl became a famous sorcerer and his first name disappeared. In his role as an ordinary citizen, he was a traffic cop in Wasserburg, a small, somewhat isolated town in upper Bavaria, with very little traffic. So he had ample time to learn an unusually wide range of tricks. He always knew a lot more than I did, and taught me a great deal, explaining complicated spells in a simple, effective way. In the postwar period he even taught me the art of poaching, which admittedly has nothing to do with sorcery, but can make protein rich food suddenly appear on the table of a starving family.

Emma was named secretary on the basis of her fine ear and beautiful penmanship (or vice-versa). That pleased her.

The Polykarp Conference focused first on the dangers of our current situation, and the need for good sorcerers to unite against the bad. We needed to join together and support one another, to free and shelter our colleagues if necessary. States have always opposed sorcerers, but at present Germany hated them with a brutality never seen before. Jews were in special danger—every conceivable ill was laid at their doorstep.

I said, "If only Indians were the cause of all Germany's problems! Then I'd be the only one they'd be after—but I'm a sorcerer and can get away anytime."

"Schlosseck was a sorcerer too," Raissa Pospischil said softly.

"Why 'was'?" several people cried out.

"He can't possibly be dead," said Lesdiguières, "he knows the most incredible ways to escape. Perhaps he's a crocodile right now, enjoying one of those uniformed fellows for breakfast each morning."

No one laughed. But we were all determined not to mourn for Schlosseck—not yet. We kept on hoping he'd survived. Whether Germany would survive, the Germany he loved, was another question.

"The Dictator is a sick man, he can't face reality and is dependent on drugs. He'll start a war within the next two years," Macintosh said, "and then it will all be over. A year or two of hubris on the battlefields and he'll be unmasked for the hopelessly inadequate devil he is. And no doubt dead soon after."

"We can't wait that long," Dreyser groaned.

"Right! He must be assassinated!" Lesdiguières said, drawing an imaginary sword and thrusting it. "This isn't about us, it's about Europe."

"We can't do that," Blüthner replied. "No act of sorcery can lead to death, directly or indirectly. That's surely clear, my dear Constable."

"I can thrust a sword without the help of sorcery, or fire a pistol. That's worked well several times."

"In this case the pistol wouldn't fire, since you'd have cast a spell somewhere along the way. How could you get close to him without using sorcery?"

Lesdiguières slowly lit a cigar, giving himself time to brood in silence.

"We're here to win people over, not kill them!" Krine Profuso said, tossing her mane of hair boldly, as if to show how personally she took this.

"Fine, but how are we supposed to win people over when we can't even tell them we're sorcerers?" Macintosh asked. "We're limited to anonymous sabotage and freeing a few prisoners. Influence people? A few individuals perhaps, but assemblies, armies and parties, humankind? No way. Using sorcery to counter the course of world events has never made sense."

That started a quarrel about the purpose of our meeting. Why were we there? Dreyser pointed out that without greater agreement on this, a "Mighty Handful" would never be formed, and that was, after all, the original purpose of the gathering. We had to act.

Blüthner took a deep breath: "First of all, sorcery certainly has significance, and secondly, that significance most assuredly includes influencing humankind."

"Without telling them who and what we are?" Macintosh said tauntingly. "I'd like to see that."

"Come now! Music, literature, and art can change an audience without the creators being known, or acting as missionaries. Sorcery does that too. We create paradoxes, coincidences that cause people to say, 'That's surely no coincidence!' We provide miracles with or without a known agent. We cause such strange things to happen that people can't believe their eyes. That doesn't make them believe more firmly in miracles, but it lets them imagine what they might be like. That's why we're here, my lady, or don't you think so?"

"Sounds like Schlosseck," Macintosh said.

"And well it might! I was his student."

Henry Grund, who'd been won over by Marxism, grew impatient.

"I have three things to say about that. First of all—"

"Wait, wait, first let Emma finish getting everything down," Kajetan Gnadl interjected. He was an experienced moderator who knew it was time for a break when people started saying "First of all." One seldom heard Gnadl's voice, since he led the discussion with his eyes, and everyone followed them. As long as he was looking at someone, they could continue speaking. At just the right moment he would close his eyes, turn his head to the next speaker, open them and nod. Of course, there was magic involved, but it was always clear whose turn it was to speak. Those who were impatient could jump in spontaneously, but they had to overcome an inner resistance. Gnadl called this retardant spell "Decorum" in Bavarian—a word that occurs in High German as well and describes a minor ban necessary for successful conversation. Even today, I recall Gnadl with gratitude every time I have to watch a TV talk show.

Emma wrote assiduously, little squeaks emanating from her pen, while all sat silent. Of course, the pages appeared blank to normal eyes when she'd finished—our minutes were not meant for the uninitiated.

After the break, discussion continued on the significance and task of sorcery, and what strategy might be developed on that basis. A man by the name of Tadeusz Alrutz made just one remark during the entire conference:

"We're here to help, but have no strategy, that's both our strength and our weakness."

That was a radical statement, totally at odds with the non-descript, somewhat glum, introspective man and his seemingly unsure and hesitant manner of speech. Everyone sat in silent thought for a few moments, then Blüthner admitted that sometimes a strategy is merely what arises from the failure to understand that something will fall into place on its own. That set Henry Grund in motion. He objected strongly. Our duty, he said, was to disrupt the inhuman exercise of power—by well-planned sabotage of the State's surveillance and administrative operations, for example. That required a strategy.

Gnadl managed to settle things down by asking me to present an overview of the Hollerith data collection system and how it could be manipulated, since I was an expert. My presentation on how sorcery could be used to alter punch cards, including a description of two-fold cards, card punchers, and registration lists, was somewhat dry, but a little boredom did us good right then. I reached the conclusion that there was only one thing to do: set fire to all the offices where Hollerith cards were stored, and if possible all at the same time. But that would be difficult, since lives would be put at risk, ruling out the use of sorcery.

Having delivered my conclusion, the group awoke somewhat and immediately began arguing about basic principles again. We weren't arsonists, Blüthner said now, nor were we striving for specific goals, but served instead the magic of life itself, something greater than ourselves.

"Then I'm starting to wonder why we're sitting around here," said the young Grund, earning an interested look from Leonore Dreyser. Several of the older sorcerers drew in their breath audibly at this. But Gnadl was quicker: "Gentlemen, it's now lunchtime, we've agreed on one hour. Don't forget what you were going to say. In an hour we'll start up again."

It may not have been the most significant hour of my life, but it was my most significant lunch break. Before leaving I removed a pebble from my right shoe. As I pulled the shoe back on, I placed my left hand against the wall. As would soon become clear, it was the wall of the men's room. I noticed with bewilderment that the wall had suddenly gone soft and was giving way. I lost my balance and fell, or better, sank in slow motion, through the wall. It was dark at first, then I was back in brightness and saw Lesdiguières enthroned on the stool. "Oh!" I cried out in shock, to which he replied "Oh là là!" Struggling to regain my balance, I stumbled forward through the next wall. I was no longer disturbing the Constable, but now stood in the adjoining room beside a bathroom mirror in which Henry Grund was looking himself over—bare down to the waist and flexing incredible muscles! I could see at once he'd used a beauty spell, no doubt wanting to look good for a change. I didn't know which room embarrassed me more. But he just grinned: "Don't worry about it, Pahroc. The Wall spell always announces itself in some embarrassing fashion, we've all been through it."

"Have a good lunch!" I cried out, stunned, just wanting to get out of there. But Grund had a question first: "That aside, what do you think of my body?"

"Unbelievable," I answered truthfully, and headed for the next wall. It led to the dining room, where a few colleagues were already sitting at tables.

"Look," Macintosh cried out in English, "Pahroc's coming through the wall!" Heads turned, and Blüthner lifted a glass to toast me as I brushed the plaster from my jacket. I sat down quickly beside Emma and tried to gather my thoughts. At first she said nothing, allowing me time to do so. Emma knew I thought best close to her—but only if she asked no questions. I've seldom met someone so sensitive. Sensitivity is a magical part of life that doesn't depend on sorcery. It has no need for Mind Reading, for example, something I'll come to later.

I had a lot to consider, for now I had to recall what I'd been thinking about as I removed the pebble and was putting my shoe back on. When the laws of physics are contravened, you need to know what set the process in motion, otherwise you can never feel comfortable leaning against a wall again. I came up with it, and Blüthner confirmed my conclusion. It's a thought that may actually appear when you've got a pebble in your shoe. I don't wish to describe it more clearly here, Rejlander or any other good sorcerer will tell you what you need to know when you're ready for it.

Now a few more basic rules for walking through walls, Mathilda. The wall softens right away, like a biscuit dipped in coffee, and is slightly sticky. When you come out on the other side, small souvenirs cling to you, red bits from softened bricks, or white dust from plaster or mortar. The wall you've passed through closes instantaneously behind you and is as solid as ever. If someone's firing at you and you've made it through, the bullets remain embedded just where they normally would be in the wall.

Another question: what can you take through with you? You can bring along anything you can carry a few meters, but it can't be a living creature—a dog or cat must be left behind.

It's always good to know who or what's behind the wall. Unfortunately it's only at a later stage in life that we can see through walls and know what awaits us. So always be cautious when using the Wall spell; listen carefully first to see if there are people on the other side. When you're escaping from a prison cell, remember you might wind up in the warden's office or be greeted by empty sky outside an eighth floor wall. You must be calm enough not to be frozen by fear and ready to take flight quickly. Make it a rule to expect almost anything on the other side. And another thing: we have a hard time walking through cast iron and can't pass through steel at all; a lattice of concrete reinforcing bars gives us a hard time too. Nor is it pleasant to get stuck in a Quonset hut or with your hand caught in a safe. You can make it through a few softer metals easily enough, as long as you're not in a hurry. Gold in particular poses no problem—but then you don't see many walls made of gold—perhaps now and then in Saudi Arabia, who knows?

Speaking of metals, I should tell you what happened to me with Schlosseck when I was about thirteen. Inside his front door, behind the mail slot, was a tin box where the post landed once or twice a day. Because his servant, Wladimir, was in bed with the Spanish flu, Schlosseck asked me to look after the mail. But the key broke off in the lock, rendering the backup key useless. I told the master what had happened, hoping to learn what magic spell would pull a bit of broken key from a lock. He smiled, went to his desk, and pulled out a large magnet. The moment he brought it near the lock, the piece of metal was drawn out. Finding solutions to problems is sometimes more fun than making them magically disappear.

Before I forget: we can't pass through glass walls, there's no magic for that. We have to break through them like any normal person, and if the glass is bulletproof we're out of luck.

The conference at St. Polykarp ended without reaching any decisions on our main goal. We founded a secret society to advise and aid one another, that was all. It showed no promise of great strength, but we agreed on signals to contact each other if we needed help, and a secret circular in which Blüthner would let the others know whatever recent news had reached him about the current situation. The fact that we didn't organize more strongly was perhaps due to Alrutz's single but influential remark that our strength lay in our lack of strategy, something I didn't agree with at the time. I never met the man again, but I've heard he spent the rest of his life helping others, without ever thinking of himself. They say he died early, for reasons that remain unclear, taking his own life to spare those who shared his burden. A strange, unlucky man among sorcerers. I've never forgotten him.

Trying to get a handful of sorcerers to agree on a single course of action failed. Opinion is still divided today as to why. Perhaps because our sort tend to be self-absorbed. Blüthner thought perhaps he should have jumped over his own shadow and followed the more aggressive Henry Grund. Gnadl felt it might have been his fault, because he was too much the traffic cop, anxious to avoid collisions. In truth, he didn't think much of the whole affair, as I later learned. Of course, it was difficult: sorcerers can't appear in public and say "Follow our lead, we're special." Sorcerers have no lobby, party, or general policy. And sorcerers can't kill with their spells, so they can't deliver any real threats. Should we have tried to reach the single sorcerer who supposedly could? But whether he would be prepared to do so is another matter. The phrase "to amuse himself" came back to me. No doubt he was callously neutral.

Moreover, a higher law fundamentally forbids sorcerers from interfering in the course of history. Given that law, were there exceptions? No one knew for sure.

Emma was happy to be flying back to Gebhardswalde, since she was worried how Waldemar, temporarily named Wladimir, was getting along without us. Besides, she claimed that Krine Profuso had given me an overly long look. I laughed and said that was for Henry Grund, who was standing right behind me. But that's how sorceresses are—they see more than is there. If I were—note the subjunctive!—interested in anyone other than Emma, it would have been Raissa Pospischil.

Meanwhile, Waldemar had handled things quite well as Wladimir, perhaps because, unlike us, he was a true Christian. That didn't mean he knew how to play the organ, of course, so a retired teacher from Zehdenick had taken that over. But otherwise he handled everything punctually and the pastor loved him.

I resumed my job and served day in and day out as a widely respected sexton. Now and then, when I had the time, I took flights around Germany. I saw synagogues burning in the cities. Since I was now a caretaker of sacred objects, it seemed to me a particularly terrible crime. Once I flew up to an arsonist, grabbed his pitch bucket, and dumped it over his head. I reached for a box of matches and he started shaking. I knew the match wouldn't light—all I could do with magic was scare him. But that's all I wanted to do.

I also took creative flights of thought. In the early morning hours I devised a new invention. It wasn't a business concept like the Schacktograph, nor was it based on an existing device like the synchronizer, it was an entirely new invention with implications for the future. Of course, it did remind one strongly of Baron Münchhausen's tales.

Humans have always dreamed of flying to the moon, but almost no one could think of anything useful to do or build once they'd arrived. Most people were just focused on getting there. I knew we'd do that sooner or later. And then? To stay and raise a family, say, was surely nonsense. But machines could be placed there, automatons that functioned on their own. And it was clear to me that a relay station for radio transmission would be needed, perhaps linked with photo or video cameras that could send back images of the earth so sharp that a rat couldn't cross a country lane without being seen. The German word "rattenscharf," which I often hear these days used in an entirely different sense, is a purely technical term taken from one of my photography patents back in the fifties.

That the times weren't yet ripe for it was clear. And there was a good deal of preliminary work still to be done. It would take time and effort to build the necessary tubes and condensers. The device, when completed, threatened to be larger than an apartment building, more likely the size of a cavalry barracks with stables. The invention would only be usable when technology existed to reduce it to the size of a doghouse, or better yet a dog bowl. But why not start planning now? Everything could be tested on earth first. And I could demonstrate that the thing worked to any physicist who wasn't too full of himself. I thought of Einstein, but he was hard to reach by that time.

So I worked away on calculations and drawings before the sun came up, then hid the circuit diagrams in a spare pyx in the sacristy cupboard. The need for a radio station on the moon was obvious: greater peace on earth, since preparations for any war could be spotted from space at an early stage. Who would dare to attack another nation in that case? I even developed a plan to construct artificial moons on earth and put them into orbit—the main thing was to make sure they didn't bump into the real moon.

Times were bad, but working early mornings on my invention left me feeling cheerful all day, and I made good progress. Several months passed in which we lived in peace, although the times grew steadily worse. The war dominated everything, first against half the world, later the world as a whole, and with every victory, belief in the "Endsieg"—the final victory—grew among the heel-clickers. As if the world would ever put up with them. I was in no danger of being called up as a soldier, since the congregation had declared my position essential, and their declaration been approved, at least for the time being.

On a Monday in July 1940, we bicycled with the children—Felix already on an old girl's bicycle, Fay and Titus on the racks—into the woods to gather mushrooms. We'd found a good spot with lots of mushrooms that we were keeping secret till we had gathered them ourselves. When we returned with our bicycle baskets full, we couldn't find Waldemar anywhere. We looked in his room and found nothing but a sheet of paper on his desk covered with a puzzling red scrawl that I could make nothing of. Our neighbors told us that our brother, Wladimir (as he was officially known), had been accosted by three men in leather jackets. They took him to his room, where sounds of a struggle and cries were heard. When they came out again, my brother was in handcuffs and bleeding from his forehead and mouth. The leather coats barely responded to the villagers' questions, but mentioned military duty and asked about us, too. Fortunately, we'd told everyone we were going to a circus in the next village. The men waited two hours, then disappeared with Wladimir.

I didn't believe they'd seized him for the army—something else was going on. Now I took a closer look at the scrawl in Waldemar's room. I was right—Waldemar had smeared a drawing in his own blood. It looked like a confused tangle of strokes, but with a little imagination I could make out a leg, and then a knife held against it. The puzzle was solved: Schneidebein! I wondered why the thugs had let Waldemar sit at the desk again after what had surely been a brutal interrogation. Perhaps they'd made him sign a confession, and he'd pretended to wipe his bloody fingers off on another piece of paper before he took the pen. They didn't see that he was drawing something.

I was horrified. In spite of Emma's pleas, I wanted to fly straight to Berlin (invisibly, of course) and have it out with Schneidebein. But first I had to get my family to safety as quickly as possible. One thing was certain: the men would be back.

I hid Emma and the children with friends in a neighboring village and called Blüthner from a telephone in the village post office. I gave a false name and spoke the words we'd agreed on if we needed a new place to hide:

"Wealth and work! Do you have a position available? I'm looking to change jobs." Had I been seeking a hideout for someone else, I would have said "A friend is looking to change jobs."

"You have a family?" Blüthner was asking if we needed a place for all of us.

"Yes, a wife and three children."

"Fine, let's talk things over at the library." I was to meet him at St. Polykarp.

"When would you find that convenient?" Blüthner continued.

"As soon as possible."

"Good, let's say 4978 then."

That wasn't a salary suggestion, it was a meeting time: the end of the 4978th hour of that year, less three. In this case, it meant tomorrow, the 26th of July, 1940, at one o'clock minus three hours—the time was thus set for ten o'clock in the morning. That was one of the St. Polykarp formulas to arrange times for urgent meetings—sorcerers can calculate quickly, you see. It's a useful trick, too, Mathilda. It confuses any unwanted listeners-in and spares us all trouble.

Possible surveillance by spies and microphones was an eternal source of discomfort. These days, we accept the fact that we're being electronically monitored at all times and simply live with it. The main problem remains unchanged: what the controlling body doesn't understand strikes them as suspicious—and there's a lot they don't understand. Which causes those under surveillance to try to be as clear as possible to those listening in: they no longer take unusual paths.

Blüthner found a solution for us and told me about it in St. Polykarp.

We left everything behind in Gebhardswalde. I was the only one who risked saying good-bye to Pastor Schnabel, and I didn't find it easy. Schnabel was a fine figure of a man, helpful, with steady nerves and the keen senses of an Indian. No doubt he was halfway glad to let me go; he was beginning to find me a bit uncanny: too many unexplained things were going on, and the occasional inexplicable ability. He surely sensed that I was no true sexton. But I had been a useful one. He would deeply miss my organ playing, of that I was sure.

Blüthner's chauffeur took us to an empty villa on the slopes high above Dresden. It wasn't a place to stay for long, since too many Party spies lived in those very areas. Felix and Fay couldn't go to school there without running risks—after all, children tell the truth. It would be all right for a few days. On one occasion we visited the Dresden zoo together, like a normal family, and studied the predators and the snakes.

Then I really did fly to Berlin. I took on the form and uniform of an especially fat minister with a fancy chest-full of medals, and visited the large prison where opponents of the regime were kept at the time. I entered the building and arms shot up on all sides in the "German salute." I raised my baton graciously a few times, just like the real minister did. I asked in an imperious tone for the men's room, was led there, and never came out again. Instead, I turned invisible and began walking through walls, searching for Waldemar among the prison cells. I didn't find him, although I saw scores of prisoners waiting to be interrogated. I turned myself into a guard, opened an exit door, and ordered them to take off. How far they made it in their prisoner's garb, I don't know. I knew I hadn't necessarily helped the situation.

Meanwhile, there was a great hue and cry because the Party Marshal hadn't emerged from the men's room. And then I saw Schneidebein approaching, who of course could see me, even though I was invisible to the others. He pulled out his pistol and I threw myself at the nearest wall. He fired as I was almost through. Unfortunately, at the instant the bullet arrived, my right arm was still in the room. I fled with a flesh wound that kept me from using the Long Arm for weeks.

I returned to Emma. In the meantime, Blüthner had found us another place to stay. He picked us up in his Horch 670. The splendid twelve-cylinder monster was black and polished as bright as a concert piano. He drove us to Upper Bavaria himself, where Gnadl would put us up at Wasserburg am Inn. When a roadblock with uniformed men appeared ahead, the car suddenly sprouted a pennant with a Party symbol. We men now wore uniforms, Blüthner's plain because he was the driver, mine a splendid black with buckles and silver buttons, matching the Horch. No one dared stop us. The entire range of magical possibilities had recently opened to Blüthner and he enjoyed making full use of them.

In Wasserburg we found Gnadl, the traffic cop, who was up on everything and had already arranged our lodgings. He had known a certain Josef Gruber, a quiet man with no dependents who ran an electrical appliance shop and hiked through the mountains on weekends, often with Gnadl. Early one morning Gnadl found him lying on the floor behind his counter. They'd been preparing for an outing, but instead all Gnadl could do was confirm that Gruber was dead—sorcerers can do that as reliably as doctors. He thought of me immediately, since he knew from Blüthner that I was seeking a new life. So he kept quiet and made the body disappear without a trace, which was easy for him. He also arranged for the burial, a solemn affair in the cliffs below the cross on Mount Hochplatte. The tombstone bore no inscription of course, and there were only two mourners—Kajetan Gnadl and I. No one in the little village missed the dead man—because from then on, I was Gruber.

I managed to look just like him. I knew much more than he had about electricity, so I had to be careful no one noticed his sudden increase in knowledge. I was also friendlier by nature and took care to let that appear only gradually. I sold flashlight batteries, kept a supply of light bulbs handy, repaired radios, or installed wiring. Emma was able to remain herself. We constructed the whole story like a novel: Gruber had taken in Frau Pahroc and her three children because their apartment in Berlin had been bombed. Herr Pahroc was no longer with them—he'd left and hadn't been seen again, perhaps he was no longer alive. With Gnadl's help I managed to smuggle punch cards for the entire family into the registries and create all the necessary documents—I chiseled the life of Frau Pahroc and her children in Hollerith granite.

The children knew Josef Gruber only as a kind uncle—a role it was difficult for me to play. All they knew of their papa was that he was living in a hideout somewhere nearby and visited them secretly from time to time when Herr Gruber was away. I had to insist they tell people in Wasserburg their father had left them and they hadn't seen him for a long time. I was heartsick at asking them to lie. But they did it perfectly once they realized that if they babbled too much, bad men would come after me. They still remembered what had happened to Waldemar in Gebhardswalde.

Speaking of babbling: while I was writing this, I watched you and realized that babies babble on their own at some point, just as they learn to walk or discover the joy of totally destroying things. Now, in 2014, you know over a hundred words and are always ready for a little conversation. You've also discovered you can make music. You sing long songs to your doll, and she praises you or sings something nice herself—and you do all that on your own. Of course, you know your grandpa likes to praise you, too: for how you speak, sing, paint, even for the way you jump around his desk so wildly. But I'm critical as well: pay attention, perhaps you'll learn to speak, sing, paint, and jump even better. And then I'll praise you again. That's my way of setting you on the right path. For you ought to become truly good at something some day, and it shouldn't just be sorcery. Silly praise never gets you anywhere, but clever criticism does. Grandparents know that better than parents, and old sorcerers better than young.

We had a pleasant stay in Wasserburg am Inn. The Dictator had acolytes and spies there too, but fewer than outside Bavaria. It was a rural, catholic region and the brown Party's worldview was widely held to be "a bunch of baloney"—which sums things up perfectly. The town was old and picturesque, and had always loved technology, which pleased me. Wasserburg was the birthplace of the engineer who invented the Lanz Bulldog, Fritz Huber. One thing this good man said deserves to be carved in stone: "A tractor can't be one-cylinder enough."

Emma didn't need to learn Bavarian, since she remained an official Berlinerin. But, since I had to be Gruber, I didn't dare speak High German. Fortunately, he was a man of few words. So in the beginning I simply remained silent and no one suspected anything. In my free time I practiced the language of the alpine foothills with Gnadl, particularly the lively movement of the throat it requires. For the rest, there were Bavarian lexicons and grammars. Titus was the quickest to become bilingual, with no help from books. Gnadl taught me more spells in Wasserburg, and sometimes Emma and I went hiking with him up mountains with poetic-sounding names like Hochgern, Kampenwand, and Geigelstein. On Hochplatte I addressed a few words to Josef Gruber, thanking him for allowing me to assume his identity and promising not to do anything to harm his reputation. I took his silence as consent.

The strain of looking like the electrician day in and day out for weeks and even months on end was wearing me out. I hadn't the strength for it. When I was very tired, Gruber's appearance would suddenly slip off and I would be back and visible as Pahroc, a very ticklish situation. At least Emma could remain herself, which was important for the children.

After long consultations with Blüthner, Gnadl, and Emma, I decided to make a final attempt with Schneidebein. After all, we'd been playmates as young sorcerers. I had to try and sway him from his inveterate hatred. If that didn't work and the conversation went bad, I might have to threaten him— he couldn't afford to have anyone find out about his magical gifts. The Party was open to charlatans, but there was no way they'd accept a real sorcerer.

Blüthner suggested protecting Emma and the kids from being harassed or kidnapped by Schneidebein. There was a spell that could only be cast by several experienced sorcerers acting together, the more the better. We were sure that all those who had been at St. Polykarp for the conference would join in. It was a type of protective circle that could be drawn around a mother and her children. Blüthner called it Mother Shield because it didn't work for fathers. I'd never heard of it, but warmly agreed. Emma only needed a few instructions for the spell to work, and Pospischil agreed to advise her. We also invented a will for Josef Gruber, naming Emma as his heiress. The real Gruber had no children or siblings, and his parents had passed away. Even so, we weren't entirely comfortable: perhaps if this odd fellow had lived, he would have left his house and shop to a colleague, or to the Society for the Prevention of Cruelty to Animals.

If Schneidebein did manage to kill me, at least he wouldn't be able to get to my family. If I needed to escape from him, and managed to, he would run me down in the Reich sooner or later, whether I was underway as Gruber or Pahroc. The only place I could flee to was the Eastern Front, where there were hardly any spies or thugs. So "Josef Gruber" would have to be officially drafted by the war office and sent to the Front, with immaculate documentation from the punch-card system. That was the only thing that would explain Gruber's absence from Wasserburg. Nothing else was likely to work: drowning, falling down a crevice on a glacier, going crazy, leaving for parts unknown? Schneidebein would have pursued any mysterious disappearance throughout the entire Reich. But being called up for military service was no mystery. And no one at the front would care what Gruber looked like back home. I could live in my own skin there. Of course, I'd have to manage to survive. But that—I thought—would be no problem: after all, I was a sorcerer.

On a mild fall day I left for Berlin. After a three-hour flight I stood, unprotected and on my own, as Pahroc, at the entrance to Schneidebein's administrative headquarters. I gave the guard my full name and asked to speak with Herr Schneidebein. We're childhood friends, I said. He's been expecting me for some time.

The guard telephoned and I was asked to take a seat in a waiting room. After half an hour, tired of waiting, I rose and walked to the window. I saw a long limousine with a Party flag pull up by the guard. The chauffeur opened the back door and an imposing figure in a black uniform laden with medals and ribbons emerged. He saluted the guard briefly and entered the building. His face made a strong impression with its large aquiline nose and eyes that slanted in different directions. But I sensed immediately that he'd made his face unrecognizable to normal people, so they couldn't remember it. A sorcerer! He hadn't seen me at the window—or had he? I sat down again.

Ten minutes later I was taken by elevator to the top floor to see Schneidebein. The door to his office was twice the height of a normal man. My escort clicked his heels, shot his arm into the air, and withdrew as I entered.

"Well look at that, Comrade Pahroc dares to appear unmasked! I find that quite courageous."

"Hello, Schneidebein."

His desk was huge, with a stainless steel top. Behind it hung a portrait of the darkly sinister Party leader. There was another person in the room as well, a uniformed figure at a smaller table by the wall. A secretary, no doubt, for a typewriter sat before him.

"Where is Emma?"

"Somewhere safe."

He gave a wicked smile. "Oh, somewhere safe! And how long do you think she'll stay safe, now that you've shown up here?"

"Schneidebein, I've come to . . . But is there somewhere we can talk in private and clear this up?"

"I have no secrets from my secretary." The man at the table turned and nodded almost imperceptibly toward him. Because his eyes slanted in two different directions it was almost as though he were looking sharply at both of us at once. I recognized the face. It was the man who had emerged from the huge limousine a few minutes earlier and passed by the rigid sentry with a careless salute.

"Fine with me," said Schneidebein. "Herr Bab . . . !" He coughed.

The secretary looked at him questioningly.

"Griffzich, give us a moment to ourselves."

"Yes, sir!"

The tall man left.

My hearing was excellent. Who was Herr Bab? Evidently Schneidebein had two secretaries, one named Bab and one named Griffzich.

Now I could say what I came for. I did so, though I had the strange feeling that Griffzich was somehow still in the room. Invisible? That was impossible, sorcerers can always see each other. But questions still remained. For example, how could an ordinary sorcerer's servant appear as a high-ranking functionary in a fancy limousine and then be a secretary taking dictation? I put all that aside for the moment.

"Schneidebein, I want to apologize, most sincerely."

"Most sincerely! I'm glad you said that, otherwise I would have thought you were joking."

If he'd asked what I was apologizing for I would have been in an embarrassing position—but he didn't. I didn't want to bring up Schlosseck or Waldemar right away.

"I'm here to ask you to stop harassing us. We were friends once, and Emma and the children have done nothing to you. We live in fear now, and rather poorly."

He looked at me in surprise. Then his gaze softened.

"Good. I'll talk with you then. For old time's sake. But on one condition: you have to tell me where you're hiding now. You've got to trust me that far."

I nodded, looked him in the eyes for a long time, and then said softly:

"I'm sorry. I'm not in hiding."

"No?"

"Not at present. Schneidebein, please understand."

I could have made up some story or other about our hiding place, but he wouldn't have believed me for a moment. We knew one another too well: we wouldn't trust each other from here to the door. And the sense that the eerie secretary was still present was even stronger, I don't know why. At any rate he wasn't far away. Strange. Why had he called him Herr Bab first and then Griffzich?

Bab, Bahb, Baab? Perhaps Babel, Baboeuf, Babenberger?

And then it came to me: Babenzeller! The notorious Babenzeller Schlosseck had told me about. The same name that had sounded like "Bambin Zélé" when the Constable de Lesdiguières had said it—we'd cleared that up in St. Polykarp.

I considered leaping through the wall and escaping before Schneidebein even responded. It might be my last chance.

TEMPORARILY TURNING TO STEEL

February 2014

Dear Mathilda, I wanted to tell you more about my 1942 encounter with Schneidebein, so I searched recently for the waxed cloth notebooks where I wrote everything down afterwards. I couldn't find them anywhere in the apartment, nor in the basement, but I did run across all sorts of things of interest—a crate with the complete prototype of my Schacktograph, some wax records, and a few other devices: a demodulator receiver, a 1962 "golf ball" typewriter, manufactured by the successors of the old Hollerith GmbH firm, and my first computer with "floppy disks" and diskettes. There was also a dot matrix printer with a supply of ink ribbons that would have lasted a decade, from around 1990 to 2000, if I hadn't switched to an inkjet printer, then later to laser. Also my first mobile phones, quite clunky, and a wireless radio with all the parts. If I live another hundred years I'll start a museum. I could call it "The Museum of Electronic Antiquities."

But I couldn't find the notebooks, which is too bad. In the postwar years I recorded a lot of other thoughts in them too: about Schneidebein and me, about God and the world and death, about Stalingrad, about those two terrible wars, the first from stupidity, the second from malice—I would have liked to read through them again. Could waxed cloth notebooks be a favorite of Pankow rats? There should have been a few scraps left over from the meal. Or did Schneidebein steal them to prevent their publication? If so, it's not important now, I can still recall every word that was spoken that day in Berlin without them. There's a magic spell to store everything, especially conversations; it functions like a gigantic recorder. I've gotten into the habit of using the spell every evening. But I don't recommend it to anyone who prefers a life without burdens. If you decide you want to learn it, ask Rejlander; she can tell you how it's done. I taught it to her just a few days ago. She did say she hoped she'd forget it some day: there are memories she'd rather not carry around with her. Rejlander and I see each other more often these days and compare notes on the practice of sorcery.

But back to my wartime conversation with Schneidebein. Whenever I recall it, I'm thankful for every hour my life was free of fear, hate, and malice. That's why I'm telling you about it.

When I asked him to leave us in peace for the sake of our old friendship, Schneidebein just gave me a poisonous look. "That's far in the past now, and a lot has happened since then."

"All right—what exactly?" I asked. "I sidestepped you once when you asked me to join the Party, and I played a small trick on your boss a little later. I apologize for that. But that's not why you're so angry: Emma chose me. You should do the noble thing and accept that." I was still trying to be diplomatic.

"You've made it clear that you're against us. You've committed sabotage and discussed plans for assassination with your comrades. I know that from a trusted source. And since you've used the word noble—our nobility is based on consistency. We don't put up with sorcerers who do battle against us."

"Your State doesn't put up with sorcerers under any condition, and you're a sorcerer. The State just hasn't realized it yet, and that's because no one's told them. Sorcerers shouldn't be servants of the State anyway."

"I'm familiar with Schlosseck's thoughts on the matter! I, on the other hand, support historical development at its strongest source. I follow its dynamics! You have no idea what that is."

"I certainly do. I'm a technician. I'm thoroughly familiar with dynamics. For example centrifugal force: whatever's not in the exact center is hurled out! That's just what will happen to you. And when it does, you'll do well to have helped a few people. You'd do best by starting with Schlosseck and Waldemar."

Schneidebein grinned. "They're already beyond my help."

"You had them murdered?"

"Eliminated—as was my duty! Who do you think you're talking to?"

Rage overcame me and diplomacy was shoved aside.

"A mediocre sorcerer serving con-men and murderers! That's who!"

He turned red and gasped for breath, seething with rage. I was too, and still caught up in my horror: So he'd done it! Waldemar had died because of us, for us, even. Loyal, honest, friendly, clever Waldemar! And perhaps nothing would have happened to Schlosseck, had he not been my teacher. Schneidebein's hatred was that strong. And I was probably next in line.

I thought things over. If the mysterious sorcerer who remained invisible even to me truly was Babenzeller, perhaps I could approach him directly, even seek his protection. A daring idea, but not entirely misguided. The fact that he was there with Schneidebein didn't necessarily mean that he wanted to destroy me. A great sorcerer serves no one, neither a Schneidebein nor the State. And was Babenzeller truly evil? Perhaps he maintained that reputation simply to keep others from constantly seeking his help. His uniform was a masquerade, that seemed to me certain. I also recalled what Schlosseck had suggested: "He's amusing himself." Perhaps it would amuse him to let me live. I took the chance.

"And because you're mediocre, you try to be evil at least. But you'll never be a Babenzeller, no matter how hard you try!"

"Babenzeller? Who's that supposed to be? One of Schlosseck's phantasms I presume."

"You don't know him? The most powerful sorcerer of all? You're lying, surely. You're probably one of his students, but one who's not worthy of him. Unlike you, Babenzeller stands above the State and your stupid dynamics."

I was slightly surprised that Schneidebein remained silent and let me finish speaking. Was it because he sensed that his invisibly present master wanted to hear me finish what I was saying?

The effect of my ploy remained unclear; the eerie presence remained hidden. Or was I wrong and this Griffzich was merely a secretary? I tried a second time.

"By the way, I've made a discovery that will decide the outcome of the war once and for all, and if you kill me, you'll never know what it is. If the slightest harm comes to Emma, the children, or me, it will belong to my father's nation. You'll soon have to deal with them in any case, and that will mean your defeat. A copy of my plans is kept in an armored safe at a notary public in Washington. It will be delivered to the Pentagon the instant they lose contact with me."

At that moment "Griffzich" reappeared. He was sitting at the secretary's desk again, but now he seemed taller and more massive than before. Only his face remained unchanged. "How amusing!" he exclaimed.

I bowed. "It's a pleasure to meet you Herr Babenzeller!" I said. I'd hit the nail on the head.

"Good day, Pahroc!"

"Does my invention interest you?"

"No, but your impertinence does."

Accustomed as I was to the Bavarian dialect, I knew one thing at once: he was from Upper Bavaria.

Now Schneidebein spoke up again, and made his second mistake: "I'll eliminate him, Herr Babenzeller, if you'll allow me."

"I won't allow you. Can't you see I'm talking with him?"

Schneidebein turned red.

"And by the way, I don't like being called 'one of Schlosseck's phantasms'—or Griffzich—who, if you please, is Griffzich?"

Schneidebein turned white. He changed colors so quickly I thought some magic spell must be involved.

"An old name for Death. It just came to me . . . I just wanted . . ."

The sinister man turned to me: "Before you two start: Yes, Schneidebein is my student. What makes you think he's mediocre?"

"I was trying to annoy him. But just him, not you! May I ask what you meant by 'start'?" I asked. "What are we supposed to start?"

Babenzeller threw a glance at Schneidebein, who then lit into me. He tried to land a left to my face—using the Long Arm from the other side of his huge desk. But I saw it coming. As the blow arrived, I lost weight and floated away like a feather from its force, so that it missed.

"What was that supposed to be?" I said mockingly, still floating, "a schoolyard memory from kindergarten?"

I knew the moment I regained weight he would strike again, but I was prepared for that too. As his fist landed, I was a tiger baring my teeth and biting down. One of the splendid predators in the Dresden Zoo had served as my model. I'd studied it carefully during our visit, little knowing how well that body would serve me. Schneidebein screamed in pain. Of course, I didn't dare bite his arm off—that might have placed him in mortal danger. I sprang on top of his desk and went for his throat. He leaped up and stumbled back against the Führer's portrait, which promptly fell from the wall. Did he really have nothing to offer but the Long Arm? Had he learned nothing in the past twenty years? I was wrong.

"Good, very good," Babenzeller nodded. He was praising Schneidebein and now I saw why: the metal surface of the desk had turned glowing hot in a fraction of a second. I roared and sprang toward the ceiling so violently I would have injured myself smashing against it if I hadn't had the presence of mind, in spite of the pain, to employ the key thought that softened walls and ceilings. If I'd hit hard, I probably would have fallen back onto the hotplate of the desk's surface and burned myself badly. But the force of my leap propelled me into the attic area, where I licked my paws and changed back into Pahroc. Schneidebein hadn't come after me, which meant he couldn't fly yet, perhaps not even pass through walls. But halfway through the tiles of the roof, as I tried to emerge and fly away, I was held fast by Babenzeller.

"Not so fast! First show us what you've learned."

"Why?" I asked. "He knows nothing but Heat."

But at the same time Babenzeller became Schneidebein and said, "Big mistake, Pahroc!"

I was stunned for a moment. Then I saw that he was slightly wall-eyed. I just laughed. "I'm not falling for that!" I cried. "You're too great a master to get mixed up in a fight between two lesser ones—it's not fair!"

But a strong force pulled me back into the office. Schneidebein was sitting there as before, and Babenzeller on a chair beside him.

"One request, Herr Babenzeller!" I said.

Schneidebein rose to continue the battle, but his master held him back.

"What is it?"

"Would you please change your outfit, if you don't mind? I'm sorry, I just can't take that uniform seriously."

I saw him smile for the first time.

"The nerve! As it happens, I was about to change anyway."

Suddenly he was wearing a Stresemann stroller—dark jacket, gray vest, silver tie, and striped trousers.

"Now get back to it—you're wasting my valuable time!"

Schneidebein was surely as amazed by his master's behavior as I was, but he spent less time thinking about it. While I was still distracted, he caught me off guard with the Leather spell, which I'd only heard about till then. Suddenly my belt started to tighten, slowly but with great force. I tried to unbuckle it, but it was too late. I wheezed and struggled for air.

"Well done!" Babenzeller said in praise. "Just the right thing!"

It looked like I was going to have to give in. What could I do? Making myself lighter or flying off wouldn't work here, I had to get thinner quickly somehow. How gladly I would have turned into a stick or wooden beam, but I'd not yet learned the difficult art of transforming myself into an inanimate object. Get thin, I thought feverishly as the belt drew tighter and tighter, slim down! And then the saving thought arrived: Turn into a snake! That I could do, so I fell to the ground and became a snake. A six-foot long python that stretched under the desk—it was clearly Dresden Zoo's day. A smaller, slimmer snake would have made things even easier, but I could still twist out of the tightening belt. I wrapped myself around my opponent's leg and worked my way up, coiling and squeezing. He hadn't been ready for that. Something snapped, and I heard his scream. But all at once the leg was gone and there was nothing to wrap around, Schneidebein had disappeared completely. I turned back into myself quickly and looked around for him. Was he invisible—to me, a sorcerer? Impossible. But why couldn't I see him?

"That's far too . . . !" Babenzeller hissed. "What did I tell you?" He was apparently speaking to his student. But what did he mean "far too . . ." Too much? Too little? Too small? Too big? Yes, too big! I looked at the desk top and saw that Schneidebein knew a spell I hadn't mastered yet: Miniaturization—changing into a much smaller creature. It's a far better camouflage than invisibility, which doesn't work with sorcerers. Just in time, I saw that a locust was now sitting on the desk top, half hidden behind the intercom, next to a glass and carafe of water. Yes, a desert locust, too large indeed to remain unnoticed. Before it could turn into something else and come at me, I grabbed the glass, turned it over, and trapped it. It tried to jump, but wasn't fast enough. One or two legs seemed injured. Locusts have a hard time when they have to face tigers and giant snakes. I would never have thought of doing that with the glass, by the way, if I hadn't been in the habit of trapping insects that way at home, then slipping a postcard under the glass and letting the insect go at the window.

Only then did I realize I'd won the battle. The trapped locust turned back into Schneidebein, but now he was the size of thumb, jumping up and down and banging on the glass with his little fists. Sorcerers can't pass through glass or steel. And to lift the glass by his own strength, or break it, he had to grow larger. But as long as I held my hand on the glass, he couldn't. Even if he'd turned into an elephant, it would have been a tiny one.

"Upon my soul, such dynamics in a glass!" I said. I was still in a dangerous situation, but at least a small taunt seemed appropriate.

I assumed that the master would now put an end to his student's humiliation. Surely he would. But how? Would he use sorcery to kill me? It was rumored that he could. But all he said was: "Get out of here before I turn the glass over!" Then he added softly, "Head for the front!" There was no way Schneidebein could have heard that through the thick glass.

"And will you track me down?"

"I've got better things to do. But Schlosseck is some-one . . ." he cast a dark look at the tiny man under the glass, "Schlosseck is someone I would have liked to know better."

"One last question."

"No, get out of here!"

I did. I took a direct path through the wall of the sixth floor, made myself invisible, and rose as high into the heavens as I could. I took my first bearing southward from the clock tower of the Tempelhof printing house, and only when I'd reached it was I sure no one was following me. As I steered toward Fläming Heath—recognized by initiates through the elevation of the landscape—I started to feel more at ease, though I was dazed by what I had just been through. Using spells in battle is terribly tiring because everything has to happen so fast. I prefer magic at a slower pace.

But for now I was enjoying a victory I would not have thought possible in Babenzeller's threatening presence. Mathilda, no matter how small your chances seem, always be ready for anything, even victory. If you must, then fight it out. The safest and most fruitful approach is to steal whatever you're fighting over through guile or kindness. That's no victory over an enemy, it's a victory over the God of War himself. But if you must fight, set fear aside, be bold, and amuse yourself if you can.

Throughout my flight back I meditated on Schlosseck's death, and wondered how Schneidebein could possibly have managed to kill him. Blüthner, who had ears everywhere, told me

about it later. My teacher had turned his back on Schneidebein to show his contempt. He was often careless in reveal-
ing how little he thought of someone. He clearly meant to
provoke Schneidebein, but not drive him to murder. Perhaps
he didn't say a word, just let his back speak for him. And that
dog Schneidebein simply shot him from behind with an ordinary army pistol.

I needed to think more about Babenzeller too.

He remained a mystery to me, and still is to this day,
though I've learned a few things about him.

That strange change of clothes. Surely he didn't mean
to tell me that a soldier could become a civilian by magic
in a matter of seconds. That takes place without the help of
magic, especially when wars have been lost. I think he was
trying to show something else: his distance from the regime
that Schneidebein was bound to. But why had he broken off
our exchange so brusquely? Perhaps to avoid confronting
Schneidebein with the fact that he had fallen from his good
graces.

What was he doing in Schneidebein's office in the first
place, and why had he entered in a uniform that befouled the
world? Why did he want to see Schneidebein and me go at
each other?

The only mystery I could clear up at once on my own
was his temporary invisibility, even though he was still in the
room. He'd reduced himself to the size of an insect and was
too tiny to be noticed. He confirmed that to me later, in East
Prussia. He'd been sitting on the back of the chair as an ant.

And equally puzzling: if he was as evil as everyone
thought, why did he let me go? Did he enjoy his bad reputation? Or had he been evil once and then changed? Did he
want to talk with me again later and win me over somehow
(to evil perhaps), or was he deeply unhappy and looking to
me for salvation? In that case, he'd have to protect me from
Schneidebein—that thought offered some hope. The more

mysterious a person is, the more ideas and even certainties rain down about his nature and what he seeks in the world.

As I said, I saw Babenzeller again at the end of the war. He offered an explanation for his behavior that at first surprised me. He said he'd actually been eager to hear more about my invention. I'd claimed it would "decide the outcome of the war once and for all." That would arouse anyone's curiosity, not just a sorcerer's. Moreover, he was impressed by my boldness, which he called "chutzpah."

He'd respected Schlosseck highly, though he obviously considered him an idealist. He wasn't one himself, but power and death weren't simply an amusement for him—Schlosseck had been wrong about that. I watched this supposed Satan save people's lives. I'll write more about that in its proper place. We're still in Wasserburg for the moment.

When I came within sight of the city by the Inn River, it was already dark. In fact I couldn't actually see the city, only the ribbon of the river glistening in the moonlight. Like all other cities, Wasserburg was blacked out to protect against bombing raids. I floated down invisibly toward the electrical appliance shop, entered the building as Josef Gruber, and only then became Pahroc again. The children were long since asleep, and I spent half the night telling Emma everything that had happened to me in Berlin. Our hopes were now raised, but I couldn't continue playing the role of Josef Gruber, the strain of remaining transformed for so long was damaging my health. I decided to arrange for my induction into the army and head for the front as soon as possible. No place in the world was safer for fleeing sorcerers—safe from persecution of course, not from enemy soldiers.

Before I left, at just the right time, I learned three important spells that could save my life in battle. First, Gnadl taught me a spell that enabled him to climb about in the mountains for days with no provisions. He called it the Camel Mode, be-

130

cause camels can cross entire deserts without food or water. They store those up ahead of time, and when they've made it through the barren stretch they tank up again. This spell is quite similar. I sometimes wondered about the enormous quantity of food and drink Gnadl could consume without falling prey to a digestive block that lasted for days. The Camel Mode is not for epicures, since they enjoy dining as often as possible. In times of need, on the other hand, or facing forced marches, one tries to eat something extra ahead of time, if possible. Of course, there are usually physical limits. Gnadl's spell expanded those limits, and I made good use of it.

The second survival spell turns a large part of one's body temporarily into steel. Blüthner advised me to learn this extremely difficult and highly problematic magical art. He hadn't mastered it himself, and the only person he knew who was an expert at it was the Constable de Lesdiguières. In response to our request, the great man came to Wasserburg in person. He did not appear as the elegantly dressed cavalier we'd seen in St. Polykarp of course, but was camouflaged instead as a remarkably old French forced laborer, working by day in an armament factory downriver. At night he would leave his barracks and fly in invisibly for practice sessions.

I received his instructions in a gravel pit behind the high banks of the Inn River, because the spell could be quite noisy—if you lost your balance while you were made of metal, for example. It takes a great deal of concentration to turn even a part of yourself into something inanimate. But the Steel spell is far more demanding. True, you can learn at some point to make yourself look like a safe or a blacksmith's anvil, but you remain living tissue, with circulation and respiration. A living being, even if to all appearances it's an armored safe, can be shot or struck dead.

It's an art of self-protection with a single advantage and several disadvantages. If I protect my arm, my entire upper body, or my head with the Steel spell, those parts of the body are not simply encased in armor, but become solid steel instead. Thrusts slide off, knives snap, bullets ricochet off through the air leaving barely a scratch. If someone hits me with his fist, he's in for a hospital visit. But it works only if I turn to steel at the exact moment of the attack, not too soon, nor too late. No one can remain in that mode for more than three or four seconds, since it causes great pain. You protect yourself against the pain of an attack by the greater pain of the spell, a questionable exchange—unless it saves your life. You can still move during the spell, but only those parts of you that have not turned to steel.

The heart, circulation, respiration, the brain, the senses—all living functions have to be temporarily stored in parts of the body that haven't turned to steel. That requires an enormous degree of concentration. Depending on what's involved, your sight and hearing get worse, you think less clearly, you can barely cast spells. The only way out of this is to spring back quickly into your normal physical state. You can't change into some other object, like railroad tracks or a water hydrant, you remain human. Nor can you turn invisible or lighter, both are out of the question. So, dear Mathilda, if you turn yourself partly into steel, don't sit on a rickety folding chair, don't stand on a boat dock that's old and weak, and for heaven's sake don't go out on the ice of a frozen lake—you can imagine what would happen. Nor is it advisable to use the Steel spell when you're in a rowboat or sailboat.

You're welcome to learn the Steel spell, Mathilda, but I hope from the bottom of my heart that you never have to use it. I practiced it diligently and even invented a simple method to follow my progress. Metal conducts electricity: I would take a small light bulb, a flashlight battery, a little wire, and test my conductivity.

Lesdiguières served in the First World War. He knew what it was like to leave cover and head into enemy fire.

Many years ago, he too had gone into hiding at the front. He'd been revealed as a sorcerer and was forced to abandon his chateau in Grenoble. So he turned up first at the front and later in Paris, where he painted pictures on the bank of the Seine. No one seemed to notice that he couldn't paint, nor took any special notice of him. One day he began casting the Euphoria spell on people who saw his work—suddenly they loved his paintings, and paid higher and higher prices for them. Now rich, he bought back the chateau from the heirs of the owner who'd disappeared, and at some point began to look just like him. That fact that he himself was the former owner was of no interest to anyone—it never even occurred to them. A splendid coup, a masterful example of long term success. But it's only logical that such sorcery takes time.

I asked Lesdiguières about Babenzeller. He said the man deliberately cultivated his horrible reputation, but that he wasn't straightforwardly evil. And he really could do all sorts of things. Even sorcerers could never be sure if he was in the room.

"And he can take on another person's appearance to perfection. He was with us in St. Polykarp!"

"Then Schneidebein knows about St. Polykarp too?"

"No, he doesn't. Babenzeller is tight lipped."

"He taught Schneidebein Miniaturization, at any rate, shrinking your body to the size of an ant."

"You should learn that too. It's good protection when Steel is of no further help."

"Who can I learn it from?"

"Not from me. My entire nature runs counter to growing smaller, nor can I do so. But see Macintosh, she's a master of the spell. I'll tell her she should teach you. She'll probably even visit you. Scottish ladies love any excuse to travel."

"Thank you, Monsieur, that's very kind of you. By the way, who did Babenzeller appear as in St. Polykarp?"

"Krine Profuso."

"That can't be! The little one from Zülpich?"

"Exactly. The real Profuso died in 1934, but I was the only one who knew that. She was descended from the Merovingian dynasty on her mother's side."

"She flirted with me! Or rather, he did."

"I know nothing about Babenzeller's erotic tendencies. He may be open to anything."

Babenzeller remained on my mind.

Macintosh arrived in the guise of a Swabian artist with a sketchbook. She spoke incredibly good German, having absorbed the complete works of Goethe in both German and English—dictionaries bored her. She stayed in Fletzinger Bräu and wandered back and forth through Wasserburg to sketch its beauties. She would land at night on our bedroom balcony and teach Emma and me the Miniaturization spell— we were both ready for it. We concentrated on the specific thoughts you need to make yourself tiny—that has to come first, otherwise there's no way to become an ant, housefly, flea, or louse.

Macintosh drilled us on the dangers tiny creatures face: people tread on them unknowingly, or knowingly come swinging flyswatters. Every tiny being has a myriad of enemies: moles, hedgehogs, aggressive ants, hungry birds, geckos with sticky tongues, snakes, lizards.

"You'd do well," Macintosh said, "to study a little biology. Find out what enemies feed on specific insects, and take a good look around before you turn into one. And another piece of advice, since you'll be staying in military barracks, don't choose to be a flea or a louse if they're spraying DDT."

"Spraying what?"

"Dichlorodiphenyltrichloroethane."

"Of course, my lady, perfectly clear."

"And be sure not to sleep that way. Small pests must be prudent and ready for anything."

I swore solemnly to do as she said. Clever, wonderful Macintosh! Had she not been such a lady and protected by so many keep-your-distance spells, I would have put my arms around her and given her a kiss.

Our next visitor was the beautiful Pospischil from Vienna, camouflaged as a nurse from a rest home for wounded soldiers, who flew in nightly from Chiemsee to give Emma guidance on Mother Shield, a disinformation spell similar to the one that protected St. Polykarp: anyone who approached a mother and her children with evil intent suddenly lost their concentration, felt an urgent need to be elsewhere, and forgot what they'd originally planned to do. Emma could also trigger this temporary mental confusion in a specific person. If the person arriving was an enemy, she was protected. If not, and Emma had made a mistake, the person would simply lose the thread of what they were saying, then pick it up again later. Emma learned quickly. She practiced on the postman and various customers at the shop. Of course she only tried it once on each person. She didn't want to send anyone into a depression. She could soon cast the spell perfectly. Pospischil parted from her with a kiss and was glad to be returning so soon to her Vienna. But she wouldn't have missed her time as Florence Nightingale: "I always wanted to know what it would be like to nurse wounded soldiers."

The Dictator had already marched into several countries and taken them under German control. The success went to his head, his roar over the loudspeakers grew increasingly triumphant.

"He's going to conquer the entire earth," Emma said, "first the northern hemisphere and then the southern, then there'll be nothing worth living for."

"Except each other," I replied.

Seven-year-old Titus heard that. He was in primary school and had a strongly nationalistic teacher in jodhpurs. The teacher wanted to learn from the children what was being said about the regime in their homes.

"How many parts will the German nation consist of after the final victory? Well?" He was probably thinking of the names of the various continents. Several pupils raised their hands.

"Titus?"

"Two: the northern and the southern hemispheres."

Moved, the teacher said nothing and wrote in his grade book: "Titus, oral response: A."

If I wanted to disappear into the chaos of war, I'd have to get moving. I was certain Schneidebein was still set on revenge, and my fear that he would find us grew greater with each passing day. And I still wasn't sure if Babenzeller was helping him. I paid night visits to the army registration office in Wasserburg and the Munich District military command post, and Blüthner visited the army's "Department of Automated Reports" for me in Berlin. I'd given him a brief course on the Hollerith system and he knew what to do. Sorcery can administer a kick in the rear even to bureaucracies. The induction notice for Josef Gruber arrived within a week.

Emma and I were both deeply saddened by our parting. I didn't know when I'd be able to return, and the memory this awakened of my father's departure for the First World War weighed heavily on me. Emma was in an advanced state of pregnancy. It was a soldier's farewell, one taking place a hundred thousand times a day back then, except that we were certain we loved one another more than hundreds of thousands of others. We hoped that the war would soon end in defeat, for that would surely be the end of our troubles with Schneidebein as well. And I wanted to be there when the baby arrived—perhaps our fourth child could use the Long Arm.

Leaving the children was particularly hard. Felix, who was ten by then, cried with the rest. Saddest of all was having to ask them to be good and to continue telling people that they didn't know where their father was.

Gnadl went with me to the assembly point. His stiff leg was keeping him out of the war. In fact, it wasn't stiff at all—on the Wilder Kaiser ridge it had been just as flexible and muscular as the other one. Gnadl was only an invalid during medical exams and recruitment tests. He was able to make his leg appear bent and misshapen on the x-ray screen. Nowadays, as I write this letter, modern technology seems able to imitate sorcery to some extent: cars perform totally differently on carbon emission tests than they do on the streets.

First, I was taken for a brief basic training course in a suburb of Görlitz. I'd arranged this on my marching orders, since the city was sufficiently distant from both Wasserburg and Berlin. In a Bavarian barracks someone might have known the electrician Josef Gruber and reported that I couldn't possibly be him. And I had to avoid Berlin anyway, since that whole area would surely be a minefield for me.

For most fathers drafted in wartime, marching and combat training were torture, but not for me. Anyone who can float gets no blisters marching, and when "Volunteers step forward!" rings out, turning invisible for a brief moment helps.

Then my train headed for the Eastern Front. I assumed that my old and newly-learned spells would allow me to remain unscathed, and that there were still home leaves from time to time. Then, for a few weeks, I would no longer be the Gruber at the front, who could look like Pahroc, but the Bavarian Gruber they were used to in Wasserburg—something I would have to deal with. Leave did come around and I got to see our newest child, little Carola, though the village assumed she was Josef Gruber's illegitimate baby. I felt as bad about that as Emma did. The little one was truly sweet, but she couldn't use the little Long Arm. We came to terms with the fact that our children couldn't cast spells, but only charm us—which wasn't too bad, was it? And we had each other again for a few short but perfect days of happiness. It's incredible how love can shield us from terrible things, even when it doesn't have much time. And the children were happy that their father came to visit them occasionally during Josef Gruber's leave—always when Gruber happened to be away. They were used to the fact that the two men didn't get along and stayed out of each other's way. Then the sad day arrived: Josef Gruber had to return to the front, and their father also stayed away. Over time they began to sense that there was some connection—they weren't dumb.

Was this damned war never going to be lost—was the regime never going to crumble?

When my troop was in danger of being surrounded outside Stalingrad, I took it calmly at first. I had no idea what I was in for. Mathilda, I wonder if I should tell a sweet eighteen-year-old girl like you, reading this letter in 2030, all of the things that happened at the front. I know how my own dreams were poisoned as a youngster by all too drastic depictions of war—I would feel a rage rising when anyone began such a tale.

In the end, you can simply say that war is hell, that terrible things happen, that you'll have ample opportunities to betray your own morals, and that there's little chance you'll come out of it proud of yourself. Reason, sensitivity, openness to conversation, a love for peace—all such qualities are pushed aside in war, considered dangerous nonsense. It's as logical as it is bleak: unless you shoot at anything that moves on the other side, you increase the likelihood that your comrades will die.

At some point all I wanted to do was flee—though thanks to Lesdiguières' spells I was in less danger than others when shells came raining down. But I was far from safe. The Steel spell gave me confidence on my way to the front. But it was of use less often than I thought. Once, when an enemy soldier had emptied his magazine at me, I instantly turned back to flesh and blood, and shot him while he was reloading. It gave me no pleasure. On the contrary, I was so disgusted with myself I could scarcely stand it. I can't help saying it. I realize no one can understand who hasn't experienced it himself: the brutalization necessary to survive, and the self-hate that comes with it, a feeling that never fully disappears.

It wasn't fear of death that finally led to my desertion, and it wasn't just my love for Emma and the children—I simply couldn't continue killing people. I planned to escape at night, when there weren't so many bullets flying around. But it was far too cold to fly. I would have to find somewhere warm to land almost immediately. I hadn't yet learned to heat walls or metal objects till they served as sources of warmth, though it had been made painfully clear to me that Schneidebein could. In Russia I had ample cause to envy his ability.

But in the end I took off anyway and rose into the air—invisibly, of course. The cold crept into my bones and even my brain, and soon I could go no farther. I was forced to land in the midst of Soviet troops and become one of them. At first I remained invisible, but I knew that couldn't protect me in the long run. So I became a Soviet soldier. I knew the language, and I picked my model the same way Gnadl picked Josef Gruber—there were plenty of dead to choose from. I was an ordinary soldier from Minsk, waiting for the weather to turn warm enough to fly. Till then, I had to shoot at German soldiers—I aimed as poorly as I could, but still faced the living nightmare that I might accidentally kill someone I knew.

I tried to take off again, but with over thirty degrees of frost I couldn't get farther than our original position, which at least offered a few places to warm up. I nearly sat down at a German campfire as a Russian soldier, but caught my mistake in time. Then the pain of having to fire my gun resumed. I'd rather go home and deal with Schneidebein than wipe out more lives here, I thought. At some point I met a young man in the trenches whom I immediately recognized as a sorcerer. His name was Titus, like my younger son. Talented, lively, musical, his father composed operas. He talked for half an hour about his sailboat on the Starnberger See, a Rennjolle, and invited me to come sailing with him some day. Dead calms were unknown to him—he could conjure up his own private breezes. Only decency and fairness, he said, prevented him from becoming world-famous for never losing a regatta. At that very moment he was struck by a sniper's bullet and died in my arms.

It's a great shame we're not permitted to undo a death— the most we can do is occasionally delay one. And bullets are simply too fast. Once they're on their way, there's no time for a protective spell. Protective spells have to be set up well in advance.

I'll make it short: a further flight attempt, this time equipped with two hot water bottles and innumerable layers of clothing, finally carried me in the dark of night out of the encircled area and far beyond the front. The feeling of being free at last was indescribable. I took shelter in a peasant's cottage, claiming to be part of a scattered group of partisans, and even joined in a few acts of sabotage against railroad lines— but no shooting was involved. When warmer weather came along I rose into the air again and hoped to reach Bavaria, Emma, and the children with as few interruptions as possible. But my navigation suffered from my poor knowledge of geography. All I could do was check the position of the sun and head in a generally westward direction. The landscape beneath me was mostly empty, so I had some trouble finding settlements where I could sleep, eat, and recover. Now and then I saw a train I could follow, and let it lead me to a city. The results were not always pleasant. Once the trip ended at a prison camp where frightened men, women, and children were being driven from train cars. A portion of them headed toward barracks and buildings—the majority were gassed immediately and died a painful death. I passed invisibly through the wall into the death chamber and saw it happen. I drew back shocked and shaken. I could do nothing, nothing at all. I was lucky to leave the camp suffering only nausea from the small dose of poison I'd inhaled. But no doubt that wasn't the poison—it was what I'd seen.

Dear Mathilda, we all want to go on living and we're glad when we survive hardships and disasters, or aren't among the victims of mass murder. At least, that's what we always say when asked—we're glad. That's easy to say, and we're expected to thank God too, which we do, it doesn't hurt anything. It's more difficult to formulate the two poisonous questions that now hang over our lives and can never be answered: Why do such terrible things happen, and why did I escape them? Why didn't I die with the rest? We're not "glad"—or not just glad, that's the wrong word.

You're not even three years old and I'm writing you about such things. If I weren't so sure this dreamy little girl will turn into a thoughtful, grown woman who wants to hear the truth, I wouldn't dare continue.

I was miserable and increasingly weak, and meanwhile the weather had turned colder. I used all my remaining strength to get as far west as I could. But then an accident occurred that affects only sorcerers. In the middle of my flight, time sprang forward two years without taking me along.

When I awoke I couldn't figure out what had happened. I'd followed a train—that was all I knew. Now I was on the ground and couldn't remember ever landing. When I saw myself in a window I was shocked. I was badly emaciated, my clothes were ripped and had been clumsily resewn—when had I patched them? And a star-shaped piece of cloth had been sewn onto the left front side of my jacket—what was that? The window was in a building next to a factory entrance. I couldn't recall having seen a factory from the air. I entered the grounds and someone asked me where I was from. I replied that all I remembered was seeing a train from above. I didn't know who I was. That was a lie: I knew very well I was Pahroc.

"You saw a train from above?" asked the man.

"Yes, strange. What's today's date?"

He answered and suddenly I realized I'd fallen into one of those cracks in time Schlosseck had told me about, what he called the Heisterbach Effect. Two whole years were simply gone! Fortunately it wasn't three hundred, like the monk at the monastery. I could remember everything up to my flight west after the prison camp. And I realized Emma and our three, no four, children had been waiting for me for over two years. The youngest must be two and a half by now.

"Are we still at war?" I asked.

"He's in shock or something," the man said to a companion, and then to me: "Yes, we're at war. But come along with me now."

So for a few weeks I was taken on as a worker in a small armaments factory. It was one of the few places, perhaps the only place, where Jews were treated relatively well: food, warmth, and something like fairness. An island in the midst of hell.

None of my colleagues have yet studied what factor sets off the stoppage of time for flying sorcerers. I first connected this mental blackout, like a film that breaks, with being cold, but then it occurred to me that what I'd seen in the camp had produced a sort of paralysis of the senses, a temporary death. Did I fall to the earth like a stone and lie there for two years? That couldn't be. Why were my cloths so worn, if not from the wear and tear of daily use? And where did the yellow star on my breast come from? In addition to this, I certainly had memories—just not of real life, but of a wealth of dreams instead, of Emma and the children mostly, sometimes peacefully engaged, sometimes facing terrible dangers. Today I'm almost certain that the Heisterbach Effect is connected with mental trauma and despair. Not many people know this, so I urgently advise you, dear Mathilda, not to fly when you're feeling down, or shocked about something, or in deep depression.

The armaments factory kept a long list of the names of those who were to be spared assignment to the poison gas factory. The courageous owner wanted to save them. He set up a major scheme to bribe the murderers, and to take the workers he was protecting with him to another factory further west. For all practical purposes, the list included every Jewish worker in the company. I didn't want to be put on the list and said I could take care of myself. The owner didn't understand what I meant—how could he? To avoid his anxious questions, I decided to depart that night on a six-hour flight westward. The air was progressively worse. The smoke of burning cities reached me even when there were only forests and fields below. And the smoke smelled terrible. It wasn't just firewood burning in those cities, but fabrics, lacquer, oil, and rubber—I don't want to say what all was burning, but it was everything. It was a corrosive smell that ate into the soul. I'll never forget it. I know I'll recognize it at once if it ever reappears. The nose's memory is pitiless.

Anyone who spends time traveling about the world profits from his old geography lessons—if he's paid close attention. Unfortunately, I'm a bit weak in this area. In attempting to avoid the smoke and the bomber squadrons, I drifted too far to the north and wound up in East Prussia. I didn't know that province at all and only realized where I was later from station signs I remembered. There were numerous lakes, small villages, and farms, and it looked like freedom reigned over it all. But one often has this impression when a landscape is broad and rather sparsely settled. It can be deceptive and in this case it was deceptive indeed.

Several times I saw long columns of people on country roads, heading west with horse carts and baby buggies. I floated down, appeared as a civilian, and learned little more than I had seen from above. They were fleeing from the enemy's army, and the front wasn't far off. One column had no carts or horses. The people wore clothes that were much too thin, they were dead tired, and sick—and they weren't moving of their own free will. Armed men in uniforms were driving them on. If they spoke to one another they were shot. Whoever fell was left to die. They were Jews who had been scheduled to die in the camps. As the front lines drew closer, the camps were closed and the inmates driven westward—with no other purpose than leaving them dead, one by one, on the way. It was clear the murderers wanted the Soviets to find only scattered bodies along the country roads, and not ten thousand killed en masse in the camps.

Now I flew as straight westward as I could, since I planned to follow the coastline as far as Hamburg. I knew what markers to use from Hamburg to Passau, and from there it was only a short jump to Wasserburg. First I had to get to the sea. The winter had been so severe that the shore waters of the Baltic were still frozen. I saw another death march: hundreds of people from one of the abandoned camps, most of them women, were being herded along the shore by armed guards and then driven out onto the ice. At first I thought they were taking a shortcut across the frozen cove, but then a fierce volley of shots rang out. Here too the criminals were set on leaving the victors as little proof for mass murder as they could—bodies on a sheet of ice would disappear at the first thaw. The uniformed men were walking about twenty meters behind the prisoners, firing at them. Rage boiled up in me. I turned into a large bird of prey, a golden eagle I'd read up on once, years ago. I plunged my talons into the face of one of the guards, took on my own form, and ripped the machine gun from his hands. I could fire that weapon in my sleep. I readied my weapon and prepared to mow down all the thugs. But it merely went "click": in my excitement I'd forgotten that I couldn't kill with the aid of spells. It was amazing enough that I'd been able to change into the bird of prey, with what I'd had firmly in mind. But there was nothing to be done now—my death seemed certain. The other uniforms had noticed that something was wrong with their comrade.

At that moment a voice beside me said:

"I'll handle this. Step back!"

I didn't see the man who had spoken, but the voice sounded familiar. A thick cloud of steam rose around us. It obscured the murderers, but their screams could be heard. The ice was melting beneath them. When you sink in water you can't keep shooting, especially in water that cold. The fog disappeared as quickly as it had come, and now, in place of the band of soldiers, there was only a large hole in the ice. I'd dropped my weapon by then and resumed my floating state.

The prisoners had thrown themselves onto the surface of the ice when the shooting started. Now they staggered to their feet again. Some of them started to go on across the cove, others headed back toward the shore.

But many shots had already struck home. At first I could only help one person, a woman. I carried her back to shore on foot, because in spite of her emaciated body, she was still too heavy to fly with. A few people were already coming from a village to help those still out on the ice. They'd heard the shots and a stranger had turned up and described the situation. They brought thirty more back to shore—fifteen of them survived. The police state had lost at least some of its power over souls. Their pity was aroused, and people acted in ways that just a year earlier they would have hesitated to, out of blindness or fear of punishment.

I definitely needed a rest now—more precisely, a bed. Near a stove, if at all possible. I was taken to a house on the side of a hill where an elderly man with a large nose showed me to a bed, then stoked a tile stove, and laid in wood. He turned to me and said: "The war will soon be over. A few days more."

I recognized him: It was Babenzeller!

"That would be nice," I managed to say.

"Now get some sleep, Pahroc. We'll talk tomorrow."

I collapsed on the bed and fell asleep. Or perhaps the other way around: I fell to sleep and collapsed on the bed. At any rate, I needed no help from magic spells.

MIND READING

March 2014

When I arose, I found a razor blade and a piece of soap on the window sill. As I shaved the stubble from my face, I gazed out onto the sea and saw they were still trying to find drowned killers at the ice hole in the cove. But no doubt they were dragged into the depths by the weight of their weapons, ammunition, and steel helmets.

Babenzeller arrived with a pot and cups: "There may be a spell to make real coffee, but I don't know it." At any rate, the drink was hot. He was wearing a dark suit with a white shirt and bow tie and highly polished shoes. Did he have a servant? In the midst of this war?

"You're a mystery to me," I said.

"As you are to me. You disappeared for two years, fell out of time itself. I can usually find anything I care to look for, but in this case I was stymied."

"And did you find my family?"

"Of course."

"Did you tell Schneidebein?"

"No, I—left him to himself."

"And why were you looking for me?"

"Your wife asked me to. She's a woman few men could say no to."

"How is she?"

"Bad. Her father was arrested and killed. They claimed he was involved in some sort of conspiracy. Her mother died in a bombing raid. And someone named Gruber is missing."

"Does Emma know you found me?"

"I told her last night."

"By wireless?"

"I have my own methods."

By the way, he never told me how a sorcerer can telegraph someone without wires or a sender, and securely to boot. To this day, I still don't know. Babenzeller was deeply interested in technology, and had a good knowledge of engineering. I told him my love for such things had cooled somewhat during the war. I'd seen too much weapons technology and the results it produced.

"But you said you'd invented something that would change the course of the war. Something stored in the safe of a notary public in Washington . . ."

So he still wanted to know about that. I explained my ideas about satellites and high resolution photos from space, and why I thought that would lead to peace. But as for the safe, I said, I'd made that up.

He was a bit disappointed.

"Fine. Something of that kind might be decisive in future wars, or even prevent them. That would depend on the transmitters being small and lightweight enough to be shot into space. But how could that be done? Electronic tubes take up space. You're heading down a blind alley, Pahroc."

I feared that too, but I'd been hoping for a little more admiration. I changed subjects and tried to learn more about him. He replied with surprising willingness. Perhaps he was even glad to confide in a younger, relatively bright colleague.

"Is it true you were at St. Polykarp?"

"Yes, Blüthner knew about it. And the Constable. He's known me for decades and we get along well. He even helps me maintain my bad reputation."

"Why did you come?"

"I wanted to be in on things, assess what was being planned, perhaps even contribute something incognito."

"Now I have to ask you something, Herr Babenzeller. When I first met you, you had on one of the most hateful uniforms I've ever known. Just what is your relationship to the State?"

"The history of nation states is largely the story of successful con-men. And they aren't going to die off. States are necessary, unfortunately, but one should never submit to them entirely. Look at what they do! They try to alter human nature, to re-educate the masses. Democracies work particularly hard at that. States want no god higher than the State. Still, we're aware of that and keep our eyes open. Anyone who's lived in a State like our present one will always seek powerful friends abroad."

"But you can kill with spells! Couldn't you render those raving madmen powerless?"

"No. Sorcerers can never alter the course of human history. That's not just a rumor. When I was in St. Polykarp Blüthner and Lesdiguières were hoping that I would at least try."

"And did you?"

"Yes."

"And the black uniform?"

"Was part of my attempt."

"So it seems you're not of the side of evil."

"I like to give the impression I might be."

"You're reputation is certainly a bad one."

"That's just what I enjoy. I'm the ghost—the evil clown. I strike terror everywhere—healing terror."

"I prefer to strike others as pleasant, if I can."

"Granted! I try to be pleasant on occasion too. As you

149

may have noticed. But we need evil as a stage presence. As in the theater. But not just there, otherwise things get boring. And when things get boring, tru`e evil multiplies—murderous evil. Do you understand?"

"No."

"OK, fine."

I understood him better in hindsight. He thrived on opposition, and he created his opponents through provocation. He especially enjoyed provoking righteous idealists, sanctimonious men of power, and arrogant moralists of all political persuasions, particularly those in democracies. But honest people touched his heart; he even loved them, especially if they were courageous. He felt among friends with technicians, and trusted electricians in particular, a profession he characterized as foreign by its very nature to any sort of hypocrisy.

I asked him the question that had been troubling me since Berlin: "What would you have done if Schneidebein had defeated me?"

"I would have protected you. Your demise was not in my interest. But I don't want any more students, let me say that at once, I'm anything but a good teacher. You have to be born to that, and have the patience of a jackass."

I asked if he would teach me just one spell, as a sort of souvenir, something he thought might come in handy in the near future. I was thinking of something that might help feed my family. But after thinking it over a moment, he said: "Mind Reading! That could soon be of great use. But of course it's problematic when food is in short supply; casting the spell makes you inordinately hungry."

I replied that I would only use it sparingly anyway, but that I'd like to learn it. He showed me how, but it took me much longer to fully grasp than other spells. Babenzeller was an impatient teacher, but that wasn't what slowed me up. Mind Reading is extremely difficult because people think in so many different ways. Some think primarily in words and sentences, some mostly in images, some think linearly, some go around corners, some think crossways or at an angle, and from time to time that all happens at once in the same person's mind. Human thought is surprisingly confused.

Now we've reached the theme for this letter. It's relatively easy to read the thoughts of literate people, particularly writers and philologists, because they're always trying to find the right word (even for things they don't want to say). It's easiest when they want something like "beer," "bratwurst," or "a cigarette"—the words immediately stand out. But in the case of involved syntax, and even conjunctive modes, mind reading gets harder because there's no longer any central image, it's all just words and grammar. That's how intellectuals make their way through life: along an endless row of words, interrupted on occasion by punctuation, and sprinkled with subordinate clauses that run counter to the main ones.

Those with image-rich minds, on the other hand, painters for example, dispense almost entirely with keywords, but their inner images are easy to recognize. In their case, I don't see the word, but the clear outline and color of the bratwurst and the beer instead. Of course the pictures don't hang side by side in their heads, framed perhaps, but flow from one to the other, each dissolving in turn, reflected by both outer and inner motions of the pupils, like a rapidly moving film I must follow.

The hardest part of all is waiting, for often there are no thoughts for long periods of time, even in the brightest minds. In those who are indecisive, at a loss, or torn between possibilities, we find nothing but chaos for hours, even days on end. It pays to remember that disorder is the normal state of things. Even among those whose success depends on the effect of their public speaking, the situation is no better: we regularly encounter mental snowstorms, only apparently structured by the constant return of identical blocks of melodious text.

Babenzeller advised me not to expect too much from mind reading. But he found it useful when dealing with a determined liar, for in the act of lying, a liar is also forced to concentrate on the truth he's trying to avoid—which can then be easily read. One can also use the spell to find reliable, loyal comrades, and good servants, for their minds are always clear and easy to read. Sometimes in life, for the sake of their intelligence, one also needs those refined comrades whose minds are hard to decipher. In those cases one has to weigh the pros and cons carefully.

"There's something scary about that," I said. He knew at once what I meant—no wonder, he could read my mind:

"Pahroc, you don't like thinking that other sorcerers can read your mind—me, for example?"

"Yes, that's it."

"Mind Reading can be counteracted by Counter-Mind Reading, it's as simple as that. When you cast Counter-Mind Reading, I can no longer read your thoughts. And of course you can't read mine."

"So you've taught me something I can use to protect myself against you?"

"Yes, my dear boy, you can take pride in that."

"Did you teach that to Schneidebein too?"

"No, I didn't. Perhaps he's learned it somewhere else in the meantime, I wouldn't know. And I have no wish to find out."

"One other thing: Schneidebein said he'd heard about plans for an assassination. From whom? Who could have told him that?"

"No one! Dictators fear nothing so much as assassination, and they blindly accuse almost anyone of making plans. Schneidebein knew nothing about St. Polykarp, let alone what I was planning."

I went for a brief walk in the village and tried out the new spell a few times, but with little success—the villagers remained opaque. At any rate, I now knew I still needed a good deal of practice, and I still had reservations. Perhaps I would be able to set them aside, perhaps not: Mind Reading is an indiscrete spell, it seemed best to reserve it for emergencies. It can be of use when someone forgets what he was going to say—then a sorcerer who's reading along can help out. But in general, invading someone else's mind seemed embarrassing.

I told Babenzeller that.

Babenzeller shrugged: "Of course people have the right to expect others not to peek at their cards. Thoughts are only truly free if you can hide them from others. But I've grown callous in that regard. What I can do, I do. A man with no evil intentions has nothing to fear from me. Another thing: if being indiscrete bothers you, you shouldn't be turning invisible or walking through walls. By the way, can you see through walls yet?"

I said no. He said he'd show me that spell when next we met, if I wished, but we didn't have time now. He wanted to take off and had to dress warmly, since it was freezing. He gave me a compass so I could fly across the sea without losing my way.

As we were parting, it seemed to me that the cast in Babenzeller's eyes was more pronounced than usual.

"Can you fly well with your eyes like that?" I asked.

"Very well. My strabismus gives me no problem when flying. Nor anywhere else—I can correct it entirely to avoid being recognized. There's only one annoying thing: when there are several people in the room and I ask a question, everyone answers."

"Another thing: where do you actually live?" I asked.

"In secret, even from colleagues," he laughed. "And you won't find out if I have a wife and children."

I realized I was blushing: that was what I was just about to ask.

"But I make an appearance now and then, when it suits my fancy."

"Thank you for everything, Herr Babenzeller!"

"No thanks necessary. I've found it amusing."

He turned invisible to ordinary eyes, to avoid offering a target to some bored person below with a rifle. Then he rose into the air: I could still see him of course. I gazed after him for a while, then he crossed the disk of the sun and was lost to my sight as well.

I checked on the woman I'd carried to shore. She was sick and worn out, but fully conscious and otherwise unharmed after the massacre. Someone had collapsed on top of her, and the dead body had served as a shield. She wanted to know my name and I gave her the first one that came to me: Piechatzek. I'd seen it once on a sign in the elevator in the building where Josef lived on Eintrachtstrasse. I lied out of caution, since I wasn't sure to whom the grateful woman might mention the name of her rescuer. Schneidebein might still be lurking about somewhere. I couldn't assume his thirst for revenge had diminished.

For that same reason, Babenzeller had strongly warned me not to return to Wasserburg until the final collapse and occupation of the entire Reich. I intended to follow his advice.

Of course, I couldn't remain where I was. I dressed warmly, rose in the air, and followed the coast southward to begin with. But then I remembered a further word of advice from Babenzeller: to remain over water as far as possible until I reached an area that was firmly in the hands of the Americans or the Brits, then stay with them until they occupied Wasserburg.

That wasn't easily done: flying over the sea was hard on the eyes. To keep going you had to find a marker. If the only thing available was the horizon, the eye had nothing solid to focus on, but kept seeking a fixed point, and quickly grew tired. Now and then I could use ships. There were many underway from the Prussian ports, trying to carry refugees from the Soviet armies to safety. I even set down on one, but it was so crowded with people that after a brief pause, I gladly returned to the air. I made up my mind never to fly over the sea again except in an emergency, and to take longer journeys of any kind by plane.

With aching eyes, I landed on a large Danish island occupied by German troops. The Soviets were conducting bombing raids because Germany still refused to capitulate. I left again as soon as possible and flew on southward through falling darkness and swarms of bombers arriving from the West. I saw the glow of the burning cities and the clouds formed by millions of strands of tinfoil trickling down from the planes to confuse anti-aircraft radar.

Continuing on this path, I finally reached Hamburg, a once beautiful city. But it was heavily damaged, and raids were still ongoing. I landed because I was hungry, thirsty, and needed to rest. The city had not yet fallen to the British, but they were gathered with overwhelming force in the surrounding area.

My dear Mathilda, any blockhead can start hostilities, but it takes far greater intelligence to bring them to a close. Three Germans—two soldiers and a civilian—were headed toward the British line on foot, carrying a white flag. They were trying to find someone in authority to prevent the shelling of a factory that was now nothing more than a sick-bay—and even included British prisoners. Since the Germans had misused a white flag recently to spy on British positions, they were fired on. The three survived and were taken prisoner. I made myself invisible and joined them. I not only heard their conversation, I read their minds. They had no evil intentions and had been authorized by the military command in Hamburg to request the factory be spared. They made their request to a young British captain who was, however, suspicious—I read his mind too. Of course, it's not easy to read what a Brit is thinking, even if you have a halfway decent command of their language. But the mind of this Brit had a solid core of images, he was well-informed, extremely clear, candid yet cautious—what the Berliners call "a bright guy." His brain first processed all the reasons for suspecting a trap. He found far fewer reasons—in fact none—to trust them. But he wanted to trust the men, I could read that too. He knew that his general had prepared an order for the total destruction of Hamburg by air—he was not about to lose another British soldier in door-to-door combat with whatever insane defenders still remained. I stood beside the captain and said in English:

"Courage, man! Focus on the civilian, you can trust him."

Since he saw no one, he thought an inner voice was speaking to him. And since that happened so seldom, he believed it. That was Hamburg's salvation—but I'm jumping ahead. The captain took the civilian aside and asked him to carry a message from the British General to the German military commander. It offered fair conditions for the peaceful surrender of the city. Delivering such a message was of course highly dangerous. The civilian, an elderly Hanseatic businessman, knew he would be strung up at once if a fanatic caught him carrying such a document. But with guile, courage, and his white flag, he made it back through the barriers. The military commander, a reasonable man, accepted the offer and capitulated. In the end, Hamburg traffic cops showed the British tanks the way to the city hall.

Those two men, the courageous bright Brit and the brave old Hamburger, deserve a special monument, and their story should be told to anyone who wants to enter politics without any precise idea of what it involves. Nor should one ever wait for a sorcerer to appear—we can't be everywhere.

I met that captain again, years later. He told me he'd heard someone say "Courage, man!" back then in the unmistakable voice of his Scottish grandfather. Since then, I've known I speak English with a Scottish accent, something I clearly owe to my teacher Macintosh.

Once the battle was at an end in Hamburg, I thought it safe to fly again, in part because the Dictator had apparently killed himself after a final fit of raving madness. So I no longer followed Babenzeller's advice, but instead headed straight south to reach Emma. Two days in a half-destroyed city were enough for me. What the bombs had left behind was terrible to behold. People were ill and living in misery, lacking the documents needed to apply for work and a place to stay. Many were too honest to deal on the black market with others who were better at bargaining or more brutal. Hardship ruled, and hopelessness, even though the hail of bombs had ceased. Many committed suicide, often those most actively involved in what had happened, but also those who'd committed no crimes themselves, but had lived too long in the midst of evil. Mathilda, you'll see—or hopefully you won't!—how the will to live is weakened when you're surrounded by thousands who are suffering.

I didn't turn invisible for the flight, but shrunk down to a hooded crow instead. The trip was still dangerous—guns going off everywhere. Babenzeller had been right to warn me. There were low-flying airplanes with mounted machine guns firing on people, even on a young boy who'd gathered some firewood and was bringing it home on his bicycle. When I landed beside him he was already beyond help. I just had time to read his last thoughts: he wished he was a grown man, a dangerous one, who could go after the pilot who'd shot him.

Now I flew on without longer stops, alighting only briefly on a church steeple or in the top branches of a tree, ignoring cold, hunger, and fatigue, till I reached Wasserburg that evening. I was shocked to see several airplanes circling above the city. I heard the loud lament of the air raid sirens—was an attack underway? I was in despair. I had to reach my family and at least die with them. But not a single bomb fell. Was the spell protecting Emma keeping the pilots from bomb-ing Wasserburg? What I didn't know at the time was this: the planes met daily above the easily recognized loop of the Inn River before heading back to England. They had long since dropped their load of bombs on the Obersalzberg, the Dic-tator's "Eagle's Nest"—it was unlikely he was there, given that he was already dead, but perhaps no one had told the pilots yet.

By the time I descended to the door of our house, the planes were already gone. I turned back into Pahroc and knocked at the door. It was after midnight. My heart was pounding like mad. It was pounding with love and nothing could slow it down.

Emma wasn't totally surprised, she'd already received word from Babenzeller that I was on my way. But joy alone was enough to weaken our knees. It was good that we could lie together. I pressed my frozen body against Emma until I was warm once more. Only then did I realize how tired I was.

I slept into the afternoon. The children had heard that Papa was back and stood—all four of them—around my bed, looking at me. Presumably each saw something different, but they all could see that I loved them. Emma came with coffee. I asked if she'd learned the Real Coffee spell. She said there was no such spell, but she'd visited the local Party Office as the mother of four children to request that the city surren-der without opposition—she could do that because she was protected by the Mother Shield. But it turned out no one was there—just the coffee.

"Eisenhaus kommt!" cried little Carola. That was a ral-lying cry at the time, but of course it wasn't Eisenhower but Patton whose troops were approaching Wasserburg. Now Fay had a question. "Are we named Schnittwitz from now on, or is it still Pahroc?"

"Pahroc, of course," I replied. "—Peace will be here soon."

Gnadl had asked to see me that morning—he already

knew I'd landed in the city. He said he needed help. But Emma told him I was flat as an end moraine in bed and shouldn't be awakened yet. He'd come about cutting detonation cables on the bridge over the Inn River, to keep final victory fanatics from blowing it up. They'd placed explosives on the bridge days ago, but a stout-hearted Wasserburger had stolen them in the night and buried them in his garden. Unfortunately, the trigger-happy dynamiters had more explosives and had mined the bridge again.

Emma gave Gnadl my entire stock of wire-cutters (none of them made it back). The good old bridge still suffered some damage, since a forgotten charge on the south side exploded. The destruction was idiotic, since Patton's soldiers never intended to cross the bridge. Too bad about that—they should have tried harder to awaken me. I can cut a wire a hundred meters away with a spell that leaves no external sign.

In the living room, I found the table and chairs covered with strange maps. Instead of showing cities and countries they consisted of a series of complex intersecting lines. At first I thought they might be marine maps with shipping lanes, or flight paths for bombers—or for sorcerers. They were old dress patterns, waiting to be picked up by neighbors. Dressmaking was now an important source of income for Emma. With one quick glance at the patterns, Emma could turn to her scissors and sewing machine and never take another look.

The Americans advanced from the northwest along a spit of land, and in the blink of an eye had reached the center of the old city. Even fanatics gave up at that point and took to their heels. They came to citizens' doors asking for civilian clothes, stole boats, and rowed across the river to escape somewhere into the woods.

Meanwhile, news spread that Emma's husband, believed permanently missing, had turned up again and was a trained electrician like Josef Gruber, who was unfortunately dead now, or in a Russian prison camp. I spent my days repairing radios from Wasserburg and the surrounding villages, mostly old models from the Party era that had gone bad. Sometimes I used spells because I lacked the necessary tubes and people were in a hurry. Everyone wanted to hear if a ceasefire had been signed, and they listened through the night.

Emma told me how things had gone while I was away. For two years, her greatest fear had been for me. I explained how my life had been suspended à la Heisterbach, and that sorcerers were susceptible to the effect when they were flying under the pressure of some terrible shock. Emma told me in turn how she and the children had made it through. Mother Shield had protected her from Schneidebein—perhaps—and other dangers, but it had also prevented her from leaving the Wasserburg area: that would have negated the spell. And in any case she didn't like being given what she called "a leg up." That was typical of Emma: she was thinking of all the mothers who weren't protected, and thus exposed to all the terrors. And she was proud of everything she'd accomplished through her own efforts or with the aid of spells: the electrical engineering exam she'd passed, for example. The Learning spell provided her with the necessary technical knowledge, and a concentrated Beauty spell ensured the good will of the Chamber of Skilled Crafts.

She also reported that Gnadl had fulfilled the role of a good and faithful uncle to the children. He'd even kicked the ball around with Felix, which could have aroused suspicions that he was faking his handicap.

I was happy beyond words to be with Emma again, and in my own body as Pahroc. I shared the wonderful silence with those around me: no more planes strafing, no more shots being fired. I contacted Blüthner and asked him to remove the Mother Shield. From now on, I would be protecting Emma. And then, at long last, Germany capitulated.

To many, this seemed anything but a liberation. Many preferred the term "collapse," as if a building had been destroyed by an earthquake, or "defeat," which was technically accurate, but hardly the word for such a hellish fall.

Emma told me about Babenzeller, too. At first he'd seemed so sinister that she'd asked him why the Mother Shield didn't keep him at bay. But at some point she became convinced he was my friend and only wanted to help.

I listened with astonishment. Babenzeller called me his friend? I would not have called him my friend up to that point, though I admired him. At most, I'd have admitted that he'd behaved like a friend. My dear Mathilda, that's something one just has to accept: there are things one can't explain, and yet they exist. Some friendships are like that—even the most important ones, it seems to me.

"What did Babenzeller do to help you?" I asked Emma.

"He searched for you, found you, and managed to let me know! And he could conjure up food stamps. Of course, I almost never used them."

"And what else?"

"What else? Please don't try reading my thoughts! He taught me that too, as further protection. And now I'll have to use it against you, because you think you have to fish around inside me."

She was close to tears—I noticed that, at least. I took her in my arms, kissed her, and asked her forgiveness. Wars don't just spread unhappiness and death, they also arouse suspicion and stupidity. And they corrupt the magic of love, in sorcerers just as in others. Our mutual trust, our wordlessly shared feelings, had suffered something akin to a loose electrical connection since my return. Now that connection was restored, and everything fell back into place. From then on, I read Emma's thoughts only in her eyes and left her free to have secrets—helped by my belief that these were few in number. I sensed what was most important without sorcery, and our love was unconditional again, a gift not given to all couples after the war.

Emma contributed far more to our household income through dressmaking than I did as an electrician, since business had fallen off sharply at the appliance shop. She sewed everything from undergarments to cotton dresses to winter coats, using tarps, curtains, parachute silk, sheets, and army blankets. She was only limited by her ancient pedal sewing machine. Electric models were now available elsewhere, and I was working on assembling one. But it would have been of little use, given the daily power outages that lasted for hours. Under Pospischil's guidance, Emma had perfected all the spells a single mother with four children might need during the war, and she could employ them better than ever now. If needed, she could turn into an invisible snowy owl and listen in on conversations throughout half the town, learning where things could be found for free. She flew over the countryside as a kestrel or sniffed about the forest as a bloodhound—not a strawberry patch, not a colony of mushrooms, not one abandoned car with usable cables escaped her—and she harvested limitless supplies of bear's garlic. She discovered all sorts of loot: wool blankets on a truck, potatoes, medicines like aspirin, or a large keg of soup seasoning a field kitchen had left behind in the woods during redeployment. We filled all the medicine bottles we could find with it and did a brisk business on the black market. I admired Emma—she was far better at organizing things than I was.

"Criminal procurement," "petty theft"—such terms are far too unkind for what we did. I prefer "conjured up supplies."

One early summer day, in the midst of a sea of flowers, I was detained by two American soldiers and taken to their headquarters. I was suspected of having been a Party member or worse, since no one could say where I'd come from in the final days of the war, nor where I'd been during the war itself. I was interrogated, and since I couldn't possibly tell my true story, I declared that I'd opposed the Regime and had been pursued by them, mentioned Gebhardswalde and the name Schnittwitz—which they checked—and that I'd then moved my family to Wasserburg and chosen to lead a life outside the law, repeatedly harbored by "good people" I wasn't at liberty to name. My responses weren't entirely consistent and didn't satisfy the investigators. Then their superior officer appeared, a prematurely gray young giant of a man with horn-rimmed glasses, who said with a smile: "I'll take over on this one!" It was "little Jakob" from Eintrachtstrasse, who'd made it to America in time and had now returned as an officer to get to the bottom of things with the Germans. He believed my story and asked about Schneidebein. But I had no idea where he was hiding. I assumed—but couldn't tell Jakob, who wasn't a sorcerer—that he'd used a Change spell to alter his appearance and escape detection. And I knew only too well that he couldn't keep that up for long. Nor could he live here in his original form as a normal citizen now that he had lost his State. Perhaps he was a rat in the hold of a ship on its way to South America, planning to play the role of emigrant and resistance fighter, then buy a plantation with all the money he had extorted and stolen—I wouldn't put anything past him. But I doubted the plantation would flourish.

Jakob now called himself James, but wanted me to call him Jakob. When Emma showed up to speak with me—finding me had been child's play for her—he was pleased, had coffee served and asked all sorts of questions.

We spoke for a while about "Germans" in the plural, but soon stopped. Jakob asked if many people felt guilty about those who had been murdered. It was Emma who replied:

"I hardly know anyone who does. Almost everyone says they knew nothing about it or that they had to simply accept things and follow orders or their families would have been in danger."

"And was that danger truly so great?"

"It was great enough to frighten them. Far worse is how many people there were who more or less agreed with what was happening. True, only a minority knew the actual extent of the crimes, but most knew and heard a great deal and could figure the rest out for themselves."

"Does anyone feel guilty?"

"A few surely do in secret, but most believe that with all the ruins and hardships they're being punished enough. They say it's time to put an end to it and move on."

Jakob was confident that the murderers and criminals would be caught and punished, but he also wanted to discover how many secret supporters of the dictatorship still remained after the death of the tyrant.

"When we ask, everyone is innocent, only democrats and philanthropists remain," he said. "You'd have to be able to read minds." Emma and I exchanged faint smiles.

"Fine, and what would you do if you could?" I asked. "If you could see that someone or other still favors a dictatorship or persecution of the Jews?"

"I realize of course that no legal judgment could be reached on the basis of reading people's minds. But those people could be put under special surveillance, and prevented from holding positions of any authority. What would you do?"

"People can learn. And they can be helped to learn. I would work for good schools and start good newspapers. And make sure everyone has enough to eat. When you're hungry, you don't learn much."

"I like the idea. I think we should try something like that," he said. But I thought he was just being polite. Any sound mind would come to the same conclusion, and in those days the Americans were of sound mind.

Jakob made sure I was released immediately and could return to work. In that same year, a serious, truly good American newspaper for Germans was published in Munich, with Jakob as one of its founders. I visited him there several times, and on each occasion received a carton of cigarettes. That was better than money—you could actually get things for them.

Even when I repaired appliances, I preferred to receive food or cigarettes in place of cash, even though I didn't smoke. I got the ice-cream machine going again in a pastry shop, and when the owner said he couldn't pay me yet, we made a deal that my whole family could eat ice cream there for half an hour. He agreed, and I strongly suspect he regretted doing so. The children devoured dip after dip, Titus leading the way. On our way home he asked, "Are we going to get all the ice cream we want every time peace arrives?"

The schools remained closed for months, leaving the children to play all day. So we decided to teach Felix, Fay, and Titus ourselves. I gave "Father Lessons" and Emma gave "Mother Lessons." It turned out that we were cut out to be teachers—both of us! I never lost sight of the joy of pedagogy, and later helped many others, mature students, for the most part, learn a few things.

We were particularly worried about abandoned arms and ammunition, which seemed to exert a magical attraction on ten-year-old Titus. They lay in wait wherever they had been tossed aside by German soldiers. They were particularly easy to gather in the shallows along the river. Even fifteen-year-old Felix couldn't resist tapping the powder from rifle cartridges and using it for "fireworks." Since our injunctions weren't sufficient in themselves, I read all I could about pyrotechnics and its dangers and passed it on. So both Felix and Titus learned all they needed to know about why we'd forbidden them to play with munitions, and fireworks were limited to the classroom. Surprisingly enough, it was fourteen-year-old Fay for whom the attraction lasted longest. Later, she became a pyrotechnician and explosives specialist, and remained a highly sought-after legal expert in court long after she'd retired, a clear result of my Father Lessons. It's too bad you didn't know her Mathilda, she was full of life and irrepressible. She's been dead for three years now—I think of her often.

The man who stole the dynamite that was meant to blow up the bridge used small portions of it to start his stove—there were still a few cold days that May and he'd read in a dictionary that it could be done. The stuff melted to a blackish paste and burned long enough to make even larger logs catch fire. But the smoke was poisonous, something I knew before the reference books did, and I warned my neighbor in no uncertain terms. I feel I surely helped keep his whole family healthy.

Then it was high summer, the finest in many years. It might well have been a verdant memory of childhood if it hadn't been for the widespread hunger. Groceries were available only to those with food stamps, and were strictly rationed. Each of us placed our weekly bread ration in some special spot in the house, as safe from mice as possible, and scratched our initials on it. Carola was long since convinced that mice could read letters. My crust of bread bore no initials, but was placed so high on the wardrobe that mice didn't have a chance.

In late autumn, lodgers who had been bombed out of their apartment in Berlin were assigned to us. They were modest and friendly, and we exchanged letters with some of them for years afterwards. But we had our problems with them too: life in the countryside requires knowledge and discipline. City folk have to learn how to keep a house cool in summer and warm in winter. We explained things to them, but their habits were stronger. It wasn't till we assigned them the task of tending to the tile stove that they finally understood when to open doors and windows and when to close them.

We were thoroughly happy not to live in a large city, where there would have been no farmers to make friends with, nor any interesting places nearby to hunt mushrooms. Mushrooms grew in abundance in 1945, at times right in the midst of discarded weapons and grenades. Nature, a master at crowding things out, soon covered war and violence with new growth. People did their best, in their own way, to do the same.

Since Emma could easily stand in for me, both at the counter and with small repairs, Gnadl and I took another trip into the mountains. Gnadl was no longer a traffic cop, but was trying out public transport instead. He carried bridal couples to the church, pregnant women to the hospital, and coffins to the graveyard. Of course there was no petrol, so he'd converted his old Adler Diplomat limousine so it could run on wood gas. A tall stove was mounted on the rear where wooden logs, beech mostly, were burned at low temperature. They didn't catch fire, but were heated from below by a charcoal grill, creating large volumes of poisonous gas that drove the combustion engine. It's true the limousine had a hard time overtaking a fast bicycle, and on longer inclines it was best to exit the vehicle, fetch more logs from the attached trailer, and add them to the pile. Still, the old coach managed to carry us through the Achen valley to Schleching where we set out on our hike. We had important business among the rocky cliffs: We were poaching. There were still some guns, since the Americans had by no means found all their hiding places. Nor were they inclined to hike through the mountains in pursuit of poor fellows trying to feed their families. They'd spent enough time on foot from Normandy to Bavaria, now they concentrated on tasks they could do in a jeep. We did encounter a forest ranger once. Gnadl was sensible enough to turn invisible with his rifle and game, while I, less sensibly, dropped my gun, turned into a crow, and flew away. Gnadl pointed out that I might be identified by examining the rifle—and if I was going to turn into a bird, it should at least be a protected species!

I didn't particularly like poaching. Putting an end to lives was never my thing—the main reason I'd fled from the front was to avoid killing people. Yes, there's a difference between human and animal life: that concept plays a major role in the history of thought. But many animals share traits in common with *Homo sapiens*, even if they have no knack for philology. I, for one, don't like killing animals, and I certainly wouldn't do so for pleasure, even leaving aside the fact that it might be a sorcerer who's just turned into a stag, roe deer, or chamois. To deliver a perfect heart shot and then see that I've downed a colleague—what a terrible thought!

Gnadl tried to use the underlying rebelliousness of poaching to win me over. He spoke of the ancient rights and freedoms the common people enjoyed in the era before notions of private property and the State arose. In that, he was more Bavarian than policeman. He also raised the social issue: honest scofflaws shared their loot with the poor and hungry in the village. It was a matter of custom, not crime—illegal, yes, but justified from a higher perspective.

The criminal side of the matter didn't bother me as long as my family had enough to eat, and I gladly shared what I had with others. But I found nothing romantic in shooting roe deer and chamois. Necessity alone made a poacher of me. I was glad I could soon end that role: in the late Josef Gruber's storeroom, I found all sorts of strange glass vessels, tubes, and spirals, and in his bookcase, right next to the Bible, a few texts on distillation. Gnadl knew how to distill liquor, too—I learned all about it. I could hardly offer the subject as one of my Father Lessons, but I was soon trading fruit brandy for everything we needed, even haunches of venison. I preferred that to blasting away on Geigelstein Mountain myself. I only went there now on quite unrebellious outings with my wife and children. Or only slightly rebellious: on a rest stop high in the mountains, Titus announced he wanted to be a poacher—and definitely not a forest ranger.

The winter of 1945/46 was hard and gruesome. Many people starved to death, even in the American sector, since the food programs weren't in place yet—it wasn't until the following winter that care packages began arriving from America, and the school lunch programs didn't begin fully until 1947. And people froze to death! We still had a woodpile behind the house, but people were constantly stealing from it. There was almost no coal. Fortunately, Emma had learned from Pospischil how to heat a metal plate without lighting a fire under it. It was the same spell Schneidebein had used four years earlier to get me in trouble. It came in handy now.

Emma loved nylon stockings, and I liked to see her in them. Her legs were so pretty and straight that her seams were never crooked. But nylons were available only from American soldiers or on the black market. I wrangled over the high prices—it took several cartons of cigarettes. Fortunately Emma could make runs "disappear" by passing her hand over them. She even did that for friends at times, before they noticed what had happened. Later she developed a passion for high-heeled shoes, but by that time she'd mastered spells to create things out of thin air, or to transform them into something else. She could even change shoes as she walked, without taking them off or on, and I had to remind her not to be too obvious about it.

In 1948 Carola entered school and Felix was nearing graduation. Titus was in love for the first time and wasn't saying a word about it, particularly not to the object of his affections. It was only noticeable now and then when his ears turned red, and in his difficulties with algebra. I gave him some extra tutoring, after which he ventured to speak to the young girl. I'd discussed mainly mathematics, but that remained enemy territory. Even in primary school, zero had baffled him. This aroused my hopes that he was headed for a great scientific career, but he turned out not to be a genius after all. This saddened me as a father and an engineer, but I drew comfort from the fact that all he really wanted was to be a poacher, live on an alpine pasture someday, and be called Öhi—sons should be allowed to choose their own lives. And daughters too, but they do that anyway.

In those days few people cared whether someone had supported the Dictator or not—they had their minds on other things: the next sack of flour, maybe even a bag of coal, and at some point in the future a ham. Most of all, they hoped they'd never see another war, or ever be a soldier. And they wanted nothing more to do with politics. The younger among them, in particular, had known that world only as an edifice of lies. They clung to a different dream: private happiness, with a cottage and garden.

Reality was far more dismal. Many fathers returned home broken, despondent, and robbed of all authority, which they often tried to regain by being overly harsh and severe. Most of them kept on smoking the way they had at the front, which meant that the only reliable means of paying for anything went up in smoke while their families went cold and hungry. Some succumbed to alcohol and went even more quickly downhill.

Meanwhile, the world was divided in two, and Wasserburg was in the Western half. We tried to renew contact with our old friends, but it was difficult, even though barbed wire and lookout towers posed no problem for sorcerers. In spite of all our arts, we could not step out of our true lives, our families, and our jobs, for long. Given this situation, sorcerers in the East tended to try to improve Communism, while we in the West worked for a solid, social liberalism.

I tried to make contact with Blüthner in Saxony, and one day I succeeded. I wanted to bring our old friends together again. With this in mind, I was assembling a list of all known sorcerers living in Europe. I'd just reached Kalupner, Kalusche, and Kaluza when Gnadl dropped in and wanted to go up into the mountains together. When I returned, all the names on the list had disappeared. Evidently I'd run into a protective spell that I still couldn't counteract. Gnadl knew nothing about it. But he advised me to drop the idea of an association anyway. Sorcerers, he said, were solitary by nature. I said I wasn't yet convinced of that.

A few colleagues I knew from St. Polykarp had died in the meantime, among them Alrutz and Macintosh. Others had emigrated to America. They sent strong-walled cartons of groceries with CARE stamped on the sides. They remained part of our household for a long time—I've never seen such solid boxes since.

St. Polykarp itself no longer existed: Blüthner reported that our secret meeting place had been betrayed by sorcerers loyal to the Regime and that its protective spell had been broken. The Communists were particularly opposed to sorcerers, and unfortunately some of the Communist sorcerers had felt obliged to go along with them. The cloister library had been at least partially saved, but no one knew where it was stored now. Blüthner remained in the East. Those of us in the West could only form a small group and wait for better times. Even a plan to place a memorial plaque on Schlosseck's house in Pankow fell through because that part of Berlin lay in the Soviet occupied zone; the plaque had been removed immediately. Here too we would have to wait.

The times were dark, but we still had hope. One event in particular pointed forcefully to a better world: the same planes that once carried bombs were now carrying flour, coal, and meat to break the Soviet blockade of Berlin—a blockade intended to weaken the resistance of West Berliners and allow the Soviets to take control of the city. That was a few days after the introduction of the new D-Mark in the Western zone. True, it was in the interest of the Western powers not to allow the Soviets to assimilate the city, but the airlift showed the entire world what greatness is. I believe that every ten years or so such actions are necessary somewhere in the world, otherwise we forget that governments are capable of acting nobly.

As ruins were transformed once more into movie theaters, and films were shown again in rubble-filled cities, we went to the movies as often as possible. We traveled to Munich to see them too, sometimes with the three older children. One evening I flew to Schwabing to see a late night showing of *Les Enfants du paradis*. We sought out mostly American, Italian, and French films, but longed for good German ones as well—and they came. Three times in my life now I've seen how films took on great importance after the worst of times, helping people deal with their situation and bringing them back to themselves following eras of confusion, violence, and ugliness. Many weathered the difficult postwar years in anger, but also with patience and a willingness to help others. The first German films reflected this, but didn't try to hide the fact that the murderers were still among us, nor that many people were no longer equal to the times, because they were too old or sick, too lonely, or too psychically damaged.

I'm probably writing so much about films, dear Mathilda, because it was Iris and Stephan's wedding anniversary yesterday, and we all watched the film that Rejlander made with them and your father two years ago in Scotland. I was proud, as always, but still bothered as usual by the name "John Parrock." Yes, I realized long ago that an actor's name has to be easy to remember, especially for Americans. It's a beautiful film and I like it: not too loud, not too hectic, good character portraits. Afterwards, the party lasted into the wee hours of the morning. I stayed awake to the end, though people half my age had long since gone to bed. I danced a lot, mostly with Rejlander. Not many people dance these days—perhaps things will have changed again in your day. Most people preferred to eat, drink, and talk. I think Rejlander wanted to show she would rather dance with a 108-year-old man than spend the evening talking with cast-iron figurines who remained seated and all said the same thing anyway: "Your film is great!" She'd long since garnered all the "greats" she needed, and her love for the tango was matched only by mine.

Later that night we started a conversation of our own, because Iris had called film a magical art. Her remark offered a challenge of sorts to sorcerers, who practice true magic. Rejlander and I looked at each other and smiled. She can read thoughts, by the way, and since I'd noted it I cast the counterspell as a precaution—she didn't need to know everything I might be imagining about us. She'd probably guessed it anyway.

We were a small group; the two of us, plus make-up and sound—Iris and Stephan—and the author of the film script, Waldemar III, my loyal servant from 1972 to 1983. You may meet him some day, he's about the same age as your aunt Carola. My son had left earlier, but Waldemar IV was there too— my current Waldemar. He couldn't drink anything because he had to drive me home, but he entered into the conversation with particular passion. He knows and loves countless films—we often attend movies together. He's probably the best servant I've ever had, though I'll never forget Waldemar I, my true servant and comrade back in Gebhardswalde.

Film as a magical art? We reached no conclusions of course—four o'clock in the morning is no time for analysis. Stephan said a good film could read the mind and dreams of the viewer, which everyone except Iris thought was nonsense. That might be the dream of television producers, the current Waldemar said. A film was only good if it was itself a dream—and remained true to that dream. And there was no such thing as a single "viewer."

"If dreams weren't so confused, and could be filmed as they occur," said Rejlander, "they would make the ideal *auteur* film and"—here she looked over at Waldemar III—"remain undisturbed by the hand of other 'authors.'"

As a young boy, I once had a dream filled with battles and intrigue, dangers and heroic acts, a mixture of *The Three Musketeers* and the French Revolution. I was awakened by the alarm clock, had breakfast, went to school, came back, ate lunch, lay down in bed, and prayed: "Please God, send the French again." Unfortunately, they didn't appear—I had a silly schoolboy dream instead. Yes, that's a spell I would still like to learn in my old age: how to continue an exciting dream uninterrupted. It might even come in handy on one's deathbed.

It's difficult to say when postwar years come to an end. Looked at logically, they never do. When one starts saying "between the wars," or even "pre-war," it depends on how one feels. But there's a date that indicates 1948 as the end of the immediate postwar era: the day the new D-Mark currency arrived. That changed our lives quite clearly. I'll say more about it when I come to the Money spell.

But even prior to that date, reconstruction was gradually getting underway, which of course required massive demolition and clearing first. Whether those who undertook the work had once worn one particular uniform or another was of little interest.

I have to tell the story here of what happened to "Hamhamham": After their master had taken off, they assumed new names, calling themselves Klein, Kurz, and Wischermann. Wischermann slipped away on his own and disappeared down some hole. The other two founded the demolition firm of Kurz & Klein, GmbH. It's said they made good money.

Schneidebein, their former master and employer, as I learned only later, was by no means a plantation owner in South America by then, but was living instead under a false name in Eisenhüttenstadt.

NINTH LETTER

MAKING MONEY

January 2015

Babenzeller didn't want to tell me where he was living, but when he visited us in the spring of 1948, he let the following slip during a conversation about school lunches while we were out walking:

"We're way ahead of you in Traunstein."

That near Wasserburg, and he hadn't even told me about it! Since he could read what I was thinking, he chuckled.

"Fine, come visit me sometime! But not in the morning, I teach then."

A high school teacher? Now I was truly curious:

"Classical languages, gymnastics?"

"I'll tell you when you come visit."

Was he embarrassed by his subject? An art teacher perhaps? Or German language? That was probably it. He changed the subject to the currency reform that was due any day. We'd soon have banknotes we could actually buy something with. Was I ready to learn the Money spell? He'd be glad to teach me.

In my case, signs of readiness had already appeared, though not yet for Emma. The Money spell first announces itself by strange things happening with paper, particularly when you need a little privacy. Rolls of toilet paper were rare in those days and most people made do with torn up newspapers stuck on a nail. These were generally read before use, offering bits of news one had missed. On one such occasion, the truncated film review I held in my hand suddenly felt like a banknote, at least the paper did.

I mentioned that to Babenzeller and he nodded with satisfaction.

"The potential is there, all right. Are you ready?" And within a single day he'd taught me how to conjure money, real money of course. There's a reason why sorcerers can't learn the Money spell when they're young: it's relatively easy to change yourself—it's much harder to transform some other object.

Here's one example: by the time you're twenty-five you can change yourself into a banknote if you've learned the Change and Miniaturization spells. You can leave yourself on the table—the waiter arrives, sees the banknote, thinks you've already departed, and sticks you in his wallet. But you have to extricate yourself when no one's looking, and that can be difficult. In the worst case scenario, you may stay stuck tight in a stuffed wallet, and in an overly snug rear pocket, to boot. Then there's the added dimension of fairness: you'll hurt some poor, hard-working waiter, because you'll be sorely missed in the evening's final tally. I did that just once, in 1946, after going to the movies. I had a good meal, but was pretty ashamed afterwards.

As soon as you can transform items of approximately the same size into something else, you can create money. Of course, it's even better if you can buy something with it. Back then shopkeepers had little to offer if you were paying in Reichsmarks, so the new spell was of little use. We had to deal on the black market. Emma's dressmaking and sewing arts, my illegal distillery, the occasional radio or emergency generator repair—we managed to finagle things. But the black market demanded both patience and caution: you might get caught.

When a per capita allowance of forty new D-Marks was distributed to every West German as part of the currency reform, I had a chance to study the banknotes and coins I got in some detail. I then credited a small fortune from color illustrations I tore out of the big Brockhaus encyclopedia and cut into pieces. As an independent dealer I found it very handy to make change from a small pocketful of pebbles anytime I wanted to. I had no qualms about this, since I was cheating a State that did not yet exist. And I was sure other sorcerers were doing the same. But I should say at once that though I knew many well-to-do sorcerers, hardly any were millionaires, let alone billionaires. As a general rule, we don't accumulate large sums of capital, because dealing with it is so boring. Life is filled with magic and far too short—yes, I can say that even at 109! It's a waste of time and of life to spend more than an hour a week on money matters.

Even in the early postwar years people were trying to get hold of money; after all, it wasn't totally worthless. Many played the lottery or bet on soccer. I suspect experienced sorcerers can influence the outcome of a contest. That's something I've never considered trying—I love the game. And I'm superstitious about the lottery. It might be possible to control the order in which the numbered balls come up, so that precisely the six numbers you've selected are chosen. But a million dollar prize uses up too much of your personal store of good fortune, and sorcerers need to keep some luck in reserve. A major jackpot, no matter how you managed it, may be followed by years of bad luck—so hands off! Or if you feel you have to try such spells, be satisfied with four, or at most five, average jackpots. There's no problem if you play as a normal person, of course. But don't buy your lottery ticket with conjured funds—I did it a few times and quickly saw I wasn't winning anything, in spite of the fact that the banknotes were real—conjured money is not counterfeit. But I should add that conjured banknotes don't last forever. I didn't know that for a long time. We'll come back to this problem, because you should bear it in mind.

The D-Mark changed life in Germany in a major way, and not just for sorcerers conjuring money. Suddenly there were things to buy, at least things that had been stored in cellars and back rooms. Business increased at the appliance shop and that pleased me, even if hard times were nearing an end anyhow. When the Western occupied zone became a true State a year later, one with free elections, it meant less to most people than an economy open to private enterprise did. I found it interesting. I recalled that Schlosseck thought nothing good would ever come from any State, an opinion strangely at odds with the Reich's war banner that once flew from his flagstaff. But he was a tragic patriot, a disappointed lover of the German Empire. I was something different, a technician: I considered a State trustworthy if it was rationally constructed, and if its constituent parts had enough free play to avoid excessive friction and overheating. That seemed to me to be the case here, and so I became a Constitutional patriot, which means that to this day I automatically mistrust any politician who tries to change the Constitution.

Emma and I had a good deal of free time for the children and each other now. And I set higher goals for myself. I planned to apply for patents for my invention. There was a German Patent Office now that even had a branch in Munich. And I wanted to try again to form a sorcerers' association, with Babenzeller as its president. I thought sorcerers should be considering how they could help the young democracy.

I retrieved the Traunstein address that Babenzeller had given me, but the writing had vanished. It was clear he didn't want visitors all that badly. I've never met a sorcerer so determined to remain alone and inaccessible. That desire added to his bad reputation, since someone so withdrawn arouses hostility and all sorts of suspicions. And yet, I knew that Babenzeller was not only the most highly-skilled sorcerer among us, but also far from evil. I managed to convince a few other colleagues of this.

I flew toward Traunstein above a landscape covered in deep snow and found Babenzeller more quickly than I'd expected. There were several schools there, but it wasn't difficult to find a teacher whose questions drew responses from the entire class because he was wall-eyed. Standing at his door I feared he might be put off by seeing me, but to my relief he was pleased. We sat on his balcony in the early afternoon sun. Beyond the railway we could see the small town, looking very pretty with all its snow-capped roofs.

"We can dine at that terrace over there," Babenzeller said, "but not on the terrace itself, that will be covered with snow. In fact, Traunstein is always deep in snow. The rich mantel that should fall in the mountains winds up down here. And there are snow days non-stop at school; pupils from the countryside don't show up because the buses can't make it through." He didn't seem overly sad about any of it.

I was still trying to figure out what he taught, and was finally about to ask him, but something held me back—it seemed as if he really didn't want me to know.

He waved off any possible involvement with a sorcerers association:

"No, a clear line should be drawn between sorcerers and politicians! Politicians can't do magic, and sorcerers can't do politics. We can't stand before people and say: When we're in charge you'll no longer have to pay taxes, we'll conjure up all the money we need."

"But we can agree to make life difficult for those who oppose freedom."

180

"We can do that individually—we don't need an association with by-laws and elected officers!"

"But it's important to talk things over. Particularly what stance we should take toward progress and technology—we have to monitor ongoing developments. Otherwise, sooner or later, technology will imitate and replace sorcery. I'm thinking of mind reading and even more."

"Fine, then they will. I'm in this for myself alone, and when I'm dead I'll have no particular interest in the world anyway."

"You don't have children."

"No."

I chose not to reply. We went into town for dinner and wound up talking about Schneidebein. He was in the Secret Service now, working behind the Iron Curtain, and was considered politically trustworthy because he'd spoken out in favor of a peace treaty two weeks before the war ended and wound up imprisoned as a traitor. He had his own office again and played the role of a former member of the resistance.

"He thinks he's returned to a position of leadership," Babenzeller said, "but he's the one being led. Sorcerers who throw themselves into the arms of the State are susceptible to blackmail. But he never learns."

"Perhaps because he doesn't want to?"

"He's so utterly superficial that a façade is all he needs. But he'll tread over corpses on its behalf."

We agreed that the Iron Curtain wasn't all bad if it kept Schneidebein off our backs. Last but not least, I learned what mattered most: the moment the war had ended, Babenzeller arranged for trucks to transport the entire cookbook section of the St. Polykarp library to Austria—to a secret underground hall in Längberg, a forested mountain in Tyrol with fortress ruins and small castles, just this side of the German border, near Kufstein. He said the books were arranged neatly on shelves, and that there were reading tables, but as yet it was unprotected by any magic spell. He said I could deal with the library, he wasn't cut out to drum up enthusiasm among sorcerers. I promised I would.

Then I flew home—with mixed feelings of course. Here was one of our greatest sorcerers, a worldly-wise trickster who still remained true in his way to the constitution, yet who, at the age of sixty, could say, "What do I care about the world once I'm dead?" That's just it, Mathilda: we can't leave our elders to their creature comforts, or the best schools are useless. The future has no chance without the older generation. I should have seized Babenzeller by the shoulders and shaken him, but he would no doubt have changed shape and forced me to give up. What's the point of shaking a rhino or an elephant? I decided to create my sorcerers' association without him. He might drop in some day, if only to amuse himself. Then I'd surprise him with the news that he'd been elected President, and ensnare him with the honor.

I only flew over the border of the Zone once, to see Gebhardswalde again. Pastor Schnabel was dead, executed in the final days of the Sieg Heilers, when a dog sniffed out the hiding place of those he was protecting. The sexton who'd taken over for me was still there, but was now serving as secretary for a local group pretending to be a Christian offshoot of the Communist Party. I asked if I could play the organ, but it had been dismantled. In a state of deep dejection, I tried to at least find the mushroom patch where we'd had such a good harvest the day Waldemar was arrested. That part of the forest was now a military training ground for the occupying forces. Mushrooms no longer grew there. I departed for Berlin and tried to find Kusenberg. They told me he'd moved to Hamburg.

I wondered if we should move too. To West Berlin, or America? Or stay and grow old in Wasserburg? I'd have to discuss it with Emma. Wasserburg had only been a hideaway—if we wanted to leave we could.

182

But then there were the children to think of, who were in school and had lots of friends. And inventions to be dealt with: the Synchro that coordinated the rotation angle of machine parts, the satellite earth observation system, and something else I'd been considering more recently. Even during the war I'd thought about how easily ships and planes could be located if their radio frequencies remained unchanged too long. Of course, transmitters and receivers could switch to another frequency, but if they signaled the change on the same frequency, the enemy would simply switch to the new frequency themselves. My invention was to link timers to both transmitters and receivers, synchronized to the hundredth of a second. These would be further linked to a punched paper tape that would automatically switch them to a new frequency every few seconds—no manual adjustment would be needed. It was the birth of a secure system against eavesdropping that functioned much better than secret codes. Whatever can be heard can always be decoded over time, but not what can't be heard at all.

I wrote and drew for weeks, then sent everything to the Deutsche Museum in Munich, where the Patent Office was located back then. They spent forever checking my work, then gave me an appointment.

There sat a compassionate, melancholy man, who paused to smoke a cigarette first because he found it so hard to destroy my dreams.

"Look, the war's been over for five years now," he said, "but people keep turning up who still want to win it. If you'd come here in 1944 . . ."

I changed color quite noticeably, and when he noticed, he turned red too.

"Please don't misunderstand me!"

I couldn't stand that either. One was always running into people who said something and in the same breath begged you not to misunderstand them. I told him I'd had neither the opportunity nor the desire to make my invention available to the Dictator. All German patents had been confiscated by the allies immediately after the war, so I'd been forced to wait. And in any case my inventions were not only ingenious but useful in peacetime too. I even startled myself a little, for I was now speaking loudly. And rightly so, for I now realize that without the basic concept underlying my invention no wireless telephone system could function, nor the digital world in general. Of course, punched paper tape is no longer needed, I'll grant you that!

I find Patent Offices highly interesting places to watch people and eavesdrop. If microphones and recording devices were installed there, you could easily compose a didactic radio play on the monumental and fundamental battle between reason and disbelief. This patent agent was fortunate that I was constitutionally unable to strangle melancholics, for that day I was one myself, more so than ever.

Everything, and I mean everything, that I had spent so much time and effort developing had apparently been discovered and registered by others recently—he showed me the documents. An American woman of Austrian descent had come up with the punch-card frequency modulation system. She'd been thinking of remote-controlled torpedoes whose course could easily be altered by the enemy if they used the right frequency. Her "frequency hopping" invention allowed the torpedo to continue on undisturbed to its target. The agent claimed she was a Hollywood star and was said to be the most beautiful woman in the world. But that was of little comfort to me at the time.

I lifted my chin and spoke: "Do you need money? I've invented a way to make banknotes. You wouldn't understand the method of course, so I can't show it to you. . . ." The melancholic reached for his cigarette package and I took my leave.

My future seemed to ready itself for a new beginning on

a different front: Jakob visited me in Wasserburg with a gentleman named Dr. Schneider, who never removed his sunglasses. They arrived in such a large car that they couldn't stop at our door. Dr. Schneider ate nearly all the pastries himself and downed an unbelievable quantity of real coffee. Jakob held back in that area, but both of them smoked so heavily that I couldn't make my way through the clouds to open the window. But what the man in the sunglasses had to say sounded tempting. It appeared he'd heard of my inventions, which surprised me, and thought highly of me, which pleased me—and he referred right from the start to my academic title "Graduate Engineer."

Dr. Schneider was worried about the young democracy and the dangers it faced from the East. Jakob nodded: "We need to work cooperatively to counteract that danger in every way we can."

It was too bad, said Dr. Schneider, that my inventions hadn't made their way through the patenting process to marketing, but we must look to the future. He felt I might be more valuable personally than for my patent applications. Could I see myself as Director of Technical Innovations of the agency he had founded called the A.A.O.? It was located in a village in Upper Bavaria, with a nice view of the mountains when the weather was good . . .

"What does A.A.O. stand for, Dr. Schneidebein?" I asked, and bit my lip. What an odd slip of the tongue!

"Schneider, just Dr. Schneider," he said after a moment of startled silence. "A.A.O. stands for Abwehr Amt Ost"—Counter-intelligence East—"but let's keep that to ourselves for the time being. We work with both the government and the Americans." Jakob nodded cautiously.

"I strongly support democracy," I replied, "and it would be an honor to help you. Above all, against those still tied to the past insanity—they're still around." Dr. Schneider nodded slowly and earnestly:

"Of course, and we're thinking of that too. If a first-class security system is established, it will register everything, wherever it is. Here, read this through carefully before signing it, and take your time."

At that moment we heard a dull thump on floor above us, and shortly thereafter a second. Emma ran upstairs and returned after a few minutes, during which the dull thumps continued. She said: "You have to come, Titus keeps falling down and he looks terrible, he must have hit his head on something!"

"But isn't he hiking with his classmates in the mountains?"

"No, he's not!"

I excused myself from the two men and went upstairs with Emma. Titus was practicing Judo pike rolls. He was wall-eyed and wearing corduroys, something I'd never seen him in. I had an uneasy feeling. Emma suppressed a laugh that might have been heard downstairs. Titus panted descriptions:

"That was Yoko ukemi, sideways to the right, and this . . ."

Brumm!

". . . is Ushiro ukemi. And straight forward is called . . ."

Brumm!

". . . Mai ukemi."

"But should it make that much noise? I imagined it softer and smoother, Herr Babenzeller."

The master returned to his own form, for which I was thankful, since I preferred my son without his eyes slanting sideways and wearing something other than corduroys.

"I had a black belt once, but I haven't practiced for a long time."

"You teach sports?"

"Not directly. But I competed in Judo—I even took part in the 1934 European championships in Dresden."

"And why are you here now, appearing as Titus?"

186

"To prevent the worst from happening: Pahroc, don't join the A.A.O.! Don't sign anything, put Schneider off somehow without saying yes or no—don't say anything!"

"Why not, for heaven's sake?"

"You won't be happy there! You'll have to work with the very people you want to protect democracy from. And Schneider knows you're a sorcerer. You mean nothing to him as a technician, he wants to blackmail you into doing sorcery for him and spying on people, you can forget about inventing anything."

"How does he know . . ."

"From Schneidebein! Secret service agents all work together, even if they're serving governments at odds with each other. Those two knew each other when Germany was still a single nation."

"And I even called him Herr Schneidebein by mistake!"

"Was he startled?"

"Yes indeed."

"Go down and tell him your son is lovesick and keeps throwing himself to the floor. And postpone the discussion, see the gentlemen out with your best wishes. Believe me, it's the best thing."

I believed him. The men expressed their understanding and headed home. I sat with Babenzeller a while longer—in the kitchen, the living room was still being aired out.

"Why even consider joining them?" he asked.

"I could imagine serving a State that opposes the unlimited power of the State."

"There's no such thing. That's your idealism, and worse yet, it's illogical."

We switched the conversation to technology, a subject we'd always shared an interest in. We both loved cars. There were still patched-up old vehicles that had survived the bombing. There was also a new release of the small car the Dictator had planned as the Volkswagen, or People's Car. The

Allies only allowed its production because in terms of technology it was a long-standing joke. And then there were the sleek American cars and a few nice German models like the Borgward Hansa. Everyone was dreaming about cars, including myself and Babenzeller, and we discussed why that was.

A car is under the clear control of a single person—the one behind the wheel. Everyone faces the same direction in a car. Parents talk in front, children ask questions from the rear. During a round trip to Gardasee there's time to talk about all sorts of things—what more could one want? A car offers the perfect seating arrangement for family life. Within it, the world is both in order and moving rapidly, there's nothing better, then or now. That's why we dream about it. The number of autos was growing at a furious pace.

"But the accidents!" said Babenzeller. "Now they want to cut down the trees lining the avenues, just so drunken drivers won't hit them."

"Passengers should be forced to wear belts that let them move, yet hold them in an iron tight grip when the car strikes an object," I replied.

"Apply for a patent!" Babenzeller said. And I tried. But the results were, as usual, melancholy.

Our children gave us great joy, including those who were no longer truly children. Felix had graduated and was studying classical languages and ancient history in Munich, though I'd imagined him more as an inventor. He himself said that if there were a field called the "History of Technology" he felt he'd go far in it. I advised him to create the field. But he seemed more eager to create a family. By the time he introduced us to his pretty fellow student she was already pregnant—we liked everything else about her too. But a student marriage that included a child wasn't easy in the crowded living conditions of a city still partially in ruins. I took heart, conjured up the necessary funds, and invented a story about a small inheritance from an Indian uncle in Nevada who'd struck gold. Soon there was a spacious apartment in Schwabing in which legendary Fasching parties were held. There was nothing to object to in that—Emma and I danced along with them.

Fay was prone to heartbreak, or perhaps more accurately, prone toward men who broke her heart. There was nothing we could do about that—it was a matter of chemistry. And perhaps too her field of study—chemistry. Emma advised her to look beyond the boundaries of that field as well.

Titus was having a difficult time in school, though he was a perfectly fine boy. But perhaps a little too fine in some respects. He had his pride, and a sensitive concept of justice. A few teachers, who'd no doubt been humiliated in their own youth, were firmly convinced that it did pupils good to be humiliated now and then. Titus could be a passable rough-neck when comrades annoyed him. But this was no help when it came to teachers. Two or three pedagogues are enough reason to learn to hate school, and Titus had these same tyrants in store again when he had to repeat a year. I went through all the spells that might be employed in this case, and only one assured an end to his misery. I conjured up another inheritance and entrusted Titus to a boarding school in the mountains. Although he liked mountain climbing and skiing better than homework, he never failed a grade again, and in the end even managed to graduate from high school.

And Carola? She grew up to be a bright and pretty film editor. You probably won't be able to talk with her by the time you read this—she's quite ill now.

One day toward the end of 1953, an old man with a large nose knocked at our door: it was the Constable! Yes, Lesdiguières. His hair was snow-white, he'd lost weight and had aged greatly—as sometimes happens when you're ninety years old. We were very happy: Emma kissed him, and, to my astonishment, so did I. The children fell in love with

189

him immediately and thought he was probably what God looked like. He asked if we had any financial problems. If so, he could show Gnadl and us how to conjure up banknotes. We said we already knew that spell and owed a good deal to it. But we fetched Gnadl and spent a pleasant afternoon. Since the Constable found coffee too strong, we heated up the samovar, served tea, and the old gentleman told us everything he'd done during the war. It was like listening to a new Alexandre Dumas: whenever the German troops occupying France were forced to stop laughing, Lesdiguières had been involved. There were many heroes in the resistance, but only one master sorcerer. In spite of his old age he'd learned to speak German fluently, scouted out enemy positions, freed and hidden prisoners, transported art treasures to safety as a locomotive engineer, and provided weapons. He'd paid the German Commandant of Paris invisible visits so often, and made him hear voices so constantly, that the man gave up the idea of burning down Paris. And at times he'd laid sorcery totally aside to fight like a normal knight.

He wasn't a nobleman by the way. He wasn't related, even by way of a love affair, to François de Bonne, Duke de Lesdiguières, the last Constable of France. There was no rounded peasant girl running about, not one. But he thought that a name and title that had disappeared as early as 1623 should be revived somehow. It would be sad for it not to be.

He asked about the samovar and we told him the story of Sergej, to whom we hoped to return the beautiful old piece some day. That was the only reason we still had it—otherwise it would have long since been traded for bread, butter, flour, and ham. We figured that Sergej was living somewhere in France, and the Constable said he would be happy to try and locate him.

Within a week of his departure, he wrote that Sergej was composing operas in Paris. We set out at once. It was a splendid trip and our last together to another country. Emma, the samovar, and I spent all day on the train since flying with the heavy brass piece would have been difficult. Sergej was happy to see us and the samovar again, and we were soon settled, drinking tea followed by red wine. He played an entire opera for us on the piano and sang in a rather odd voice. Composers always sing somewhat oddly.

We grew gayer by the hour and reminisced about all those who had been at that evening dance in the Pankow Bürgerpark, about Jakob, Alissa, and at some point past midnight, even Schneidebein. It had been twenty years since that gathering in Bürgerpark, and Sergej recalled our love story: "I knew it right away—I heard an inner music with you two." He showed us his record collection, which had swelled to gigantic size in the meantime, and from two a.m. on we played only records we could sing along with. Lesdiguières had wanted to come too, but with all the stories and singing we no longer missed him. The next day we learned that he had died that night.

The burial took place in Grenoble, his hometown, home as well of Stendhal and, for centuries now, the best walnuts anywhere. We traveled from Paris by train, feeling it more fitting for a funeral. On the way from the church to the open grave, the line of mourners grew longer and longer, with people joining in from seemingly nowhere. They were sorcerers who'd arrived invisibly or flown in as birds and now, behind bushes or gravestones, were transformed into men and women dressed in black. I suspect that till the end of your days too, and for all eternity, sorcerers will recoil from entering churches—thereby missing some fine woodcarvings and a few decent sermons, not to mention the organ.

It was a magnificent burial, with many of his comrades from the days of the resistance present. They'd never known he was a sorcerer. Grenoble now has a Museum of the Resistance, and an art museum in which hangs a portrait of the real Constable, painted toward the end of the sixteenth century. He's standing in full armor while his little son plays beside him with one of his father's huge iron gloves. No one has ever noticed that the features of the true Constable are those of his self-titled successor from the twentieth century—our friend had worked his magic! I would probably have never noticed if he hadn't mentioned it himself once.

I've often thought about who among the dead are most deeply missed. I suspect it may be the honest ones, or, at any rate, those who were considered honest by almost everyone. Whether they lied, once or often, plays no role if they did so for others, or for the honor of humankind. Lesdiguières was a man of action and military strategy his entire life, even in times of peace, but never for low or common purposes.

No one was surprised that Schneidebein was absent. A sorcerer who'd killed one of his fellow sorcerers—and especially one like Schlosseck—would rightly fear public disgrace and even deadly revenge. And, no doubt, the literally devastating gaze of his former teacher, Babenzeller, who to my astonishment was dressed like a priest and disappeared immediately after the ceremony. We saw Henry Grund, Pospischil, Blüthner, and finally the person the Constable had completely kept from all of us: his wife. In spite of her veil, it was clear she was beautiful, and her hands told me she was in her mid-thirties. I found it hard to imagine back then that someone in his eighties could fall in love forever. Today, as a 109-year-old sorcerer, I can only smile gently.

As Emma stepped up to the grave and took the little shovel of earth, I couldn't restrain my tears. I didn't need to read her mind: I knew she was plagued by a premonition that she was saying farewell not only to this beloved old warrior, but to Grenoble, Paris, Europe and her colleagues, perhaps to the magic of the world itself. Grenoble, with it splendid snow-covered mountains on the horizon, was not a bad place to do so. Her sense of leave-taking was premature, for we still had a long, lovely year ahead of us. But the recognition that life is finite thrusts itself upon us when it will. It doesn't follow a script.

Emma was pregnant, though she alone knew it at the time.

Grenoble had never seen so many sorcerers on a single day, before or since. We met several new people, among them a couple from our area: our colleague Blank, nicknamed "Cheese," and the love of his youth Aurora Rehwinkel, wonderful young people who were also both sorcerers. Ever since a trip to the Philippines, she'd enjoyed going about as a Philippine porcupine, which attracted attention in Upper Bavaria, and is difficult to do, by the way. I haven't managed it to this day—for lack of a living model.

Dear Mathilda, when you read these pages they will seem in many ways like reports from a sunken world. Not only because I'm telling you about things that happened in 1955, but also because I'm doing so in 2015, from yet another distant point in your past. Right now you're hopping about before my eyes as a three-year-old, wanting me to stop writing and tell you another story. Tomorrow your mother will take you to preschool (called "kita" these days), but on this afternoon you can play with me or look at picture books while I read the brief captions to you. I avoid any fairy tales in which a sorcerer comes off badly.

Today is the 7th of January, 2015. Yesterday Rejlander and I celebrated the Visit of the Three Magi, called Kings by most people (they can accept that with a smile). The last time I celebrated the festival with a sorceress was with Emma, in 1955. I haven't lived with another sorceress since then, but for the last three months I've been with Rejlander. She has a house in Sweden and an apartment in Berlin, where I'm an almost constant guest. The house is rented.

We invited three friends over last night: Iris, Stephan, and Waldemar III, who read us something from his latest book.

Waldemar IV cooked and Rejlander baked the cake that's always part of the celebration. It usually disappears quickly, since a little figure is baked inside it, and whoever finds this figure in his piece on the plate is named "King" for the day. He, or the "Queen," has to invite everyone to next year's feast at their place.

I've kept the fact that I'm a sorcerer secret all my life—only my colleagues and our servants knew. Servants have to be told because it's important that we talk about sorcery with people who don't have the gift themselves. If we don't converse with normal people we run the risk of becoming arrogant Samurai—Schlosseck knew that. But the word "normal" doesn't really apply here: servants can't do sorcery, but they have rare gifts of discretion, and of admiration for what they can't do themselves.

Last night, Rejlander and I decided to tell Iris and Stephan about sorcerers. At first they were both astonished and incredulous, but then they grew excited and enthusiastic. We had an open, lively discussion. I wonder if the world would be better off if people knew we existed, could see us as adding to life, if they ceased to hate, mistrust, or fear us, and came to respect that we are different. Surely we might achieve what the disabled have. In America they are referred to as "differently abled," or "differently gifted." That's the right way to look at it. There's not a person in the world who doesn't have something to teach us—what they've had to learn to be themselves. "Differently abled"—yes, so are we.

The book from which Waldemar III read was already three years old (he should write a new one). It dealt with a fictional trip through time, back to his youth, to the year 1958 when he was attending school in the mornings in Traunstein and went sailing in the afternoon. He's about the same age as your Aunt Carola. When he finished I asked him if he'd ever visited Wasserburg am Inn prior to 1955. I realized how happy it would make me to talk with someone who might have known Emma back then. But apart from my son Titus (now Alpine Öhi on the Wilder Kaiser ridge), hardly anyone can say that. Your father was still an infant when she died, and has no memory of her.

Until recently, I thought I could never love another woman again as I loved Emma. After her death I felt as old as the grave, and yet life lasted far beyond that. People say life is too short, too short for this and too short for that. That's almost always true. What's less well known is the incredible amount of time we do have: time that changes almost everything, time that heals all wounds. And you don't have to live to 109 to learn that.

By the way, Iris got the little figure in the cake yesterday. So next year we'll all be together again at their place. They've become our best friends; we're never bored when we're with them. Iris is a visual being: she has an extraordinary ability to read faces, and is the best observer of other people that I've ever known among non-sorcerers. She looks into another person's eyes and knows everything. And Stefan is an auditory being: he hears everything and forgets nothing, not even the slightest tremor in a voice. Such friends are a special gift: they enrich and enlarge our lives.

I feel like bringing this letter to a close. I've said what was most important on the subject of money, and I'll tell you what happened to Emma and me in the next letter. Besides, Rejlander is changing to go out to dinner and the movies with me—that's always a good reason to end a letter. We're going to see a film about a likeable old man who's becoming increasingly senile. Rejlander saw it just before Christmas and insists on seeing it again with me. I hope I don't cry! That embarrasses me every time. For me, the rule still holds true: An Indian never cries. Perhaps there's a spell to keep from crying, but if there is, there's not much point in my learning it now.

P.S.: I wanted to add something about the deterioration of conjured money: it doesn't revert to its original state until the sorcerer who created it dies: then banknotes turn back to magazine pages or oak leaves, coins turn back to gravel, coal, or broken stones.

With regard to the possible consequences of my own death, at least I've lived long enough not to have damaged the value of the D-Mark through my own creation of currency. The D-Mark was abolished without any help on my part, and remained hard currency till the end. And the Euro? Since its introduction, I haven't conjured up a single banknote or coin, though I have taken risks, always successfully, speculating on the open market. So in this area, I'm totally free of any guilt.

Marginal note of his last Finance Minister:

Pahroc was no speculator, though he liked to present himself as such. In fact all he actually did was instruct a bank back in the seventies to purchase stock for his children each month with his pension, which he didn't need. That wasn't risky, but it was certainly successful. Rejlander.

Bringing Out the Best in People

February/March 2017

Dear Mathilda,

I'm writing again after a two-year pause. Yes, I haven't written a single line since Three Kings Day in early 2015. You wouldn't have noticed this pause had I not mentioned it, since all the letters came to you in one thick packet.

While you were still a baby it seemed perfectly natural to me to write future letters to the young woman you would someday become. Now, after this break, as you sit on the floor beside my desk drawing a tall mountain and toboggan with colored crayons, it seems strange to be talking with the child and writing to the young woman at the same time. But I must remind myself that it's not strange, but logical. You've just climbed up on my lap and are looking around on my desk. I thought about putting the letter away, but then I decided to go on writing. You asked: "What's that you're writing, Grandpa?"

"A letter. Then someone can see what I want to say to them, even though I'm no longer there."

Now I hoped for the question, "Who are you writing to?" But I seemed to have overestimated my abilities as a pedagogue. You already knew what a letter was, lost interest, and turned to the globe. The way it revolved was far more fascinating than how someone who isn't there can say something. You turned the globe faster and faster with your little patty-cake hand, but it neither hummed nor squeaked.

This weekend all of us—your parents, Rejlander, and I, and of course you—took off in the car for Chemnitz to visit the museum, then on to Schloss Augustusburg to toboggan. A grown-up always rode down with you and then you'd both plod back up with the grown-up pulling or carrying the toboggan. Finally you resolutely insisted on going down alone, and we reluctantly agreed. When you arrived at the bottom you called out for someone to come carry the toboggan back up. When we refused, you threw the sledge down on the snow and yourself beside it, then yelled up loudly to us: "Now I'm freezing to death!" It was only a question of time till one of us came to save you, and who would that be? Grandpa, of course, though by then he already walked with a cane. But I was touched by how much alike we are. I too tended to do only what gave me pleasure, and left the rest to my servant. You'll probably have some sort of servant of your own, as Rejlander does—hers is named Flamelet and she's almost a better cook than Waldemar IV.

You've just shown me your drawing of the toboggan. It has big horns and the caps are flying off of everyone sitting on it. Now you're working on another picture, a dinosaur with a long neck. "I think he has grandchildren, I'll draw them too."

Perhaps it was seeing you and your sled that encouraged me to overcome my laziness and resume my letter writing. I'd paused for a long, long time. Rejlander thought I just didn't want to tell you about Emma's death and the difficult time that followed. But the real reason is that things have been going too well for me to write! I've found the second great love of my life, after Emma, and plan to stay with Rejlander as long as it lasts. I accompany her on trips and watch her making films. I've retired from my role as hostel host— no more bed-and-breakfast in Pankow, though I enjoyed it to the end. But I still have the apartment.

Rejlander and I enjoy watching animals and taking on their likenesses. We speak the major animal languages of the world, and the languages of snakes and birds, as well. Last summer we cavorted about as deer in the woods and meadows. I appeared as a particularly attractive buck, and she as a pretty doe. We found springing about that way more fun than flying. We'd checked the entire area in advance as ravens to be sure there were no hunters—we had no desire to find ourselves on some menu.

That fall we discovered flying in flocks. We could fly beside one another as birds! You may recall that sorcerers can't normally fly side by side—they have to take separate routes. But in a flock of starlings or swallows we could swoop in circles together with a thousand or even ten thousand other birds. You don't have to fly all the way to Africa with them. You can use the period when the flock is gathering and practicing flying in formation. I would have liked to take a long trip with Rejlander this way (it would surely have been more fun than many transatlantic crossings), but she had a new film to make and was not keen. She had mastered Lesdiguières' trick of duplication and could look down on the Mediterranean as a swallow and do something else in Berlin at the same time. But unfortunately the spell doesn't result in exact duplication—one of the two is weaker, and since Rejlander preferred to go on the flight as the stronger of the two, in order to enjoy it fully, her double on the set would have given the impression of being somewhat out of her depth.

Now I've taught her how to multiply herself even further, to form an entire flock of birds for example. We each turn into a flock of starlings and take off, then form a single flock in the air.

Rejlander has reminded me several times to continue my letters to you. She says a sorcerer in the best of his years at over a hundred shouldn't put off important tasks, or they might easily lie unfinished for a long time. She's right. But I'll stop making one type of sorcery the theme of each letter: there are simply too many spells, and some you'll never run into. It's more important to me now to finish telling you the story of my life as best I can. As time passed, I found sorcery became more and more natural, but less and less central to my life. At some point what we can or could do, what we've tried and achieved in all things large and small, is no longer so important. Then our life stands in the landscape like a solitary tree, the sum of what can no longer be changed.

My grand, wonderful Emma died in 1955, a few months after the birth of your father. She simply fell down dead, which was a relatively pleasant end for her, but a frightful shock and loss for those who loved her. She'd just assured me that little Johann was definitely a sorcerer—he'd reached from his crib toward the pictures and now they all were hanging crookedly on the wall. I'd seen him do it, but it never occurred to me that he was being helped. Any sorcerer who's fairly advanced can lengthen another person's arm of course, but I wouldn't have suspected such a tender, bold action from Emma.

Emma departed this world suddenly, but she'd long sensed she would die young, and she'd asked me to bury her in Berlin. I understood that well. She'd been on her own in Wasserburg so long. And she'd never stopped feeling that Berlin was her hometown.

After her death I felt for the first time that life had no meaning, and certainly not one given by sorcery. From then on, I firmly believed that all I touched was mere "vanity and vexation of spirit"—as it says in the Bible, the book of sayings. But in the Bible it's a look backward. For me, it was a glimpse into the future. I felt so bad I wanted to die. I was on the way there, becoming sicker and weaker. I was sure I didn't need to kill myself—my grief was going to do the job for me. The end would come faster on its own.

But it didn't come, and I placed the farewell letter I'd written to my son in the secret compartment of my desk, where I forgot it.

Just at this period, my powers of sorcery developed to their highest level. I'd been able to transform one object into another of the same mass for some time. Conjuring money was just one aspect of this power. If you can turn stones and leaves into coins and banknotes, you can direct a sharp gaze at a juice press and turn it into a typewriter. I'd already succeeded in moving objects about or making them disappear. Now I was ready to create items of daily use out of thin air, without any source material. And under the careful supervision of sorcerers like Schlosseck, Macintosh, Babenzeller, or Lesdiguières, I could have learned how to turn human beings into animals or other humans, as long as they weren't themselves sorcerers.

I saw that almost anything was possible now, an irony of fate since I was no longer interested in such things. I realized my world was falling apart. I could have discussed this, and sorcery too, with Gnadl, but our friendship had suffered somewhat following an argument over the treatment of animals and other topics we disagreed on. The narrow and winding lanes of the small town lacked the fresh breezes that might have blown away such ill feelings, and those that had lodged there seemed stuck fast. The city was a little too small for two good sorcerers in any case. We continued to exchange cordial greetings, our children played together, but our friendship was no longer the same.

I only saw Babenzeller again once before he died in a scenic parking area on the Queralpenstrasse. He'd failed to pull the handbrake on his DKW "Master Class" tight enough, and when he stepped out to admire the view of the snow-covered

Watzmann massif, the car, to which he'd given the bold nickname "The Grim Reaper," rolled into him from behind and took him with it into the depths. He died without knowing what hit him.

I don't think cars should be given names anyway, including Sandman, Thanatos, and Angel of Death. It's too easy for vehicles to take it wrong and develop their own personalities. Babenzeller's death left me even sadder, if that was possible. He wasn't friends with everyone, in fact I was his only friend, for in his eyes all the others lacked something. He frightened them intentionally so they would leave him in peace. A learned man, a sorcerer without equal—and then this shocking death by means of a stupid car. That it was a "Master Class" was pure sarcasm—fate tends toward offensive jokes like that.

And what of Jakob, who'd become as good a friend again as he'd been in kindergarten? He had to return to the States at just this time—his newspaper's circulation had fallen lower and lower, although its journalism was as good as ever. Jakob had a large family to feed. I wished him well in America.

I was alone, that was a fact, and I didn't want to see anyone. Nothing interested me, not even technical innovations. My former firm, Hollerith GmbH, now represented American interests only. Operating under a new name in Böblingen, they'd brought out the first computer for ordinary people. It was called RAMAC and its hard drive weighed only a metric ton—you could practically fly to the moon with it. But I remained in a state of lethargy and no longer wished to go to the moon. I didn't even like driving a car, while everyone else was crazy about it. Driving two cars simultaneously offered something different for a change—I could do that now, making two Pahroc's out of one, and seating each behind the wheel of a Borgward Isabella. I could make the money for it with my eyes closed. But what a senseless thing to do! That little game was fit at most to lead to a spectacular crash in which I would run into myself: the result—a double death with a single grave. Only if I hadn't intended to of course—otherwise the spell would have prevented it.

No, I had no wish to go on. But in spite of this, I would try now and then, behind my own back and unobtrusively, to discover if there might after all be something I could possibly do.

Tinker about, fiddle with something, work on new inventions? No! Learn new magic spells? What would be the point? With whom could I share the joy? Schlosseck would probably have said that now was the time to get a new servant—someone I could talk things over with. But I felt sure that no one could put up with me, given my mood.

Drinking helped a little, but only for short periods. Sorcerers can hold their liquor extremely well—if they drink, things get expensive. But I didn't need to hold back, I'd have no trouble paying the bill. It's dangerous, by the way, to transform yourself when you're drunk, it makes it difficult to regain your original self, so you wind up having to sober up as a bear or wild boar—and hope you aren't something smaller that might be eaten. Except for spiders—they're usually left alone. I hate to confess it, but I crouched in a cranny as a totally stoned spider and saw stars once.

There have been many sorcerers who could no longer deal with life and perished. I was a perfect candidate to join them. But then came a day—I sat brooding in a Bürgerbräu restaurant with a beer in front of me—when a woman approached and asked in a Polish accent "Aren't you . . . you must be Herr Piechatzek, right?"

It was the woman from the death march in East Prussia, the one I'd carried off the ice half dead, one of the few who survived the massacre that Babenzeller and I had been unable to stop in time. I'd given the name Piechatzek in a moment of caution. Her name was Ewa, and she glowed with gratitude. She said she had a job and a husband now and that they would soon be emigrating to Palestine, something she was looking forward to. How was I doing? I thanked her and said I was doing fine, that I had an elevator company and several children, even grandchildren. I said that to make her happy, and when she said how much it did, it made me happy in return. Just a little. But enough to give me an idea. Helping others, and seeing how thankful they were, seemed to bring me a degree of happiness, even in my present state. If I were to help a large number of people, might the sinking ship of my life rise from the waters again? Soon after Ewa left—she worked in a hospital and had to return to duty— a news report came over the radio. A widespread uprising against the Soviet regime in Hungary had been bloodily suppressed and hundreds of thousands of people were fleeing to Austria, which could take in only a portion of them. So they had appealed to Germany for help. But help required helpers, and they were calling for volunteers. I thought how Emma would have dropped everything and headed off to lend a hand, and I knew what I had to do, regardless of how I was feeling personally.

One of the German reception camps, Piding, was located in Bavaria, near Reichenhall. First I went to the State Library and learned Hungarian with two fingers. Then I flew to the refugee camp and used conjured papers to register as a Caritas volunteer. I told them I spoke Hungarian and might be of some use. Around five thousand Hungarians were gathered there, many of whom had confronted the tanks, but there were also entire families, embittered old people, crying children. I helped with registration and food distribution, sorted donated clothing, handed out teddy bears, and, above all, talked with hundreds of people who were pleased to be able to speak their own language, even if they did find my Hungarian a little strange—perhaps I should have laid three fingers on the grammar's spine. But I soon realized that speaking wasn't what counted—listening was. The only person who can offer true consolation is one who doesn't always have to hear his own voice. Now and then I couldn't be found, for I was flying above the countryside organizing deliveries: blankets, laundry, overcoats, bathtubs, baby bottles, electric cookers. The ability to conjure money made sense once again, and when someone questioned my right to place orders for the camp, I showed him a menu from the local inn "Zur Post" and made him think he was seeing an authorization from the Upper Bavarian government with two signatures and three impressive stamps.

I also repaired radios, since news reports from Hungary were of vital importance, and used spells to heat hot plates when no electrician in the world could have fixed them.

The camp didn't just have volunteers, there were also representatives of organizations who hoped to hire workers. The German economy was growing and needed men and women. Since I'd become a trusted figure in the meantime, I was present at many discussions and could push for higher salaries now and then. I was also brought in when one congenial fellow tried to hire "fiery Hungarian dancing girls" for a nightclub. Since I could read both his face and his mind, the pimp got nowhere. A man from the Foreign Legion proved more difficult—he was after quick signatures. I told him in no uncertain terms that he needed to explain more clearly what the men could expect: action in Algeria with miserable chances of survival. Evidently he didn't understand my French, or it was too loud for a conversation—at any rate, he asked me to go outside with him. Once outside, I suddenly saw a fist approaching my face. I instantly made myself light and soft—the blow landed, but had no effect. Then he reached back to box my ears, just as I turned momentarily to steel. He held his right hand in his left and danced about. At that point he gave up and headed home.

I stayed in Piding for three weeks, till most of the Hungarians had found new homes. Then I reopened the shop in Wasserburg and fetched Carola and little Johann from Gnadl, with whom they'd been staying for some time. I was in good spirits again. I'd done something for and with Emma. I was still in mourning, but in a more active form.

I'm still not sure even today if helping others is part of the meaning of sorcery, but it's certainly part of the meaning of life. At any rate, a person gets right with himself when he takes care of others. And even someone who's in danger of losing their grip on life may help restore some order in it by helping others. At least that was true in my case. I had something to look forward to again in life.

But I had no intention of serving as a spy for Dr. Schneider in the A.A.O. When he called yet again, appealed to my patriotism and spoke of democracy, I remembered what Babenzeller had said about him. I told him that after my wife died I'd embraced faith and was going to enter a monastery. Things quieted down at once.

Babenzeller had managed to let me know where the sorcery library was stored and how I could gain access to it. He hadn't told anyone else, so I felt it my duty to inspect the holdings and make them available once again to my colleagues. One fine day I flew along the Inn River till Kufstein came into sight, and off to the west Längberg, a forested mountain with the ruins of a fortress. In a hollow below the fallen stonework, I found the small castle Babenzeller had described to me. It had two round towers with copper domes, several balconies with views of the Wilder Kaiser ridge, and a graceful annex, beneath which, deep within the mountain, stood the library. I concentrated on the key thoughts that unlocked the secret door in the forest and descended a nearly endless spiral staircase in total darkness. Arriving at the bottom, I cast a Light spell that made everything bright as day, and I soon sat pouring over the books—in my overcoat at first, since the cellar was extremely cold until my Heat spell took effect. I'd decided to search for instructions on group spells with multiple colleagues like the one that had protected St. Polykarp, or the

Mother Shield that once kept Emma safe. It was now up to me to produce something similar to protect the secret library in Längberg. And if I succeeded in bringing several sorcerers together for that purpose, why not form some sort of association or league at the same time? The fact that we'd been unable to do anything to stop the regime of terror didn't mean we couldn't try to prevent new dictatorships from emerging. There was a lot of talk about a politically united Europe—that seemed a concept sorcerers could support.

Today is the third of March, 2017. It's astounding how many different eras and places your mind can be in at the same time. There I sit in 1957 in the subterranean library, thinking about Europe, but I'm also standing here at my desk, looking at the unforgettable face of the new American president in the newspaper and thinking he might well be forgotten by the time you read this letter in 2030. Unless his behavior has served to truly unite Europe politically for once.

At the moment there's a great fear of refugees, and of terrorists who disguise themselves as refugees. They would even have us believe that all refugees are terrorists, even children. No one in their right mind truly believes that, but it's used as an argument to deny them aid, and to mask tight fistedness and hardened hearts. The "refugee problem" exists primarily in the minds of some Europeans—a more concrete problem is a shortage of mercy. Dear Mathilda, all this will surely have ceased to be of interest by the time you read it. I'm certain that those living in countries from which refugees are fleeing today will, in your day, be working peacefully and making an adequate living, and that many who left will have returned home.

In 1957, a sign that read "Closed due to illness" appeared increasingly often in my shop window, even though I was no longer ill. I'd always devoted myself to the radio and appliance business somewhat half-heartedly, and now I did so tenth-heartedly. The shop had been meant as camouflage, and it had served its purpose. I could have moved to Hamburg, where Kusenberg was living, but I soon made up my mind. Emma's grave was in Berlin, servants weren't that easy to find around Hamburg, and my older children said they'd rather travel to Berlin and visit their Mama with me. I was waiting to make the move till Carola had graduated from high school and I could turn the house over to someone trustworthy.

Titus was in Rosenheim working on a degree in Forestry, a field of study only sons of timberland owners generally chose.

"Do you intend to plant forests?" I asked him.

"No," he said cheekily, "chop them down and plant cannabis."

Titus hated to be asked questions. Any question, any at all, made him aggressive. I was concerned from the start about his exams. He was the perfect candidate for an isolated alpine pasture at two thousand meters or so, and that's where he wound up. When anyone asks me which of my children reached the highest point in their profession I always name Titus—and get a laugh when I say why. The top rank in my eyes goes to Fay, who completed a Doctorate in Natural Sciences, a degree that requires some serious brainpower.

Carola passed her final college preparatory exam and was intending to study German Language and Literature at the University of Munich. For the time being, she could live with her brother Felix. I sold the house, which I'd never legally owned, to the mountain rescue service for a token sum—the rescue service seemed a fitting heir for the silent mountaintop wanderer Josef Gruber, who was buried in the region they served on Hochplatte Mountain.

Johann was now five and a half years old. He cried when he had to leave his little classmates in Wasserburg, and they cried too, for he was always fun to be around. He could imitate grownups so well—particularly those who were ill-tempered and scary, among whom, thankfully, I was no longer counted.

The struggle between the West and East could be felt with particular clarity in Berlin. A wall was even built, right through the middle of the city, so that no further movement from the East to the West zone was possible. Most people thought West Berlin might soon be swallowed up by the East. People departed in droves for Hesse or Bavaria, leaving splendid apartments in the best part of the city empty, at prices lower than ever. I rented one of the most beautiful among them. It was on Tauentzienstrasse and was so huge that I contemplated with pleasure all the things I might do with it. Today, in 2017, five lawyers work there, often all at the same time. At any rate, there was a handsome room for a servant and I set out to find one, along with some new pursuit that would offer more flexibility than an appliance shop.

I found a meaningful and sufficiently dangerous task helping East Berliners escape to the West.

What could be more satisfying for a technician than outwitting government agencies and smuggling people? I refitted large western cars and hid my clients behind cleverly reduced luggage areas. I familiarized myself with the art of tunneling, constructed power gliders, and assembled reliable burners for hot air balloons. I employed my facility for falsifying documents more sparingly, though my travel visas and ink stamps passed the closest inspection. I didn't want word getting around that there was a surefire sorcerer helping people escape—that could prove dangerous. The wall itself posed no problem of course. I flew over that latest achievement of genuine socialism invisibly, or as a dove—I didn't even have to tire myself walking through it. I made regular flights back and forth, and along the wall as well. I explored its entire length closely and found nooks and crannies where even a non-sorcerer could get across.

I visited those seeking help in their East Berlin apartments and offered them advice without fear of discovery. Of course I was under surveillance, but as I invisibly entered their apartments I was also sitting quite visibly (and very well watched) in the Restaurant Ganymede, sipping Crimean sparkling wine.

Visual duplication is not too difficult an affair, but far greater art is required to reunite two brains with different experiences—you may start babbling nonsense or become completely disoriented. If you ever try this spell, dear Mathilda, be sure to have experienced companions with you. Sorcerers often suffer strange fates in such cases—but I don't want to frighten you, a word to the wise is sufficient.

Meanwhile, after intensive study of the books in Längberg and several visits to Blüthner in Dresden and Pospischil in Vienna, I knew so many spells that I became rather foolhardy. In the sixties, I even learned to multiply myself in greater numbers. One Pahroc could become ten Pahrocs, or a hundred blackbirds, or an anthill swarming with ants. But I rarely used this spell till I joined Rejlander—now I enjoy it several times a week.

Back then I had no idea how much danger I was in. Yes, it was Schneidebein—Schneidebein yet again! He was now in Eisenhüttenstadt doing what he'd always done—causing trouble.

I took money for helping people escape. That was a purely cautionary move, for if I hadn't done so, the people I saved would have found it strange, even suspicious; they might not have entrusted themselves to me in the first place. It took some effort to return their money or its equivalent in some inconspicuous way—by getting them a job, for example, or through some other "lucky break." I had to pull a lot of strings to do it, and often followed them clear to West Germany. That was generally more work than arranging the escape itself.

I'd found someone to move into my apartment and take care of Johann. He was a man, about forty-five years old, whom I'd helped escape. He was a real find: an amateur cook and soccer player, good with figures, a careful driver, and a modest, friendly man to boot. He also drove the boy to school—Johann was entering the first grade. Somehow he knew that I was a sorcerer, and I knew that he knew. I realized he would make a good servant, in part because Johann liked him. As a young man he'd been a loyal follower of the Dictator and even wore a black uniform. I learned by reading his mind that he was ashamed of this and felt that only menial tasks lay before him, since in any sort of career his past would be revealed and used against him. I also noted that he hadn't killed anyone. He'd joined out of conviction, not opportunism, and couldn't understand now why he'd ever done it. That he'd allowed his life to go astray in such a catastrophic way had one positive aspect: he knew how easily it could happen. Someone who's made such terrible errors is less likely to look down with contempt on the mistakes of others. I got him to tell me all this, and in return told him how I differed from other people. We came to an agreement. He served me well, beginning in 1963. I named him Waldemar II and paid him generously—I didn't want him to think I was taking advantage of his dark secret. For a moment I thought of going to the archives and falsifying the documents and records pertaining to his past, but then decided to let it go. He wasn't a bad fellow, but I couldn't do that for him. Waldemar II was a loyal and prudent servant, and I'm pleased to say he remained unmolested by government agencies without the help of sorcery. Unfortunately, he died in 1971. I would have thought such a calm man capable of anything, but not a heart attack.

Not much came of my attempt to revive the sorcerers association. Gnadl didn't even come, Blüthner was cautious because
of Henry Grund, who believed in socialism and tried to defend it against colleagues like Blüthner and me. But I did get
to know others I'd only heard about: the beautiful Caracciola
from Tessin, and De Crescenzo from Naples, a fantastic engineer who later managed to invent a great thinker and weave
him magically into the history of philosophy. At the time, he
was working for my old punch-card firm, which had been re-
named long ago. We shop-talked late into the night.

At our gathering on Tauentzien I encountered new faces,
but also old doubts and opposition. There were fundamentally differing opinions on everything: on the purpose of sorcery, on socialism and God, on the future reunification of
Germany and its current rearmament, on the atom bomb,
and certainly on Europe. Some felt a united Europe would
bring peace and warm relations among countries, others
foresaw a powerful cartel that would dictate the price of raw
materials to poor countries. And one, a nondescript colleague
with an equally nondescript name, who has long since passed
away, said something in a low voice that I find wiser today
than I did then: "Transforming events! Europe must become
a linked chain of compelling events, otherwise it will be no
more than a central insurance agency." No one took up the
remark, including me, but I made note of it. I realize today
that it was prophetic.

Then I did something I thought quite promising. I raised
a topic that had never played a role among sorcerers, but that
I felt should concern us. As I started to speak the room fell
silent, for it was something new and at the same time something old.

"We can transform ourselves," I said, "and we often turn
ourselves into animals. Each of us knows intimately the
animal we most enjoy turning into; in my case, it's a crocodile."

The audience laughed and Blüthner nodded affirmatively: "In memory of Schlosseck!" And someone called out: "Can we see that please?"

"Gladly, a little later," I replied, "I can't talk so well when I'm a reptile, and I'm not finished yet." Then I continued speaking of animals, whose speech we sorcerers understand, whose pain we share, and without whom the world would be a dismal place indeed. Life among humans only would be hell, and what would become of our children if they never knew animals? Not just sorcerers, but all humankind had reason to be thankful for them. But we were in a special position, I said, to help animals, and that was also one of our missions. We had to do battle against the unbelievable ways animals were treated on this planet.

"How? By joining the SPCA, or forming our own animal protection society?" Henry Grund asked.

"We should talk about how," I replied. "I can imagine doing things in animal form that force humans to take us seriously. Start a revolution as slaughterhouse cattle, or turn into a species of fish that's dying out and strike fear into the hearts of mechanized fishing trawlers. It's good for humans to face so-called miracles now and then. Why not provide a few that help animals?"

"Sacred cows in Central Europe too, I get it!"

I could have choked the heckler. And I realized I stood alone in my cause. I'd given a few of them something to think about, but as a whole, sorcerers were not ready for such a project, nor was the rest of the humanity.

I didn't allow my disappointment to show. I served them all coffee and cakes, organized a city tour and steamship ride, and followed up with dinner in Grunewald. After careful consideration, I decided to keep the secret entrance to the library in Längberg to myself, for I was sure that it would reach the wrong ears. I had no desire to see someone like Schneidebein in Längberg!

In the end, it was clear: there's no point in starting something just because you have a big apartment.

I felt down for several days, which wasn't helped by the news that Johann was being offered a spot as a child extra in a crime film. I was against it, since the boy already had enough distractions at school, and his grades were almost uniformly bad. But he was all for it: he was saving up for a bicycle and loved playing roles anyway. I told him he wouldn't be playing a role, just standing around in the background, but he couldn't be dissuaded. Reluctantly, I gave my permission. Even the title put me off: *News from the Wizard*.

And then I started something new after all. I'd discovered that I liked being an aid worker, taking care of people or smuggling them, and now I saw a chance to expand that role: I wanted to bring out the best in them, to make them happy. What I'd done with Emma and the children—at least when I was there—could be developed into a profession, bringing greater joy to myself and to others.

But where could I find unhappy people who would let me lead them toward happiness? I couldn't do without clients, but unhappy people want almost anything but to be happy— that's a large part of their problem. How could I lure unhappy people to my place on Tauentzienstrasse? Certainly not by offering a seminar on happiness. It would have to promise them the one thing they hoped would compensate them for their unhappiness—success. And "leadership" was considered the key to success. I had never shown myself to be a particularly good leader, but since I found the concept interesting, I decided to teach others all about it. It's well known that those who lack talent are well suited to teach things they themselves can't do to those who are more gifted. A good trainer knows what it's like not to be able to do something. And when it came to leadership, I knew that better than anyone else. It happens that 1965 was loaded with young people trying to lead in some way or other. They were "acting out," trying to be important, most to impress their parents, or because they bore some other burden they were trying to make sense of, or find a purpose in. I placed an ad in a newspaper called *The Evening Standard* that always appeared at noon (which suited me).

"Success through strong leadership. Sign up now—that's an order!" Followed by the telephone number.

And beside the entrance to my building, I placed a sign:

Berlin Leadership Academy
Ring at Pahroc four floors up on the right

I still think my "leadership seminars" weren't all that bad. My exercises taught young people concentration and conscientiousness, and they learned a few things about service and helping others. I treated with some discretion the fact that I'd run an electric appliance shop in Wasserburg and not an international company.

I had them do exercises, gave them rules, taught them tricks. Some were right, many were wrong. For example, I told them that one mustn't show fear when completing a business deal. Decisions are always coupled with a degree of fear, for they represent a trade. One gives up the advantages of the known for the advantages of change. Risk is always involved, and that causes some uneasiness. So one aspect of leadership is to engender an atmosphere of calm, and say as little as possible. Talking too much is a sign of fear. (That was rubbish: I know now that many people talk a lot simply because they have something worth saying.)

We began the sessions by asking someone to tell a story that he or she found relevant to the theme of leadership. One student recounted the following dream: He was sitting up at the front of a double-decker bus in Berlin, holding a toy steering wheel. The bus was making its way through milling traffic that the student saw only vaguely from above. He couldn't tell what was directly in front of the bus or on either side. Suddenly, he realized that he was driving the bus. If pedestrians were run down, or cars reduced to scrap metal, he would be responsible, he alone, the driver upstairs. In situations like that, the student said, there's no point in remaining calm. You have to cry out loud for help: "I can't handle it!"

"No," I said, "you have to wake up."

We discussed the dream. My diagnosis was megalomania, which happens in dreams, and is quite acceptable. Someone else thought it was the dream of a democrat who felt responsible and concerned for the public at large. A woman disagreed: it was one of those nightmares that haunt people with an entirely false notion of democracy.

Later—much later—many of my pupils ascended to high positions. They began by joining the student movement. One of them I remember particularly well, because he clarified our common goal as follows: "Leadership is never allowing doubt to arise about your abilities as a leader." A year later, he was the star of an anti-authoritarian movement and joined others in founding a commune. It was three years before I saw him again: he was the ex-president of a corporation and gave lectures on leadership.

By the end of 1966, I was annoyed by how many future leaders were refusing to enter a barbershop. Shoulder-length manes were appearing, as if to prove no one really wanted a job. Then one day students simply stopped coming. In my initial bewilderment I envisioned a collision on nearby public thoroughfares and pictured a wrecked bus. But there was another reason:

"Leadership" had turned into a bad word overnight. The students thought it smacked of paternalism. Now everything was to be discussed by everyone and then decided in common. Actions would arise from the correct historical consciousness of all, or at least of all those present. Decisions would no longer be made by a leader, only the "base" could do that. Those who proclaimed this most energetically were, of course, leaders of a sort, but they never called themselves that, for they were strictly anti-authoritarian. As a result, there was no official leader anywhere who could be held responsible for broken windows or overturned cars—to us older citizens the world seemed completely off its rails.

On the other hand, the youth movement had a certain sex appeal. It celebrated freedom and provided the stuff of myth for coming generations. We older folks felt it too, at any rate, all sorcerers did. The youngsters loved whomever they wished, whenever they wished, and could do so without consequences—without birth control pills it would have been another matter. They dressed for comfort, and not as convention demanded. No ties choking them, no more suits! Skirts were shorter and legs longer, barer than ever. I enjoyed going to the demonstrations, but only to watch approvingly from the sidewalk. Since many of the demonstrations came down Tauentzienstrasse, I could see everything from my own front door.

They smoked hashish, a pleasant drug offering a sense of peace. I tried it too, but found I had a hard time casting spells under its influence. It induced an uncontrollable chain of images and thoughts. One unplanned transformation after another followed—I turned into almost anything but what I wanted—as far as I can recall.

To the young, the social system was not democratic, but capitalistic, exploitative, and—weighing most heavily—militaristic. Had it not been for the American war in Vietnam, it's doubtful there would have been a worldwide student movement. The German variant of the youth movement was aimed at their parents' generation, who had cheered the Dictator and followed him gladly. The older generation found that unfair, or at least not very kind, and soon almost hated the rebellious students. And many of the students bore it less easily than they had expected. They continued to act as if they were fully enjoying the revolution, but you could see they were smoking too much, talking too much, and no longer listening. Within a few months, internal dissension had increased and political groups large and small were forming, each trying to be more radical than the other.

Many who had enthusiastically joined in with this new freedom at its dawning were not feeling so well a year later when stones began to fly and fires were set. Added to this was despair over the events in Prague. Socialism with a human face had been steamrolled by the Soviets, and left-wing movements in Western Europe seemed to have been flattened along with it.

What to do? Many withdrew, wrote endless doctoral dissertations of no interest to anyone, meditated at the feet of Indian gurus, or tried alcoholism. And all of them went to the movies more often. They had that in common. Films show life and all of life's errors, that's their purpose. They encourage us to talk about our own mistakes, and even laugh about them. Bad times are good times for the cinema.

Many of them underwent psychotherapy, in flight from the stress of a crumbling social movement. They no longer studied, they delivered furniture or drove taxis to pay for their sessions. I sensed that my hour had come. My dream of bringing out the best in people remained unchanged. I completely renovated my apartment on Tauentzienstrasse, put in brighter lights, hung all sorts of conjured diplomas and certificates on the wall of the largest room, and placed a new brass sign at the entrance to the building:

Dr. med. Pahroc
Analytic Event Therapy

1969 brought with it three newsworthy events: an American danced on the moon, West Germany elected its first Social Democratic chancellor, and I founded Pahroc GmbH to revolutionize psychotherapy.

Business was lively from the start, and I was soon well known. Of course, I was paid—that was part of the therapy. People tend to take good advice only if they've paid good money for it. But I asked less than other therapists, so I appeared more student-friendly. No one suspected that I had no training and wasn't a medical doctor. That didn't bother me in the least. I'd read almost a thousand books with two fingers within a week and mastered all the relevant technical terms. I could also document my training—I cast a spell on the professor whose signature graced my diploma. If asked, he would remember me, and even the subject of my doctoral dissertation: "The Eye and the Event: Recent Research on Close Attention Therapy." It's true that I had no practical training, but I was no confidence man—I was a confident man, and highly qualified.

I developed the concept of "Event Therapy" on a single afternoon, having almost more fun than I did inventing the punch-card frequency modulation system. The course was similar to my leadership seminar, but I dispensed with recounting dreams. Basically, I went walking with the patients, or on a bicycle ride. The excursions themselves were free, you only paid for the discussion sessions afterward. We would go over everything the patients had experienced on the trip. These "events" varied widely, but always involved a moment when their eyes were opened in a new way. Within a few weeks, my patients were transformed into keen observers of others and learned anew how beautiful it could be to live among people.

In my breakfast nook there's a poster that says: "Become a people person!" One of my younger guests, who came from Cologne, wrote "or a Rheinlander" under it with a magic marker—I let it stand.

I referred patients with truly serious problems to other colleagues, but my methods sufficed for normal cases of unhappiness. I don't think I cured anyone, but I opened many eyes. They learned not to brood over long-term ambitions, but to pay close attention to their feet and their breath when walking, and to realize with gratitude what was happening around them. And they were amazed at how much that was.

Interacting with these young and often very bright people gave me great pleasure, and the small belly I'd developed during my period of mourning disappeared with daily exercise.

My patients were indeed happier, without the word happiness ever being mentioned. Nor did I ever speak of success, or praise clients for their progress. I employed spells only rarely. At times, I raised someone's spirits with a Calming or Euphoria spell, or used one that relieved pain temporarily. Mysterious minor improvements strengthen one's faith, and that's of therapeutic value.

I did all this with a calm expression—I was a poker-faced druid. But that didn't make me a guru—I never surrounded myself with acolytes or disciples, though I easily could have. I'm quite proud of that: I've never been tempted to found a sect.

For years afterwards, I received thank-you letters from former patients, including two heads of government. And a great artist assured me I'd set him on the path from pain to painting. When that letter reached me I'd been living somewhere else for over a quarter of a century, but I used the Forwarding spell, which lasts for about fifty years. If you ever need it, Rejlander can show you how it's done.

Incidentally, much as I hate to say it, you shouldn't follow her lead blindly in every case. She takes great joy in beautiful and extravagant handbags. That's not only forgivable, it's perfectly normal. But ever since she perfected the Handbag spell, I've been warning her to be careful. She changes her handbag twenty times on a single shopping trip. She sees one in a store window and instantly there's one just like it under her arm, with the contents unchanged of course. Then she

220

checks herself out in a mirror and is pleased. But soon she's under the spell of a new bag. She's not worried enough about being noticed by some skirt-chaser chasing sorcerers.

The year 1973 was particularly important for me. Johann attended acting school and got his first real role—he blossomed entirely without my help. Then I met a patient who later became my servant, Waldemar III. He'd grown up in Bavaria, went to school in Traunstein, and received religious instruction from a teacher who was wall-eyed. The sound and fury of the student movement had sent him into a state of depression from which I'd gently released him. During one session he referred to himself as the "ideal supporting actor." I listened with interest, but told him the word "ideal" had a slight ring of megalomania about it, regardless of whether he led, supported, or walked on as an actor. In fact, he wasn't an ideal servant, for he remained a convinced pessimist. But at least that meant he was always on time.

Something else happened that year: I was arrested, hauled into court, and sentenced to two years in prison. In spite of the perfect camouflage I'd provided, the fake doctor title and the lies about my training had all come to light, and the fees I'd charged meant I was a true criminal. Only the evil intent of some other sorcerer could have exposed me. You can guess who that was.

My punishment was entirely justified in legal terms, and I accepted it, though there were a hundred ways I could have gotten off. But I regretted nothing, nor do I to this day. I was more modest as a result of that mishap, and perhaps a little wiser, but that's all.

I should bring this letter to a close, Mathilda, it's gone on long enough, and I'm going into the hospital tomorrow. I'm slightly nervous about it. If all goes well, Rejlander will bring you along to visit me, and I will be home again soon. At any rate, a few weeks ago I had the honor of being invited to join the gallery at Parliament to witness the election of the President. I didn't see anyone else as old as me, so it evidently wasn't some automatic honor for 111-year-olds. I think Rejlander, who's a member of the Federal Assembly, set it up, but she claims she knew nothing about it.

This fall you'll enter primary school. You're already looking forward to it. Yesterday I asked you: "What do you want to be when you grow up?"

"A pirate, an Indian chief, and a paleontologist!"

"But those are three different occupations," I said. "Which do you love most?"

"All of them! I'm a love-it-all!"

"And what will you dig up as a paleontologist?"

"A Pachycephalosaurus."

I know from experience with my son John: anyone who can pronounce words like that perfectly at five and a half will wind up on the stage some day.

"That's the dino with a hard skull." I wanted to show that I could keep up with the conversation.

"Yes, that one . . . When it meets another one it goes like this!"

You pretended you were about to ram your little head against my skull—dinosaur against dinosaur.

When I'm released from the clinic, I'll start my next letter to you right away. We'll see how many I manage to write. But perhaps I've already said what's most important—it's always hard to be sure.

Gaining Wisdom

April 2017

Ah, Mathilda, how wonderful it would be if we could simply turn ourselves into good people! Ones who are honest and true, always ready to help others, who never yield to selfish temptations. If we could conjure up a good heart. Then we would be like the angels. But how happy is the life of an angel? I'm skeptical—perhaps it wouldn't be all that wonderful.

I think that might make a sorcerer's life terribly boring. If one were automatically good, temptations would cease to exist, large or small. But either way, they're part of the spice of life: If we give in to them, we have something to enjoy, if we resist them, we enjoy a sense of purity. No, we're fortunate there's no spell for self-perfection. To be incapable of surprising yourself would be like being buried alive.

The same is true for wisdom—there's no Wisdom spell, and I don't miss having one. Although I can certainly say, in spite of my advanced age, that I'm still not truly wise. But it doesn't matter. Conservatives have the edge when it comes to the wisdom of old age anyway—they started earlier. But I've picked up a few insights in the course of my 111 years.

Most insights come from failure, certainly more than from success, at least that's true in my case. Don't be afraid of rough landings, that's the only way you learn anything. Gaining insight is almost always a painful process. But it's certainly better than hindsight.

My greatest setback was my imprisonment in 1973. Its most unpleasant aspect was that I had to give up my practice, which had been going so well. The first thing I did was try to figure out who was responsible, who turned me in. It's easier to spare yourself the pain of self-knowledge if someone else is to blame. And I discovered who the guilty party was. An East German agent told me that Schneidebein had revealed my true past as an electrician and sexton to the Medical Board and the Public Prosecutor out of sheer malice. He hadn't done so directly, but used his West German partner Dr. Schneider instead—who was still annoyed with me for having misled him about my plans to enter a monastery. But I considered Schneidebein the true agent of my humiliation. When I realized he was behind the whole thing, I was overwhelmed by memories of all the humiliations and losses in my life that could be attributed to this murderer. I was in a rage for days.

Evidently he'd even known about my efforts to help people flee and tried to have me locked up in a steel jail cell in East Berlin. Luckily, I escaped that fate without ever realizing I was in danger. Now he wanted to drive me overseas and force me to adopt a new identity. But I wanted to remain who I was, simply because I loved my children and they loved me. And I must admit I also had revenge in mind. Toward that end, too, I wished to remain Pahroc.

I accepted my punishment. I didn't fear prison itself. It's hard to keep a fully developed sorcerer jailed in a normal cell. Two years without parole? Fine, I'd parole myself later. Till then I expected to move about more freely than ever, since everyone would think I was behind bars. There's no better alibi than being in jail, particularly when you're planning a murder, and the timing was good, since that was just what I had in mind. The urge to confront Schneidebein face to face and kill him, with no magic spells involved, pounded away in my soul hour after hour, day and night. I realized the wretch would be expecting this, but I hoped I'd be clever enough to outwit him.

I was released from the clinic yesterday, and it seems I may regain full health. I hope to be around for the next few years to help you with your Latin homework. I have some doubts about making it to your graduation.

Tomorrow, Rejlander and I are heading for Längberg. We want to study the works of the great Bachstelz, my beloved portly ancestor. Rejlander will surely fly there someday with you. There are splendid walks in the area, and there's a wonderful tavern nearby.

The time I spent in prison lies forty years in the past now. I never really understood the point of jail sentences while I was in prison—in fact, their pointlessness was more apparent. Many of my fellow prisoners claimed they were innocent, and a few actually were—I read the minds of several inmates and it was easy to tell. Many were taught to feel like true criminals for the first time while incarcerated. Still, since the Dictator's era, progress has been made in rehabilitation. Prisoners who pose no real threat are now released more often, under proper security, to attend classes, say, or to see their children. And many read entire books for the first time in prison. I had more time to read, too, and lived, so to speak, in realities of two different magnitudes: the small hard one that held sway inside the prison, and the large soft one outside its walls. I alternated between the two and amused myself fairly well.

After an initial period of adjustment, I spent less and less time in jail, leaving my double behind in my cell, and running errands outside, or visiting women for hire. Everyone needs a warm, friendly body tangibly near, now and then. You can't live on memories alone. I got other important matters done on the side: for example, I employed my ex-patient from Tauentzienstrasse as a servant—he became Waldemar III. He was seeing a legitimate analyst at the time, and driving a taxi nights to pay for the sessions. I was often his passenger—I conjured up a few large banknotes and named distant destinations so we'd have time to talk. He never wanted to turn off the meter. He said he couldn't do that to Elvira and Claus, who owned the taxi. That allowed me to diagnose him as sufficiently normal to no longer need an analyst. He believed me, left therapy, and did just fine without it. He became a teacher. A demanding profession, but Waldemar had few actual duties with me. I was in the slammer and had everything I needed.

I also visited Kusenberg in Hamburg. He remembered me—because of Emma. He asked how she was, and was sad to hear she'd been dead for twenty years. I'd forgotten to write him at the time—I forgot everything.

His fantastic stories filled several volumes by then. I could only take one of his books back on my return flight, but in Berlin I had Waldemar order the rest.

Now and again I would check on Johann. He'd been playing juvenile roles at the Theater am Kurfürstendamm in the meantime. I sat in the front row in the guise of a known terrorist, and was quite proud of my son. Of course, I couldn't congratulate him after the performance in that form, the police were waiting to arrest me. I disappeared invisibly through the wall of the men's room and enjoyed the headlines of next day.

I spent my time well in prison. I worked in the uniform shop, learned languages, and developed the idea of a "European event-oriented democracy," in which everyone was expected to learn—no, wanted to learn—all the languages of

Europe. It was a question of pedagogical sorcery. I was an ardent card player on the side, and chose all the hands. I even cheated at chess, which isn't hard when you can change pieces from black to white.

I thought our penal system could be improved, and over time it has been. I still think it only makes sense when necessary to protect us from truly dangerous people. For many others, personal insight and inner transformations can be achieved more readily without incarceration. Nevertheless, I would not have missed my stay in prison—it's an important part of my life story. And I probably became a little wiser while I was there, for I no longer saw myself as the great healer, guiding others to happiness. I just planned to lead a happy life of my own when I got out. That didn't exclude helping others, but I no longer wished to make it my profession. Psychotherapy was out of the question anyway—the authorities had their eye on me.

Something else important happened to me while I was in prison: I freed myself from the tyranny of revenge.

One of my fellow prisoners, thirsting for such revenge, had committed a brutal murder ten years earlier. I read his mind and spent many hours in conversation with him. The violent youth he'd once been had long since become a stranger—he was now a thoughtful and educated man. But he couldn't free himself from that earlier act, nor could he upon his release. His victim haunted his dreams. His conscience kept gnawing at him—a tenacious adversary with ample time. I realized from our conversations that my own conscience would be awakened by murder too, perhaps only later, but without fail and repeatedly. And I assumed the same was true for the murderer Schneidebein. Surely the realization that by his acts he had forfeited his happiness forever had hit home with a vengeance, or would do so eventually. I didn't want to disturb that process.

I was released within a year and a half. My double and I had both behaved well; he, in particular, seemed thoroughly rehabilitated. Now I was free and seeking new pursuits. I could no longer be in a health profession. And no one must know that money hardly mattered in my case—I had to do something so my car and large apartment didn't strike anyone as surprising.

When Johann got his first minor role in a film, he spoke to the unit manager and I was given a spot as a walk-on. I mimed an elderly father who had to join the "Volkssturm," along with schoolboys and old men, to face the tanks of the Red Army in defense of a Berlin already lying in ruins. In the mid-seventies, an unusually high number of films were made that dealt with German history. That meant that a pyrotechnician was one of the most important members of the team. I looked on as he worked, used an invisible Long Arm to loosen a small wire in one of his explosive devices, and said: "Hold on a minute, that's not going to work!" Before the astonished eyes of the specialist, I refastened the wire and appeared to have saved the scene. "I know a little bit about weapons and explosives," I explained. A successful advertisement.

You don't have to learn anything to work in films, you just have to have some special ability. That suits sorcerers well. My career as a pyrotechnician had a steep upward curve. I restored old machine-guns, provided reliable explosions, and helped reproduce the German past believably. Within two years, everyone called me "Uncle Boom-Boom." They knew nothing of my past, since film people know only film people and don't have time to worry about the rest of the world.

I worked a good deal with prop masters. They're responsible for seeing that all the furniture and devices in a film fit the story's time-frame. Now and then I showed my familiarity with older technology and revealed that I had a small collection of such devices at home. So at a later point I left

228

Boom-Boom behind and became a Special Properties Master, earning good money at it. I conjured up most of the devices when no one was looking, then said, "Luckily, I still had this in my cellar." I could reproduce anything: telegraph offices, conveyor belts, the machine room of a light cruiser. My masterpiece was a 1920 steam-driven open plan office. There were no electric typewriters at the time, but there were models powered externally by transmission belts. The belts were attached to a long overhead axle coupled to a steam engine on the floor above. I'd seen an office like that once as a teenager: the secretaries all wore earplugs, since the ambient sound was equivalent to a high-speed German locomotive. The director had his heart set on the office. I built it without asking Production, and he was thrilled—he even wanted to call the film "Transmission." It all fell through, first with Sound and then Production, due to nervous breakdowns. Too bad, because the film would have made my set famous. My servant said the idea belonged in a book anyway.

Waldemar III was teaching high school, but when his morning classes were finished he would come to the workshop or the film set to help me. In return, I'd take a few minutes and correct his assignments using my Spellchecker spell—I didn't even have to open the notebooks. The only hard part was the red ink. Sorcerers can't normally add comments in ink to closed essay books, but after some practice I managed that, too.

Waldemar loved films just as much as I did. Visitors to a film set fall into two categories: one sort just sees people standing around doing nothing and is terribly bored; the other feels the tension and the minds at work, the thought and inventiveness behind it all. And they are never bored.

Waldemar and I also loved the people who make films. They take personal responsibility, because they must. They have to be honest about what they can deliver and what they can't, or things will get expensive and they'll be out of work.

The only people who aren't expected to know their own limits are directors. They are geniuses and can do anything they want—without exception.

1981 brought three important changes: Waldemar moved out, started work on a novel, and no longer came around as often. Johann got his first major role in a film, assumed the stage name John Parrock, and moved into his own apartment. And I decided to stop working on films and live life more philosophically—for example, to try being lazy for once. I rented out four of my eight rooms on Tauentzienstrasse, read a lot, went for long walks, and spent each evening at the cinema. People who knew me thought I was bored. They gave me crossword puzzle magazines and a Rubik's cube, a mechanical gizmo everyone was playing with at the time that made their heads spin (not mine—I found the right sequence in exactly thirty-two seconds). I was never bored in the slightest, and studied the newspapers contentedly. After five years of films set in the past, I enjoyed reading about current events. The newspapers delivered yesterday's news, and today's began early in the morning with my tenants. They occupied both bathrooms and weren't seen again for an eternity. I read the newspapers till someone called out: "The bathroom's free." I generally had to read a long time, so there wasn't much in the way of current events that I missed. For years I was no doubt the best-read landlord in West Berlin, no, in all Berlin, for under their political system, the East Berliners had no idea what was going on.

All sorts of thing passed by in the eighties:

The American president, a former movie actor (in itself a point in his favor), wanted to build a neutron bomb and force the Soviet Union into an arms race it couldn't survive.

In Berlin there was one demonstration after another (mostly along Tauentzienstrasse) over plans for new rocket installations in Europe.

Someone palmed off the forged private diaries of the

"greatest general of all time" on a journalist for a huge sum. German history had to be rewritten, but only for a few days.

In Moscow a clear-sighted man appeared—that didn't happen often—and became head of state. From the Soviet Union's point of view it was a mistake, for he always spoke the unvarnished truth.

A nuclear reactor exploded and for years half of Europe couldn't eat wild mushrooms, due to radioactive fallout.

In 1987, a television broadcast of the German chancellor's New Year's greeting carried the previous year's by accident. Almost no one noticed, since the politician hadn't changed his appearance for a year, right down to the color of his tie.

I love television bloopers! Sometimes I try to cause them myself. Making the newscaster lose his place by an intense Half-Listening spell is one of my favorite TV-damage tricks.

By the way, I'd like to know how my colleagues managed to switch the cards for Best Film at the Academy Awards in Los Angeles this year. If it was done long distance by a colleague watching television, I'd like to learn that spell. I'd enjoy conjuring up a shocking speech or two for a few presidents around the world by slipping manuscripts into their briefcases, even if I had to learn more foreign languages to do it.

I still have to tell you about the misfortunes of the Berlin Wall. It began with more and more people gathering at the wall shouting "We are the people!"—a cry aimed at the state functionaries, making clear they weren't. Others tried to leave the walled-in city in large numbers by different routes. And then something faintly reminiscent of the California gold rush occurred: countless men with shovels and pickaxes could be held back no longer. The structure I'd had so many interesting encounters with, and made a little extra money from, after seeming so permanent for decades, crumbled: In 1989 people were suddenly hacking away at various places on the concrete wall with hammers and chisels and didn't stop until nothing remained but bits and pieces. These could be sold for a good price. Those who erected the wall had thought of everything, but they hadn't reckoned with its value on the open market. The event had major consequences: Germany was soon a single country again, and everyone was so happy their heads were spinning—except the heads of those who knew how to exploit spinning heads.

Those in East Germany were familiar with the plagues of governmental mistrust, control, and spoon-feeding, but not yet with the wanton readiness of some businesses and individuals to commit fraud. And they experienced a new plague of euphoric West Germans ready and eager to enlighten them. These citizens explained their paradise somewhat condescendingly to the newcomers and felt a high degree of self-satisfaction in doing so. Out of pure joy, they cast aside as a hindrance the skepticism they had always adopted quite vocally with regard to their own system. Suddenly a free, even free-wheeling, market seemed the new Gospel to be spread. The major influence of stock corporations on the market, and whether they themselves lived well or poorly, didn't matter to them. That hardly any idea, regardless of how good it was, had a chance of being realized if it ran counter to the business interest of the companies did not strike them as problematic. Nor was it, except for inventors and the future.

The East Germans had carried out a successful peaceful revolution and had a fairly good idea what the absence of freedom felt like, but they also knew how it felt to suddenly regain it. Now they had to learn what West Germans meant by it. That was important, for example, during job interviews.

How you feel about freedom and what you say about it can be two different things. For someone who can peer inside minds, periods of adjustment to a new system are of special interest, but fatiguing as well. And because mind reading, as you know, makes one ravenous, I gained weight dramatically after the "Wende"—the turnaround that changed everything. I had to find a clothing store that carried larger sizes.

I wanted to get in touch with Kusenberg and encourage him to write a story about freedom. Unfortunately, he had died in 1983. I was sad about that, and about myself, for having plainly neglected a fine friendship.

While the Germans now turned to years of self-absorption, I decided to travel to parts of the world that until then I'd known only from films and TV. I gave notice to my tenants, sold all my furniture, and gave up the spacious apartment. There might be some spot in the world so beautiful that I would never want to return to Berlin. In any case, I didn't want to have to return because of an apartment on Tauentzienstrasse.

I also wanted to overcome my old reluctance to take a sea cruise. Up till then, I'd only used ships as way stations on cross-sea flights. Ever since someone described the sinking of the *Titanic* to me at the age of six, I'd been plagued by a nightmare in which I was asleep in a cabin on a ship and woke up much too late to find that the cabin was already below the waterline and sinking.

I embarked on my first voyage in the summer of 1990, on a German freighter out of Hamburg, a giant box stacked with thousands of containers. Captain Kaiser and his officers were German, the crew consisted of Filipinos from the island of Luzon. I knew that in advance, so I'd learned Tagalog, one of their major languages—just in case I got bored with German conversations.

Traveling on a freighter is a fine thing. I could ask the captain questions about technology and navigation whenever I wished, and the ship had everything: a swimming pool, an on-board movie theater, and a good chef. Since I was the only passenger, I was living in the owner's cabin (the owner wasn't along). It was not only roomy, but outfitted with every luxury: a rococo bureau, computer, radio set, and the best bed since Abraham's lap.

It was literally an around-the-world voyage. We were at sea—with stopovers and loading time—for six months. I wasn't bored for a single moment. I finally wrote long letters to my children and more of them than ever before. I read books, watched new films, and got to know the whole ship by heart. I couldn't enter the hold, because its metal walls kept me out, but I could still see what was going on behind them, even if they were made of sheet metal. I saw people, stowaways, hiding in several of the containers, with sufficient supplies of food and water. I even saw beds, battery lamps, and chemical toilets. But I didn't share my knowledge with the captain. These quiet people were in no danger, nor did they pose any—so why interfere in their plans?

I enjoyed life on the ship. Sometimes I felt I was born to take sea voyages. Among the new things I discovered, the most important was storytelling. I had the best possible audience one could imagine: the captain, helmsman, engineer, officers, and the German chef, too, all sat around me and listened. I realized that a long life filled with dangers is a precious thing if one knows how to tell a story. Storytelling may have been born at sea, for nowhere is attention more concentrated—not only on the ship, the weather, and the smallest interactions among those on board, but on every detail of a story, every line of a book. Gradually, I told them my entire life. My only difficulty was suppressing those parts involving sorcery, explaining events in some other way, basically inventing my life anew for the sake of the story. That was a sophisticated mental game, for sailors don't miss the slightest contradiction, and since they're not easily distracted, they tend to be pretty sharp-witted.

My primal fear of going down with the ship remained, though I took some measures to overcome it. I practiced being a fish in the swimming pool for extended periods of time. I was already able to look like a fish and swim like one as well, but the switch to gill breathing proved more difficult—I kept having to change quickly into something else. My practice sessions were a success, though they once placed me in an embarrassing position: The man who took care of the pool arrived unnoticed and began to empty it. Then he saw a fish. I couldn't possibly change back into Pahroc the passenger, so I rose from the water as a seagull and flew away. I changed back into a man somewhere among the containers, went to lunch, and joined the conversation wondering how a seagull could suddenly appear in the middle of the Atlantic Ocean and rise from a swimming pool where it had looked for a moment like a fish. Perhaps it had been on the ship since the mouth of the Elbe River because it liked swimming pools.

A proud moment was 1991, when I looked directly out of the owner's cabin onto Wall Street and felt truly at eye-level with the world's center of capital—for I could make money too.

I saw a great deal of the world through the eyes of a captain, since I was a welcome guest on the bridge. As we moved up the Yangtze River one evening, which, by the way, is a broad brown broth, Captain Kaiser cursed the huge number of fishing boats that impassively blocked his way, often lit only by a candle. Discrete toots of the horn had no effect. Only when our colossus headed directly for them did the fishermen start their diesels and pull out of the way.

Kaiser often complained about things and seemed to enjoy it. In the sandy harbor of Jeddah Islamic Port, he felt it was taking far too much time to load the new containers. The men were praying too long and too often, he said. If robots ever took over work anywhere in the world, he felt they should start in the Muslim countries, simply because robots don't pray.

He complained most about the yachts being sailed about the seas by elderly rich people. "They take so many risks!" he cried, as yet another yacht hove to in the middle of the ocean, moving along slowly because the owners were napping. "They're old and have lost all fear," he said, "but we're the ones who get in trouble if anything happens! They get attacked and robbed by pirates, storms tear their boats to pieces, and they say 'So what?' They're totally tired of life and just don't realize it."

I had an idea: "They should make yachts that can be submerged when you want to sleep or avoid pirates."

"A submarine with sails?" Kaiser smirked.

"Why not?"

"Much too heavy," he said. "To get that moving you'd need the rigging of a five-master, and that wouldn't fit on your steel cigar. And what do you think you'd find in the shrouds when you resurfaced?"

"Nourishment," I replied. "Fish! Seafood!"

He laughed and laughed. That's just why he liked to take landlubbers along—they came up with the strangest things.

But I still thought I'd develop the idea and apply for a patent: "SinkYachts, by Pahroc."

"For millionaires only," Kaiser said, and wiped away the tears. "A sub like that would cost more than a battleship."

But I didn't want to give up the idea right away; it was a question of loyalty.

Pirates were an actual danger at sea, in Indonesia and elsewhere. They could appear in speedboats at any time in the Indian Ocean or the Pacific. I took part in the exercises the captain arranged to prepare for pirates. There were iron gates that could be lowered and water cannons meant to hold them off, and if that didn't work, we were to withdraw to an inner room they couldn't find easily, one that could be locked from the inside. For greater security, I was listed as a member of the crew, so no pirate would think I was a rich passenger and demand extra ransom. Also, harbor officials in some countries demanded higher bribes if the ship was carrying paying passengers.

Sadly, due to the danger of pirates, distress signals from shipwrecks were now often ignored, since they might be traps set by the pirates themselves.

Shore leaves could also be dangerous. There's practically no place in the world where you're safe from being robbed, but in some ports it's almost part of the schedule. Thieves had no luck with me; in fact, I was just waiting for them. My money instantly turned to waste paper or pebbles, and there was no way to grab or hit me. Now and again, I doubled up: I delivered blows from above like Muhammad Ali and struck from below as a scorpion.

Others faced greater danger. Our chef was an enthusiastic jogger. He said he had to compensate for all the dishes he needed to taste. As we lay at anchor not far from Brisbane, Australia, he went ashore on an inflatable dinghy and jogged along the seafront, where he ran into a hungry saltwater crocodile.

"And?" I asked.

"I ran as fast as I could, zigzagging, because crocodiles can't change direction quickly."

"Good," I said. "How big was the beast?"

"At least two meters."

"A young one," I said. "Why didn't you just throw yourself on his snout—on his snout, not in it. It makes sense, since the muscles it uses to open its jaws are much weaker than those that close them."

"Where did you learn that?"

"Experience." I could hardly tell him that my experience came as a crocodile.

"Wouldn't it just throw me off?"

"No. It's far too astonished to find that it can't open its mouth."

"And then?"

"Crocodile steak with creamed vegetables and fried potatoes, with a glass of red wine."

At Papeete, the capital of Tahiti, a major fire broke out on board. It was caused by a fluid in one of the containers that spontaneously combusted when the temperature reached 40° Celsius—no one had known it was there. There were no injuries, but the ship was delayed for some time. I transferred to a freighter that was heading for Madagascar carrying parceled goods. From there, I traveled through the seven seas, once again in the owner's cabin on a container ship for the most part. Now and again we entered European waters. In the Bay of Biscay I was standing on the bridge with a captain named Robert, who wanted to be on a first-name basis, when a gray, heavily-armed frigate from the German navy appeared.

"*Die Bäyern*," Robert said, "just placed in service."

"Beautiful somehow, so much power," I said, "and the name reminds me of my time in Wasserburg am Inn in Bavaria. Of course, I was always opposed to German rearmament."

"Surely you can't be opposed to frigates!" Robert replied. "We need them, not against enemies, but against pirates. We're at sea. Wherever we have freighters, we need frigates too." Somehow the sentence ended with an inaudible but clearly sensed "Basta."

We were on friendly terms, as I mentioned, but contradicting Robert wasn't advisable. And in this case, I had no urge to.

And so for a good two years, I remained at sea on various freighters. I lacked for nothing, certainly not for money, all I had to do was take along a stack of magazines and newspapers, with a few brightly-colored stones, every time we left port.

Any news of importance from Europe reached me, but it never seemed as important as it might have, had I heard it in Berlin. The Soviet Union ceased to exist, the European Union was formed, but remained on feet of clay since elections in the Strasbourg Parliament had little meaning. And in Germany a few refugee shelters were set on fire, which horrified everyone. When I spoke about this with a businessman in Hong Kong, he asked sarcastically, "What's that got to do with us? To us it's like a sack of rice toppled over in Berlin."

I saw a great deal of the world. I finally got better at Geography. I'd seen all the oceans and continents—except Antarctica, because no container ships went there. I wish I could have traveled through the Northwest Passage, which is easy to do now, but that didn't happen.

I felt an increasing desire to stay somewhere longer, and not in a port city. Sunning myself on a white beach in New Zealand, near Dunedin, I suddenly realized I wanted to return to Berlin. It's strange: the longer you're away from the country that issued your passport, the stronger the desire to see it again, and in particular the place where you grew up. Yes, I was homesick. I rose high above the beach and headed toward Auckland as a cormorant. There I boarded a plane as a passenger without luggage, returning to Europe by way of Los Angeles.

Arriving in Berlin, I took a taxi directly to Pankow, and what do you know, a five-room apartment was for rent in the building where I spent my childhood. It was a little too large, but I took it and set to work to save it from disrepair. I've lived there happily ever since. When I arrived, the building itself seemed almost in ruins, but it was later renovated by West Berlin investors, who even added an elevator—I was able to stay there. The nicest thing was to be able to look out my window at the building across the street where my dear former teacher lived. It looked just as it had eighty years ago, the flagpole was still there, and the inscription on the pediment. It had been left untouched because people thought "Haus Schlosseck" had some connection with the nearby Schloss Niederschönhausen. Fortunately, this idea was held in the Dictator's era too, otherwise the name Schlosseck would have been removed in the thirties.

I'm probably a romantic among electricians, otherwise I wouldn't be attracted by ruins. After the war, I was fascinated by crumbling walls from which willows with catkins rose, and I loved Potsdamer Platz with weeds growing everywhere and only a single building left standing, and rabbits romping about. In my years helping people flee East Berlin, I loved the S-Bahn because there were so many rusty tracks leading nowhere, with the most amazing plants growing between them. All of East Germany had some of this charm, but only romantics could love it, and capitalism was about as romantic as a bulldozer. Pankow has become steadily more Western from the time I went back till today, and that's had one good result: it's colorful again.

One of the advantages of living in Pankow was that no one knew me there. On Tauentzienstrasse I was constantly meeting people from my former life: students, patients, people I'd help escape—I even met the judge who'd sentenced me to prison. No one recognized me in Pankow, so I could live in peace.

I went into action to secure a commemorative plaque for my teacher. I visited both the property manager and the county commissioner and presented them with documents on the well-known philosopher Schlosseck, including articles from supposedly real encyclopedias, all carefully conjured. I had already designed the plaque and was ready to help pay for it. My request was denied.

I made use of the powerful Chinese Notes spell: the man in charge was forced to recall my request every twenty minutes. Even this week-long hammering didn't do the trick. Casting effective spells was still difficult in the East. But they didn't know Pahroc! I saw to it that the sign by the door, which pointed the way to the building manager's office, was transformed in the eyes of any intelligent observer into the following:

The Philosopher and Aphorist
F. N. U. Schlosseck
Lived in this Building from 1906–1934

People could make what they wished of "F. N. U." Only sorcerers would realize that he must have been a great master— F. N. U. was our abbreviation for "First Name Unknown."

To show I was a true Pankower (and I was actually born there!), I also bought a car called a "Trabant." I was still a good driver, in spite of my eighty-eight years, and it was a good thing I was, since the car had almost no pickup power. When I tried to pass anyone on the highway, I was reminded of Gnadl's 1946 wood burner, and soon gave up such attempts. But it was fun driving the Trabant in the city. The car and its white-haired driver were both strongly underestimated. I particularly enjoyed beating out sports cars thanks to my better knowledge of the city—the puzzled drivers probably thought I must be some kind of sorcerer.

After a year I sold the speedster to a family in Pankow for a token mark. They accepted it gladly, but forgot to pay the mark. I noted with relief that in the East they were no longer so concerned with symbols.

I often went to concerts, and enjoyed turning myself into the conductor or the soloist. Of course, I didn't perform, I simply sat in the audience—as Daniel Barenboim, to give one example. Hardly anyone noticed, and if they did, they didn't believe it. Only once was I asked softly, "If you're sitting here, who's that up there conducting?" I was as happy as a child, and told the man I was the conductor's twin brother, but please not to let it get out.

At some point I recalled having read in Längberg about a type of transformation that included the artistic abilities of the person who served as a model. One could even take on the abilities alone, without assuming the form of the artist, but that was one of the highest arts. On a subsequent visit to Tyrol I found the book again, practiced diligently, and actually managed to play like a famous soloist for a few minutes. I had the notes in my head while I was transformed, and my fingers did precisely what they were supposed to— and were strong enough. I realized how ardently I'd sought applause throughout my life, and that I clearly hadn't harvested enough, since I was now taking every opportunity to produce a few more handclaps. I even bought myself a grand piano to play a little something for my guests at breakfast.

Of course the Soloist spell was extremely taxing—I was dripping with sweat within seconds. By the way, it seems that more than a few pianists around the world are actually sorcerers. The pitiless gaze of the television camera reveals how heavily they're sweating. I'm just surprised they can hold out so much longer than me—I can only manage the shortest pieces of Chopin or Scriabin, and can barely add "Little Hans" as an encore, a note of friendly self-irony which always draws applause. Of course there was no way I could have given a full concert.

In the apartment above, a boy was constantly practicing on his drums, often early in the morning before leaving for school. When he asked if it was bothering me, I told him no musician ever became great without annoying his neighbors, and to keep right at it, I was on his side. But he actually seems to have developed into a great drummer. At any rate, he practiced deep into the night. That gave me the impetus to travel the world again, this time on a regular passenger ship, where I could surely find a piano. I flew to Saxony to try to talk the ancient Blüthner into coming with me, but he was having his own difficulties. He'd been working on a Memory Erasure spell and under its influence had forgotten how to reverse it to regain his memory. Although he didn't recognize me, he knew that he knew me, and kept reassuring me confidently: "It'll come back to me. I'll have it by tomorrow!" I left feeling sad, and tried my luck with Gnadl. A cruise would give me a chance to really talk with him. Though he was long past a hundred now, I didn't find him. Someone told me he'd moved without telling anyone, but was often seen on the Reiter Alm, and climbed the Hintere Feuerhörndl twice a week. I didn't find him there either, though I waited for days.

So I departed on the trip alone. In December 1999, I was on my way aboard a huge Norwegian cruise ship in the Pacific Ocean. Everyone on board was in their seventies. Not a good age for me, since they were too young to exchange pre-war memories and occasionally too old to listen well.

Then came the St. Sylvester Day party. I'd developed a reputation as a passable storyteller in the meantime and so had been invited to the captain's table. When I arrived, the captain introduced me to the oldest passenger on the ship, the ninety-seven-year-old retired Col. Schneidebein. I froze: yes, it was him. He was only a shadow of his former self: trembling, sad, frightened, and confused, but that may have been due to the situation. The captain saw my look and asked:

"Do you know each other?"

I sat down and said: "Casually."

Nor did I greet him—I simply stared into his eyes. I felt a little sorry for him, but I couldn't shake his hand. He stood up, murmured something about going "back to the cabin," excused himself to the captain, and left the table. A sailor saw him climbing over the rail astern and tried to hold him back, but he jumped with no hesitation.

I had a queasy feeling. Of course, it would have been better if we'd spoken with each other. One can speak with someone one can't forgive. But that's all theory. Had he stayed at the table I couldn't have brought myself to say a word to him, nor attempt a reconciliation of any kind. I would have begged their pardon and left the table myself. The man had managed to separate me from Emma and our children for three years. And he still deserved to die for murdering Schlosseck. That's how I saw it that Sylvester evening. Actually, we resembled each other: he couldn't forgive me and I couldn't forgive him. We were both trapped. But I hadn't killed anyone, except as a soldier. I often think back on all that, even today, but I couldn't think about it then, not in Schneidebein's case. And then he put an end to it himself.

The captain ordered a man overboard maneuver. The huge ship slowly swung around and a hundred pairs of binoculars searched the waters—in vain, for it was already dark. I was asked what I knew about the passenger. I told his story, and that he was responsible for the murder of many of my friends and countless others. When he saw me, all those deaths must have suddenly come back to him, and looking at me he could see that I would never forgive him. The captain thought Schneidebein must have been planning this for some time, and did not expect to see the new millennium. And doubtless he'd picked out a good place to jump ahead of time, you don't just find one by chance.

The Sylvester party was officially cancelled because of his death, and the band withdrew. But since everyone remained at their tables drinking champagne, I sat down at the orphaned piano and played. I began with the ragtime by Scott Joplin that, more than sixty years earlier, Blüthner had played for Emma and me, or, more accurately, had played for the missing Schlosseck.

I think I wrote to you about that, I won't look back now and see. The piece was well known because it served as a leitmotif in a film set in the twenties, a comedy in which an unsavory Mafia boss who's a murderer is sold down the river

by two con artists. The audience reacted warmly to my playing, and around one o'clock one of them called out "Play it
again, Pahroc!" followed by expectant applause. I stood up
and said: "Thank you, but I'd rather play something for the
third millennium." It could only be Bach. The majority remained. Some even wanted to hear more Bach. Those were
the ones you can seriously begin a third millennium with.

Schneidebein's suicide was immediately reported, and
with that he was truly dead, both officially and by Monday
at the latest in the media. His shame was a matter of public record and his life was at an end. Even if he'd turned himself into a fish or bird and reached land, there was no way he
could return to his old self. But he was no doubt dead, both
officially and in fact, for I did not believe him capable of long
distance flights or breathing with gills. As I've said, he was no
great sorcerer.

After that experience, I was done with cruises and with trips
on freighters. I'd been running a bed and breakfast in my
apartment since 1998 and was soon enjoying playing the host
again. I didn't have a large number of guests, perhaps because
visitors don't tend to think of Pankow as truly part of Berlin—
where in fact it's the navel of the city. But I had many good
conversations over breakfast with young people, and when
my children and grandchildren came to visit I could put them
up and introduce them to Pankow, for which they showed
a polite interest. From 2002 on I had a servant once more,
Waldemar IV, whom you'll surely get to meet, since he'll be
handling a number of my affairs when I die—together with
Rejlander, of course. He's a good cook, has a deep knowledge
of films, and is one of the most reliable people I've ever met.
We sorcerers may not actually need servants, but the older
we get, the more we value loyalty, and like to have as much
of that around as we can get.

Last week I read that frogs can see colors in the dark. I

made a special trip to the zoo to take a good look at a live frog, then turned myself into one and looked at our paintings at night. What they say about colors is true! Kandinsky in particular came through, but so did the painting of Indians by August Macke. Rejlander woke up, turned on the light, and was amused by the frog. "And so nice and slippery," she said. "First you have to kiss me," I croaked, and when she had done so, I changed into a prince and followed her to bed.

Dear Mathilda, I don't believe I've become a wise man. If I'd been truly wise, I'd probably have spoken with Schneidebein.

There is no grand spell for wisdom, not even for specific moments when it would be most useful. How wisdom arises and how it feels is known only to those who possess it—I can only guess at it.

But I've often found joy and happiness in life, with Emma for a long time, and now again with Rejlander, and often between the two, when I was a free man and a sinner, or at least close to freedom and to sin.

What joy is, I can definitely speak to: it's the feeling that you're on the trail of the grand context of life, and that you're in harmony with it or soon will be. You don't have to feel it every day—seven times a week is enough. More than that would be too much.

Bidding Adieu to the World

May 2017

Dear Mathilda,

The day before yesterday you visited me in the hospital with your parents, Rejlander came yesterday, and today I'm beginning a new letter to you, just like that. For everything about sorcery should be said.

Because we were alone in the room yesterday—my neighbor was taking a long walk—Rejlander and I wept together for a while. We both noticed that the other felt like it, and when that happens you might as well do it together, the good effect is even stronger. Crying is like wiping things off with a damp cloth: it picks up crumbs on the soul one hasn't even noticed. Afterwards everything is shiny again and seems friendlier. It did me so much good that when Iris and Stephan visited that evening, I couldn't stop laughing. They were telling the craziest stories about film productions. They're still working; she does make-up and he's in sound. They also brought along a bottle of red wine. By the time the nurse arrived, we had finished it.

It still makes me feel good to think back on the conversation I had with you yesterday.

"Grandpa, where do you go when you die?"

"I don't know, I haven't died yet. But somewhere up above, I believe."

"And then you'll fall again as rain?"

"Could be."

"And then the lawns will grow."

"Absolutely.

"I'd like to run the lawn mower. Papa never lets me."

My son and I glanced at each other. I probably wouldn't have either.

Then Adele and John wanted to discuss something with the doctor and left you with me. I gazed out the open window and asked:

"Mathilda, could you pick a leaf for me from that tree outside the window? It's such a beautiful jagged leaf, the one hanging closest to us."

"But I'll fall out, Grandpa!" you replied, half in fear, half in cunning.

"Well in that case, you certainly shouldn't do it."

Then you looked at me inquisitively and I nodded.

"Try it from here. If your arm is too short we'll forget it. Yes, Mathilda, I know all about it. But we won't tell anyone. It will be our secret."

You didn't even need to get out of your chair. One grasp and you handed me the maple leaf. You're so far along, you're there! Now I just have to live a few more years, that's all.

"Thank you, that's a beautiful leaf," I said, and had trouble holding back my tears of joy.

I'm less concerned about the immediate future than I've ever been. Now everything in my life seems so clear.

If I have worries, they're about our planet; for example, technological developments.

There are technical innovations that I don't have to think about, I'm simply pleased by them. For example, a bionic prosthesis for someone who's lost a hand. He's given a mechanical hand he can move by directing his thoughts. He even receives sensations through the fingertips, and can feel the shape of objects.

They're close to deciphering the chemical and electrical processes in the brain now, and mind reading will be technically possible. People will soon find it hard to keep secrets with devices like that scanning their brains. But people will probably find a way to outsmart them.

I hear methods are being developed to smuggle specific images into your dreams while you sleep, beginning, no doubt, with images of commercial products. Blending advertisements with dreams—what sad nonsense! We need our dreams for other things.

When we leave home, our faces are photographed and scanned in more and more places. That's no problem for a sorcerer, if he knows in time. If! I probably wouldn't notice every security camera in time to change myself into someone else, Karl Marx or Karl May, or a man-size gorilla in a Burberry coat.

When I first got excited about data processing half a century ago, it never occurred to me that it might develop into something questionable. My enthusiasm suffered its first setback when this same technology served unsavory purposes for dictators and murderers. As I write this letter, dictators are looming on the horizon like a solid low-pressure front, particularly where hardship reigns. Hardships produce dictators, and dictators produce more hardships.

I view this with sadness. Seventy or eighty years ago, when I was a young electrician and inventor, I should have gone to the third world and built something there. But would that have been possible? There was a war, I had a family, and, above all, Emma.

I've changed myself, over and over. Humanly, not with sorcery! I lived long enough to do it. But, on the whole, I remained reasonably true to myself. Others did a better job of that of course. Unless we remain true to ourselves we are lost. For a long time loyalty struck me as a dangerous notion, given the criminal reign we experienced. I regained only gradually the sense of what it means to remain true.

During a shore leave in Ashdod, Israel, I studied Hebrew for a short time. In that language the same word is used for both truth and loyalty, and that led me to ask if the two might actually be one. No philosopher would put it that simply, but I'm an engineer, so I may. If you're not particularly interested in theory, go ahead and skip forward, at some point you'll think about these things on your own anyway.

I'm not talking about absolute truth, but the one we encounter in everyday life. It's created when we set out on a path, and do so along with others. It doesn't matter if we lose our way, the path can be emended. But it cries out to be followed, and without faith that won't happen. We remain true to the idea of taking the path, together with our companions, and we ensure we do by remaining firmly on it. That's the simple truth of the path. We know something else too, unfortunately: it's not eternal. At some point it's replaced, there will be new paths, and new traveling companions.

Our brains are structured in such a way that, despite the mind's ability to produce endless objections, courageous decisions are made in favor of an idea to which the mind can remain true. The mind also produces "truth." We accept everything that supports the idea, and reduce anything that undermines it to fine print. If we did not, we would remain in a state of permanent indecision, unable to take a step forward, wretchedly unhappy, paralyzed by our doubts. Just as the balance wheel of a clock ensures that it doesn't run too fast, in spite of its tightly wound spring, loyalty to an idea ensures that it runs at all, and will keep on running. There you have my engineer's model of loyalty.

The idea can be anything: a path, an invention, a concept for a film, a theory, a hypothesis. We need to be true, above all, to our own ideas. That goes for love too. At that evening dance in the Pankow Bürgerpark, I met Emma. There was nothing particularly special about that. But then the idea "Emma" emerged, and I remained true to it, otherwise nothing much would have come of it. You could almost say I invented Emma, and she me. We just didn't apply for patents.

I've met more than a few people who were happy so long as they remained true to their idea, regardless of whether or not it proved successful: Waldemar III's material for his novels, Schlosseck's concept of Germany, Blüthner's vision of sorcery's task for humankind, Gnadl's model of poaching as a way of life, and a friend I haven't even told you about yet, Eberhard, with his concept of control.

He was from Pankow and we got to know each other on a foraging trip during the hardships of 1918. As a fifteen-year-old, he was already talking about his idea to anyone who didn't immediately take to their heels: The entire world was being controlled, control ruled everything. In this idea lay the key to the order of the universe. He seemed to believe in some gigantic machine, today we might call it a supercomputer, one not made by man and controlling everything. But in those days I was only interested in machines I could construct and build myself. I pointed out that "controls" were everywhere, from a light switch to the emergence of new species on the planet. Recognizing this didn't prove anything in itself. He smiled and said: "You still haven't understood me."

That was a striking thing about Eberhard: he was calmness personified, and his calm came from his conviction that he was on the track of a basic principle. Nothing could provoke him, not even suggesting he was deeply religious and had been talking about God all the time without realizing it. Later on he heard that cybernetics, systems theory, and a good deal else had been around for a long time. He nodded at this: Yes, all those were initial steps in his direction, but he'd moved farther on. Throughout his life he regarded every report, every event, from the perspective of control, making notes, filling folders and filing cabinets.

Now, the wonder of Eberhard was that he was not fanatic or doctrinaire about his theory. His calm loyalty to a world-idea made him a curious and wise contemporary and friend. He remained fearless and benevolent, even toward those who lied, stole, defrauded, murdered, or started wars. They simply had not yet understood the principle of control. That's what I call remaining true to an idea. In the end, he became a highly educated man and a typically poor but happy German Adjunct Professor—and found a loving wife who was happy but not poor.

Life holds a joy in store that can't be conjured up, even with the help of cookbooks from St. Polykarp's. As if sitting by a stream, one has to wait for it to come drifting along, then offer it a friendly invitation to stay a while. The tribe of my ancestors bore the name Pahranagat, which means something like "He who puts foot in water." It's a good name, since being open to happiness means simply sitting by a stream and putting your foot in to stay fresh and alert. Nothing more is needed—not fear, not power, not privilege, and certainly not the ambitious goal of bringing out the best in people. You can teach people a number of other useful things, but the best way you can help them be their best is by simply being there, being happy yourself, and waiting quietly till they ask you how you did it.

Happiness may last a long time, but it eventually fades. It floats on by, or flies off like a flock of birds. But it's hasn't fully disappeared. You can still watch it, and you shouldn't be too upset if it decides to land somewhere else—it doesn't like being bored.

Mathilda, as you've no doubt guessed from the things I've been meditating on in this letter, and probably long before, I never could do sorcery, let alone be a master sorcerer. That's my truth for now, for this morning. But what you've read is my story, all the same. Something about it must be true, or I couldn't have told it. Perhaps you'll be a little angry at your grandfather for spinning such tales, but think of the child you were while I was writing these letters. Not only do children like listening to stories, they like to make up their own, and the wilder the better. I understand my friend Kusenberg better now. He was a playful child who managed to oppose the power of adults with humor. And he did so without awakening their scorn, without allowing anyone to bully him, and without being trapped forever in childhood. He was an independent, confident adult.

It's amazing how many young people manage to do that today. Without feeling guilty or pressed to justify themselves, they live playfully and invent the most unbelievable things. They began that way as children—we all do—and were never cruelly forced into the roles of adults. They were simply lucky. Perhaps they had good parents and teachers. At any rate, they picked up something that made them immune to fear and paralysis. I was the same way, but in my case it took a while before I allowed the child in me more freedom.

A man from Hamburg was in the bed next to me until this morning. He is a river pilot on the Elbe, who was operated on for a slipped disc. Given the intense pain in his back, he had a hard time doing his job—which included jumping into a boat from the last rung of the pilot's ladder in heavy seas when the ship had reached open waters. That had become torture for him. He's happy now because he finds joy in his work again. He can jump. But he would have kept on even with the pain, of that I'm certain. True as gold, the Germans say of such a man (as if gold were ever true to anything). Best of all were the stories he told of ships and sailors.

He was released this afternoon. His parting words were: "Till the day," the standard farewell in Hamburg. And when I thanked him for the pleasant company and good stories, he said, "T'was nothing."

I replied "Auf Wiedersehen," though people rarely see each other again after a hospital stay, even if they've shared their stories. "Adieu" would have been better, first because it's French, and second because it doesn't commit you to something that's not going to happen. "Servus" means both hello and goodbye, and sounds more like a request than a greeting, which has always bothered me a little. The Bavarian "Pfüat di" would be all right, but "Gott" needs to be added or non-Bavarians hear only "protect you," and respond with "protect yourself!" You often hear "Tschüss" in the hospital, but that means the same thing as "Adieu."

Well, let's stick with "Adieu" then.

Waldemar III wanted to visit me tomorrow, but I begged off, in spite of how much I like talking with him. At the moment, I have no need of a well-meaning pessimist. Even when he stays silent, I know he thinks I'm in a bad way.

I'll be here through the weekend, on Monday I can go back home—evidently they can think of nothing more to do with me. Then I'll be sitting at my beloved desk again. It's hard to write in bed. Starting Tuesday, I expect you'll visit me at home. Maybe it will be warm enough to go out for ice cream.

Those were Pahroc's final lines. He died during the night of March 10th–11th, 2017, in the hospital—he wanted to die at home, but he didn't have that good fortune. He'd known about his condition for months.

AFTERWORD

by WALDEMAR III

Reykjavik, 25.07.2032

I've been asked to write an afterword for this book, and I do so gladly, for I have good reason to hope that it finds many readers, not only now but in the future, and, above all, in the past. That last bit may sound odd, but I'll try to justify it.

First, as to myself: From 1973–1983, unbeknownst to all but a few, I was a servant to the electrician, inventor, pyro-technician, psychotherapist, and sorcerer Pahroc. In a few days, I'll celebrate my ninetieth birthday. As with all my major birthdays, I'll celebrate it in Reykjavik. I'm a retired author, so for the most part now I only write forewords and afterwords for works by others. Enough about me.

After Pahroc's death in 2017, Rejlander, his second wife, gave me letters to read that he'd written to his granddaughter Mathilda (born 2011), letters she was meant to read only as an adult. Since Pahroc's final servant (Waldemar IV) died just a year after his master, it was Rejlander who passed them on to Mathilda in a folder two and a half years ago, on Three Kings Day, 2030. Upon reading them, the young woman had no objection in principle to their publication in book form, but at first that seemed completely out of the question. Sorcerers are more mercilessly persecuted today than ever before. And anyone involved with such a publication risks imprisonment and electronic mental monitoring, as happened some months ago to poor Rejlander. She's still alive, but with no brain activity to speak of, nor any prospect of regaining her powers as a sorceress.

A year ago she visited the secret library for sorcerers in Tyrol with her new friend, an Arab named Ibn Ruschd, and nineteen-year-old Mathilda. They were studying the works of the masters to see if the course of history could be altered. They were already thinking of arranging to publish the book ten or fifteen years earlier in time, in a past that still might be won over to the role of sorcery. Such an intervention would have one major argument in its favor: it would save Rejlander from her present fate.

I should perhaps relate how things could come to this pass. It wasn't that the great sorceress fought too strongly against a political system obsessed with normality, or joined in an attack on the Dictator—her misfortune took a much more banal path. Rejlander's habit of carrying a different handbag every few minutes when she was out and about in the city had not escaped the security cameras, and one day led to her undoing. She was identified as a subject practicing sorcery and locked in a trap of steel and reinforced glass. Then her memory was scanned and manipulated. The process is irreversible, and in fact only one possibility exists to save her—a return to the time in which her future still lay open. Various switches could then be set differently. Publishing Pahroc's letters in the year 2020 or 2021 would be one of several measures by which today's repression could be undone—by ensuring it never happened.

In preparing to write the afterword for this book, which I fervently hope may be published, I've reread my copies of Pahroc's letters and studied them all carefully again.

The very first time I read them I was shocked by something—in his final letter Pahroc confesses that he never was a sorcerer, that he'd just made it all up. Since, as his initiate and servant, I witnessed what an ingenious and artful sorcerer Pahroc was, I can only explain this curious confession in one way: He recognized the future dangers sorcery faced and wished to protect his granddaughter. It was meant to deceive unauthorized readers, spies, and possible traitors. As an inventor and electrician, he may have foreseen the future development of brain technology in much more detail than his letters indicate. Nevertheless, he would be horrified and saddened if he knew what was going on in the present world. More precisely, in the Western world.

The European experience has been a transforming event, but a discouraging one. The democracies have not survived the war against terror. Nor has that terror itself, but that is scant consolation. Dictatorships now set the tone because they're in a position to blackmail almost anyone. One embarrassing revelation follows another, but there are no consequences. True power resides in the internet companies, which have long since found democracy annoying and get along better with new dictatorships. And our dreams—those of non-sorcerers—consist only of political thought control and commercial advertisements. Pahroc foresaw it all.

In the seventies of the previous century a man raced through Berlin writing on every surface he could find that he was being scanned and tortured by radio transmitters. He was ahead of his time. Today we wear copper wire headcages to prevent having our brains hacked electronically. Some people, including men, wore burqas so the headgear couldn't be seen. They claimed it was for religious reasons, but burqas have long since been outlawed for preventing faces from being scanned. As a result, many people bandage their heads. The number of alleged skull injuries has grown sharply, and doctors wind up in prison if they issue medical certification in such cases. And above all this stretches a sky that's always overcast. It's now advertisements from one horizon to the other.

In contrast, the Arab lands and cities that were once destroyed by crises and wars have been rebuilt, the universities are indeed universal, and their societies flourish under matriarchy. Mathilda, who's studying both mathematics and medicine, can imagine living in Damascus, one of the freest cities in the world. Of course, it's difficult to get there now, since the number of emigrants from Europe seeking asylum has risen sharply. In fact, Mathilda would gladly remain here, since she's inherited her Uncle Titus's alpine pasture on the Wilder Kaiser ridge. But she knows that the life of the mind requires not just isolation, but also the proximity of free people.

From my present vantage point I can well understand Pahroc's last letter. The wellbeing of his granddaughter (and also Rejlander!) was more important to him than the truth when he wrote his letters. Mathilda sent reports to me, Rejlander, and other friends on several occasions—by email, so the authorities would see them too. In them, she describes Pahroc's letters as a curious play of fantasy that might at best give literary pleasure. No one can cast spells, she said, herself least of all, and she was glad of it. She had understood Pahroc's warning and taken it to heart, far more effectively than her beloved teacher Rejlander.

When I celebrated my seventy-fifth birthday in Reykjavik, Rejlander was among my guests, though Pahroc had only recently passed away and she'd withdrawn from society. She brought along copies of his letters to Mathilda. Apart from me, she only entrusted this information to two other friends of her husband, Iris and Stephan. But they hadn't made it to Reykjavik—they were under contract and shooting a film. Mathilda asked Rejlander if she could publish her letter of 28 July, 2017. Rejlander said yes, and felt it would make a good introduction to the book as a whole.

While in Reykjavik I had a long talk with Rejlander about the film she wanted to make some day about Pahroc. As happens with many who come to feel at home on the set, the medium had never lost its hold on her. It was even in her genes, since she's related to Oscar Gustave Rejlander, who was a pioneer of art photography long before the invention of the Maltese Cross mechanism—that's the gear drive with a "stop-and-go" movement, without which there would be no films.

But there will be no film about Pahroc unless the Past Time spell works.

Our plans in Reykjavik also included a memorial plaque for Pahroc's birthplace in Pankow, placed there in 2020. Since that same year, a similar plaque for his teacher Schlosseck stands on the building opposite, easily read by anyone. I designed them both.

It would be wonderful if sorcerers could be a part of our lives again. Their main purpose, after all, is to enrich the world of our dreams. If sorcerers were completely effaced from the earth, fairy tales would disappear too, and all child-like qualities in adults. So many beautiful, crazy stories (including that of Salvation) would be lost, along with "what if"—the best part of the conjunctive mode. In all magic there dwells a beginning, a small entry into the best of all worlds. That joy is not the sorcerer's alone, it's always a joy to others.

If sorcerers could have formed an alliance in 2020 or 2021, in Europe and around the world, perhaps with lodges like the Freemasons, perhaps openly as clubs and lobbying groups joined by open minded "normal" people, they would not be playing the role of victims today. But after two failed attempts, in which Pahroc took part, of course, they simply lacked the courage to try again, and still lack it today.

Rejlander's friend looks something like Dustin Hoffman—I'm deliberately choosing an actor who was sufficiently well known in 2020. Ibn Ruschd has a life story that deserves to be told, with settings like the following: an inflatable boat in the Mediterranean, a refugee camp in the Upper Franconian countryside, a small computer shop in Bamberg, a job with a broadcast technology firm in Munich—and that's just a small sample. For Ibn Ruschd is a sorcerer specializing in time travel, and often comes from great distances. There's strong evidence that in 1855, as the pastry chef Hamzeh, he helped write Bachstelz's *Introduction to the Fine Art of Cookery*, then catapulted himself to the year 2015 as a young man and mixed in among the fleeing boat people. Why did he do that, instead of flying on past it all as Caliph Stork? I think he enjoyed crossing the sea safely as a sorcerer in 2015 in that sort of dangerous vessel. But he's said to have arrived from much farther back in time and to have somehow furthered the career of the philosopher Aristotle. I asked him once whether he intended to stay in Germany or go back. He said he was staying. He's not going to leave Rejlander in the lurch, though she no longer recognizes him. She calls him Pahroc, so perhaps that's who she still remembers.

In the writings of Master Bachstelz, Ibn Ruschd has found hints that it may be possible to produce so-called "era gaps," which loosen events from their context and situate them elsewhere. It's true that even great sorcerers can't intervene in the course of history, that's an unwritten law, just as no one may be killed using sorcery. But evidently there's a higher authority that allows exceptions when they seem justified. Otherwise Babenzeller could never have used the ice-melting spell to sink a firing squad in the Baltic Sea. He knew that there were exceptions. Bachstelz knew it too, and hoped to succeed in carrying out a highly honorable project.

Bachstelz was planning nothing less than preventing the Thirty Years War. He thought it might be possible, if the first printed Bible translation of 1534 could be set back to 1400. I beg the reader's forgiveness, but as a former historian I must go into greater detail here: It's conceivable that with an earlier appearance of the printed Bible the Reformation might have occurred sooner, but it may also have never happened at all, for it was a reaction to the pitiful condition of the Catholic Church at the time. That condition, said Bachstelz, may well have been totally different if a printed, readable Bible had been available sooner.

If so, it was a matter of finding a publisher around 1400 for a printed Bible. Bachstelz seems to have chosen an unusual path in this case: since he mistrusted Catholic institutions, as well as the cloisters, which came to mind first as possible "publishers" in those days, he chose instead the Likedeeler—yes, those pirates. They were "God's friend and the world's enemy" and proud of it. As independent, wealthy financers, they alone could support the project at the time. Bachstelz thought it could be cleverly arranged: Klaus Störtebecker, who enjoyed the protection of Duke Albrecht I of Bavaria and Straubing, Count of Holland, Zealand, and Hennegau, would be only too happy to find some new way to annoy the magnates of the Church and the Hanseatic League. He was the ideal man for the job. A Bible translator had been found as well, a Dutchman from Zwolle versed in old languages, who also happened to be one of the early inventors of printing. According to Bachstelz's plans, he was to produce printed songbooks and then bibles in Gouda in 1390. That the first printed Bible was now to appear in Holland did not bother the master greatly, nor the fact that the time shift meant a few famous stories had to be dropped—about Störtebecker's demise for example: He probably would not have been captured near Helgoland (there's nothing to interest a publisher there). Nor would he have been beheaded on the Grasbrook, let alone walked past his comrades headless. It's more likely that, with the help of the Gouda Bible, he would have made the Likedeeler a powerful force to be dealt with in

Europe. Bachstelz even foresaw that Störtebecker and Jakobäa von Straubing-Holland, of the House of Wittelsbach,
might have drawn nearer personally, so that instead of Jean
de Valois (the future king of France, who passed away too
soon to take the throne), Jakobäa might have taken Störtebecker for her husband! With him, she could have become
a great symbolic figure for the renewal of the Church—and
for the life of the community as well, since this development
would have cleared the way, against much resistance, for a
completely new status for women. Luther, Zwingli, and Cal-
vin would no longer have had to play major roles: with Jakobäa Störtebecker's impact, their work would have long since
been done. And if the Church had remained the sole church
for Christians, they could have spared themselves the Thirty
Years War. Something like that must have been what Bachstelz had in mind. As we know, he died too young to put his
ideas into effect.

Last week, at the secret library, Mathilda assembled almost all the sorcerers who were not being held by the authorities, since such a radical re-setting of time requires the joint
effort of a larger group. Ibn Ruschd went over the process
with all of them again. Not everyone agreed at first. There
was general nervousness, for it was at heart a matter of saving the whole of Europe. But then Mathilda gave a speech
that left everyone's ears ringing. The decisive statement was
said to be this:

"Sometimes a generation of sorcerers is destined for greatness. You can be that generation. You must be, or you will be
the last."

The sorcerers are now prepared; they share a common
will. But I understand the time shift may simply be too difficult for sorcery. The plan won't fail because of me—my
afterword is done. I've even provided a title for the book that
might awaken interest among discerning readers in the year
2020: *The Joy of Sorcery*.

But I've been a pessimist for almost ninety years. It wouldn't surprise me if books were published, but couldn't be made public.

Sten Nadolny was born in Brandenburg, Germany in 1942. He is the author of eight novels including *The Discovery of Slowness* and *The God of Impertinence*. *The Discovery of Slowness* has been translated into more than twenty languages and become a modern classic of German literature. Nadolny has won several literary awards including the Ingeborg Bachmann Prize. He lives in Berlin.

Breon and Lynda Mitchell have been collaborating on award-winning translations of German novels and short stories for over three decades, including major works by Franz Kafka, Heinrich Böll, Günter Grass, Uwe Timm, Sten Nadolny, and Marcel Beyer. Their most recent translation was the English libretto for Gottfried von Einem's opera *Der Prozess*, performed in concert at the 2018 Salzburg Summer Festival.